Dear Mollie & Tom!
For both of you.

Indu

Indu

JAHED RAHMAN

Library of Congress Control Number: 2015906133
ISBN: Hardcover   978-1-5035-6289-9
                   Softcover   978-1-5035-6290-5
                   eBook   978-1-5035-6291-2

Print information available on the last page.

Rev. date: 05/26/2015

To order additional copies of this book, contact:
Xlibris
1-888-795-4274
www.Xlibris.com
Orders@Xlibris.com
697805

CONTENTS

My Words ix

Prologue.. xi

Progression 1

Stepping 18

Recount 32

Finale 144

To

Beloved Sons and Daughter: *N*umayeer, *R*ahier, and *P*riya

MY WORDS

I AVOWED IN my maxim of the autobiography titled *Bends and Shades* that I am not a writer. *Bends and Shades* was my first publication. That induction of mine in the ingenuity of writing impelled me, unknowingly though, in taking a perky first step in the long ladder of writing. The outcome is *Indu*, my second publication. I am writing not to become a writer. I write for my own pleasure.

Indu is a fiction premised on very common and equally ethereal reflection of real-life situations in most local surroundings of Bangladesh and eastern part of India around late 1940s and mostly up to mid-1960s. The background relates to, revolves around, and fringes against the backdrop of prevalent political, social, religious, and economic paradigms: their complexities, their impact, and the real-life challenges and limitations in facing them.

The story relates to early growing-up interactions between two subjects of opposite gender hailing from different religious, social, and economic strata. Notwithstanding animosity caused by competing religions and much debated but unexpected partition of the geographical area (India) to constitute independent countries, the two early teens bonded emotionally. The comparative social standings, educational attainments, economic eminence, and major religious differences had no impact on that warm and evolving relationship. In that phase of emerging youth, such unambiguous feelings and mutual likings were too personal and overtly sincere to be affected by outward stances of the larger society.

Indu and Shetu, two growing up early- and mid-teens, used to have regular interactions with their innate warm feelings bonding intensely. Not surprisingly, and as it happens in most cases of nascent feelings unknown to growing-ups, that snug emotion had occasional hiccups too. Both such happy and agonizing experiences had an effect on Indu intuitively, while Shetu, though slowly harboring an enhanced liking for Indu as she was growing up, would just shrug most of them off outwardly. That relationship and contact sustained impetuous physical separation due to partition of India in 1947 and consequent migration of people. That included Indu too.

While remnants of those words and exchanges, and equally feelings and likings, continued to influence actions and decisions of the married life of Indu in the genial setting of her in-laws' house with a very frustrating conjugal life, Shetu, in the setting of the new country, quietly and unknowingly parked those in a subtle corner of his mind and moved on in life.

Some of those words and feelings of the growing-up phase, experiencing afflictions caused by partition of India in 1947, unpredictably resurfaced in both their lives at a much later phase through startling occurrences and involuntary thespian events, some of which were orchestrated by old friends of Shetu, and a filial understanding and support of the daughter promoting unequivocal confession by Indu.

The story recaps time-tested reality: growing-up experiences and emotional penchants are more deeply rooted in the minds and thoughts of any young girl, notwithstanding the passage of time. While such experiences always cause a serration in the mind of any young boy too, the related yearning often is submerged in the challenges of learning and life. But the same is never tarnished away. It may resurface even at a later phase of life if circumstances so warrant.

The story of Indu is a testimony of that reality with the exception that neither the earnest desire of her nor the desperate effort of Shetu could result in having a much desired reunion.

I am thankful to all those who earlier read my autobiography and conveyed kind words. That encouraged me in taking this nominal first step to write the second one. Supportive acts and encouraging words of my wife, Shaheen, motivated me in undertaking the second writing effort. Her patience in tolerating my shally dally with much required household chores, in the backdrop of living in North America, was particularly helpful.

Jahed Rahman

PROLOGUE

INDU, A VERY attractive preteen girl of a low-caste Hindu family, grew up in an underprivileged habitation commonly known as *Bera Bari*. That settlement was at the western periphery of Anandapur, a semiurban parish of Noakhali in Bangladesh. Bera Bari habitation generally was a settlement of *Palki* (traditional means of manually carried transport) bearers. Besides being low caste, the habitants of the settlement were facing insurmountable sociopolitical and economic challenges and hardships. Some of such problems emanated from the partition of India in 1947: noticeable migration of educated and well-off Hindu families from newly established country Pakistan to India after partition, rapid evaporation of faith-based traditional social safety nets, and unpredictable nature of emerging security concerns. That was aggravated due to rapidly dwindling income profile because of redundancy of Palki as a mode of transport.

Indu was the only child of a Bera Bari couple but had to struggle on a daily basis because of constraints her parents and neighbors were encountering. From early morning to early evening, the parameter of a day in a least developed setting, Indu, from her very early childhood, had to listen to and live with negative attributes historically grounded on primacy of social systems and prevalence of religious edicts, like relevance of ordained privilege structure (caste system embodied in and fundamental social setting of Hindu religion) and the *will of Bhogoban* (the Lord), respectively. The poverty syndrome of the family accentuated that. She, like most of her compatriots from similar background, had no social access to and relevance in a predominantly Muslim habitation.

Conversely, early teen son of the surrounding, Shetu, grew up there merrily as the offspring of a respectable and well-to-do Muslim family. Shetu's preoccupation at the early phase of life was his school, interactions with friends of neighborhood, and playing mischief with younger siblings. When alone or based on seasonal variations, he played at home with his indigenous toys and tools. That sort of life pattern with seasonal variations was the norm for most of the children of his time. Climate changes mostly encompassing the summer months of April–May, rainy months of June–August, and very cold winter months of December–February had their respective influence on the type and nature of related activities.

Early noontime of April–May is generally a very quiet time in Bangladesh because of hot and humid climate condition. Things slow down. Family elders even take naps following a relatively heavy late lunch. In one of such days, Shetu was engrossed with mock practice of various maneuvers pertaining to his play toy locally called *gulti*.

Gulti is a modest handy triangular wooden frame of the shape of letter *Y* with rubber belts (in some cases with flat elastic substitutes) of few inches flowing from both upper ends of the frame and tied to a leather base at the middle. The shape of the leather base is similar to the outer cover of a small avocado when cut into half lengthwise. Small stone is placed in the leather base, and the rubber belt is extended by pulling the leather base toward the body while holding the rear end of the frame with a solid grip by the other hand. As the pull is complete, the tensed rubber bands are softened quickly, and the stone is released to hit the marked target. That normally is a small bird or fruit, or similar items. Children of Shetu's age profile in early 1950s used to enjoy playing with gulti.

In the midst of such engagement, Shetu was astounded seeing a boy of his age slowly climbing the mango tree at the northwestern edge of their homestead. That particular tree was known for a very special type of mango, which just prior to being ripe used to have a mouthwatering and affable mixed taste of sweet and sour.

Shetu, instead of drawing attention of others, carefully approached the site by passing a number of other trees. Hiding behind a *korai* (rain) tree, Shetu noticed a very slim and fair girl of about nine years guiding the boy by sign language toward a particular mango she wanted to have. The boy was having difficulty in reaching the mango, as the stem was very thin. He decided to shake the stem vigorously to ensure an early disconnection. The boy's concentration was on that, as he wanted to get out of any embarrassing situation that might cause if any one of Shetu's household catches him in that sort of action. The girl's focus was manifestly on getting the desired mango soonest. She quietly jumped from time to time, throwing up hands in desperation occasionally. Soon the mango fell on the ground. The girl was very happy and took careful steps forward to pick it up with symbolic gesture toward the boy to get down. As she was about to pick up the mango, keeping her head down, and the boy was positioning himself for a quick descent with body and face toward the main torso of the tree, Shetu, following the girl from behind, caught her right wrist with the mango in her palm.

The girl instantaneously suffered a trauma with shame and embarrassment ubiquitous on her face. She just froze, did neither move nor make any physical effort to disengage, and always kept her eyes down, while the boy was in a silent static position with both hands in a circuitous position of the main trunk of the tree and his one leg anchored on a stable stem. Shetu did neither accuse the girl nor accost the boy. He just kept on holding the hand of the girl having the possession of the unauthorized mango. Shetu came out of that state of mind only when a drop of tear from the eye of the girl fell on his wrist. He quietly released the hand and walked away without even looking at the motionless boy still on the mango tree.

The girl and her accompanying boy disappeared soonest, escaping from the unthinkable ordeal they could have otherwise faced. Shetu, however, did not think much, but something in himself drew him to the spot after a while. He was taken aback seeing the mango near the position the girl was standing. He took hold of the mango and placed that in a safe place of the kitchen but did not mention the incident to anyone.

Shetu was almost finishing his afternoon meal on returning from school the following day, and both he and his mother were surprised to see a Hindu lady standing near the entry door of the kitchen. She greeted Shetu's mother by saying *"Nomoshkar"* (a common Hindu way of greeting with respect). Behind the lady clad in a handwoven mundane white saree with thin blue border and prominent *sindoor* (vermilion) on her forehead was the girl of yesterday standing with apologetic physical expression. As on the previous day, she was dressed in a frock (a knee-length cotton dress) but, as a change, was having two tightly made rather thick braids flowing by the two sides of her tender neck, serving the unintended purpose of frame for the very beautiful facial structure.

Shetu's mother recognized the lady as one from the nearby settlement even though there was no regular contact. She offered a *peera* (a rudimentary wooden seating tool with small support structure affixed underneath in the four corners). The lady accepted the peera with a sense of gratitude and placed that on one of the flat banisters of the kitchen steps. The girl was behind her holding one end of the *anchal* (tail end of the saree) of her mother, more symbolic of obedience and a sense of security. Shetu, after finishing his meal and washing his hand, positioned himself near the entry door of the kitchen, slightly bending toward the vertical wooden frame of the door.

The lady, addressing Shetu's mother as *Ma* (for mother), opened up by introducing the girl, saying, "She is Indu, my daughter. I have come to seek your forgiveness for something done by Indu yesterday at your place."

Shetu's mother was taken aback and said, "What happened? I am not aware of anything."

That took Indu's mother by surprise, and she reacted by saying, "*Dada Babu* (brother [meaning Shetu] with salutation, "Babu" conveying socially desired respect irrespective of age) did not tell you anything?" Indu's mother then detailed what happened yesterday pertaining to the mango and said, "We rebuked Indu for doing something very wrong and have come today to seek pardon. That is why I also brought her."

Shetu, all along, was looking at Indu while she occasionally looked at him with expression conveying both regret and plea for pardon but most of the time kept her eyes down. Shetu politely affirmed what Indu's mother narrated and said that the matter was so a trivial one that he did not think it meriting any other consideration. That was the reason why he did not tell that to anyone including his mother. More so, Indu even did not take the mango, which he later brought and kept in the kitchen. He brought the mango and gave to his mother.

Shetu's mother then lovingly called Indu in, hugged her softly, handed over the mango, and said, "If you want anything from our place in future, tell your *Didima* (grandma)," meaning herself. She further continued, saying, "You can come anytime to our place and play with our children. You should not feel shy about it."

That was a remarkable response that made Shetu happy and enabled Indu and her mother to be at ease, totally forgetting the predicament that initially shrouded their visit. It was of tremendous moral boosting for the very poor Hindu lady living in dominant Muslim society of a new country called Pakistan. Being a minority haunted by recent communal atrocities on both sides of the border of truncated mother India, the Hindus of Bangladesh (at that time East Pakistan), more particularly the poorer segment, were enduring a pressing psychological ordeal about their future. The leaderships of All India Congress took care of the interest and security of educated and wealthy segments of Hindu population of Bengal while dividing the province between new countries of Pakistan and India. Consequently, the Congress totally ignored and abandoned the poor, the unlettered, and the deprived section of the same population who were located in East Pakistan (Bangladesh). That was the setting of the time. That was the background for the sense of incredible relief that overwhelmed Indu's mother. She never expected that sort of understanding and response.

Indu's mother made a request before leaving. She said, "Ma, we are having real difficulty in accessing safe drinking water. If you permit, Indu will come every day to take *jol* (water) from your tube well (hand water pump), and to redress the ordeal, Indu would take a shortcut through your property in negotiating the site of the tube well." In her response, Shetu's mother not only consented but also explained that the tube well is meant for the community. Many families come to take water, and Indu too is welcome.

In the days following, it was routine for Indu to be at Shetu's place in the afternoon with a small *kolshi* (jar) and a *gamcha* (handwoven cotton scarf) on her tender shoulder. She would meticulously wash the kolshi in the adjacent big pond, place it under the extended nozzle-type feature of the hand water pump, and start pumping the water by pulling up and pushing down the long handle affixed by the side of the main iron-cast longer structure of the pump. When the jar is full, Indu would carefully remove it to a safe distance to ensure that the jar was not touched by anyone. She would then systematically roll her gamcha to form a steady base for placing the kolshi on her head in journey back home.

Within a few days, Shetu found out a strange coincidence. Indu meticulously comes to fetch water at a time when he returns from school. Shetu's cordiality with Indu gradually developed, centering the small talk in and around the location of the tube well. He always felt blissful and at ease with her, though had no idea at that age about any sensibility.

Going to Shetu's home daily to fetch jol was initially a repetitive assignation for Indu. With the passage of time, that, what was supposed to be a routine one, gradually took the silhouette of intent expectation in the inner mind of Indu. Notwithstanding deprivation all around and depressed setting of her life, Indu fondly looked forward to each late afternoon visit to Shetu's place and spent some time with him. That slowly made her so happy that she started easily sustaining daylong hardships and frustration with a smiling face. For an early teen girl, any specific sensuality, as normally could be ascribed to such feeling, was not germane.

Both Shetu and Indu used to be in their own world during that brief time they were together daily. They neither took note of nor were bothered by respective religious affiliation, which was the prime focus of political primacy and bone of contention in social priorities of the time. Likewise, quirkiness with other standard criterion of relationship such as financial status, social standing, professional and occupational uniformity, and level of learning did not hinge on their daily interactions. They were just happy and enjoyed being together. They did not have any expectation. Their daily interaction was not premised on inert specificity of any sort.

Shetu's yearning to meet Indu recurrently was premised on his simple fondness for her: not utterly because of her physical beauty, dazzling complexion, flowing long shaggy hair, and wide-open eyes with astounding ability to connect, but more pertinently for her amiable demeanor, politeness in communication, and serenity in listening. The last one was cherished by Shetu much, as he could unleash words of knowledge and wisdom, either learned or heard from elders, without any retort, and he enjoyed a sense of self-gratification.

That was not the case with Indu. Contrary to her family setting, upbringing, and educational attainment, she was startlingly blessed with a prying mind. From the early phase of growing up, Indu unwittingly mastered the art of enriching her knowledge and thoughts from the words and statements of others. Thus, she always enjoyed thought-stimulating avowals, which Shetu would invariably unchain whenever they were together. For her, and at that early teen age, Shetu epitomized all that she did not have in her very improvised social locale and intellect-oriented mind-set.

Though products of diverse conditions, the two—one in midteens and the other in early teens—intertwined contentedly against the backdrop of insurmountable adverse equations. They were totally oblivious of those and continued enjoying their daily meeting and discourse. The routine responsibility of Indu to fetch jol (water) from Shetu's habitat paved the process.

Shetu discovered Indu's susceptibility to certain acts based on prevalent religious injunctions and practices. For example, no Muslim was permitted to enter the kitchen or prayer room of a Hindu family irrespective of the level of caste of the latter. Likewise, any food or drink item to be taken by a Hindu used to be treated as unholy if touched by a Muslim.

One day, the tiny brother of Shetu innocently touched the filled water kolshi of Indu. She immediately emptied the kolshi, washed it afresh in the adjacent pond, and refilled the kolshi by pumping the tube well, saying occasionally, *"Ram, Ram"* (the revered name of Hindu Lord), and then walked away. Shetu got the clue. Whenever he wanted Indu to stay longer, Shetu would touch the filled water jar, and the process of her departure prolonged. Occasionally, this was repeated more than once. But interestingly, Indu never expressed any displeasure for that or made an issue out of this.

Shetu also observed that whenever she was at ease with herself or wanted to express discernible happiness, Indu will silently sing first two stanzas of then-popular Bangla (anglicized word "Bengali") song, *'Chande chande dulia nonday ami bono phoolgo'* (In rhythm I sway in a jubilant way of a wildflower in the woods). She used to do that for herself. Once asked, Indu said that this was what her mother used to sing every time Indu was taken to bed to sleep at night.

Seeing Indu near the tube well base on a particular afternoon, Shetu came to meet her but unpretentiously carried with him a book of poetry. On that day in the school, Shetu was told by the teacher that he would have to recite the first three stanzas of the poem "Bidrohie" ("The Rebel") written by Kazi Nazrul Islam, later on the national poet of Bangladesh. He was practicing the same to orient his diction according to the direction of his teacher so that while following rehearsing process and in reciting on the day of upcoming school event, he could perform well in front of others. As soon as he saw Indu, Shetu came to meet her, forgetting to leave behind the book.

Like all other days, both of them got engaged in discourse at a place near the tube well location. Unlike other days, the discussion of the day revolved around the book in Shetu's hand. In response to Indu's simple query about the book in hand, Shetu explained the background. The reaction of Indu took Shetu by surprise. Indu looked straight at Shetu's eyes and lamented that though she knows the alphabets well, she can't properly read, forget about recitation. Indu continued, saying, "I am from a very poor family. My parents can't afford education beyond *patshala* (informal early primary school). There is no evident priority for education in the family. Parents just await our growing up and then discharge their responsibility by marrying us out." The subsequent statement of Indu, stating that "partition and migration dimmed that possibility, a very intractable one for girls like me," was more intriguing.

Shetu was dumbfounded hearing about marriage-related concerns from a girl of Indu's age, more so against the backdrop of larger issues of partition and migration. Within his mind, Shetu consoled himself by relating the words of Indu as those possibly she overheard many a time when parents and family elders discuss the consequences of migration. He bypassed the issue of marriage and partition but proposed to help Indu in reading, in writing, and eventually in recitation. They agreed that Indu would come to Shetu's place every Friday (weekly school-off day) noontime, and Shetu would teach her. There was no need for Indu to buy books. The process was continued by using books of Shetu's younger siblings, and occasionally they used to take part. Shetu and Indu also started spending times together, sometimes in the company of Shetu's siblings, in playing games.

That teaching and learning endeavor could not be a structured one in that phase and placing of life of either, but it had its focus, regularity, and earnestness with fun part of relationship continuing unabated. One such day, Indu came in with little homemade tamarind pickle wrapped in a leaf. She was enjoying that, occasionally taking a bite and putting that in her mouth by the first finger of her right hand. On that day, it so appeared that Indu was more relishing the pickle than concentrating on the task she came for.

As Shetu would not like to hurt Indu, he thought of sharing the pickle to finish that quickly and then concentrate on doing what was to be done. So he asked for a part of it. Indu was taken aback, as she had the impression that boys generally do not like indigenous pickles, more so tamarind one. It is the domain of girls to like acerbic eatable items and spicy mixes of those. As an immediate reaction, she put in her mouth whatever she had on the leaf while some residue from a previous stub was still in her first finger. Before Indu could understand anything, Shetu grabbed her first finger, put that in his mouth, and started sucking it in order to finish the pickle episode.

Indu was taken aback. But she neither objected nor took any initiative to disentangle until Shetu voluntarily released her first finger. She was almost in a standstill position, something similar to the first time Shetu grabbed her hand with the sweet-and-sour mango in possession. All that she did was to look straight at Shetu's face with a quiescent internal feeling never experienced before. Outwardly, she was even oblivious of reactions of others if anyone steps in. Conversely, Shetu was very relaxed and happy to see that the pickle diversion is over, creating a more conducive setting to continue with the study matter. The lingering taste of tamarind pickle, as could be sucked from Indu's finger, made him happier nevertheless.

Some periods thereafter, another similar incident took place, which was not thought of by either of the two, even remotely. Keeping the first finger of his left hand below the main frame of the wooden pencil, Shetu was sharpening the same with a half broken shaving blade to help Indu in her pursuit of reading and writing. His balance tilted and slightly cut the first finger of the left hand, and consequently some blood oozed out. Seeing that, Indu impulsively took his left hand and put the finger in her mouth to take out the oozing blood and impetuously swallowed that. She then ran out, plucked some leaves of local *ganda* (marigold) flower plant, smashed those with a stone, and put that on Shetu's finger, bandaging the same by a tattered piece of cloth that was near Shetu's playthings. Indu's prompt actions made both of them happy, as the oozing of blood stopped.

During a holiday, Shetu showed up at Indu's home for the first time without any plan. Seeing him coming and his calling of "Indu" rather loudly, more to let her know about his presence as he was unaware of exactly which one of the many clustered houses belonged to Indu's family, elders came out momentarily, felt embarrassed, and retreated quickly. That was not because of Shetu's appearance but their lack of basic facility to welcome him. They were thus gazing at him from a distance.

Indu soon came out and welcomed him, saying what an event it was, as the son of a relatively well-off family came to her thatched home. She then asked Shetu to take seat on the most indigenous bench made of thin but longish frames of betel nut tree placed horizontally in front of but reasonably far away from their home.

Shetu, by this time, started feeling uncomfortable too, as some of the habitation elders by rotation were apparently glancing at him from sort of semihidden positions of various houses.

To ease any feeling of discomfiture on the part of Indu, Shetu volunteered to explain that returning from the nearby Catholic missionary school, he took the shortcut and was passing by the side of the enclave where Indu's family lives. His unplanned visit to Indu's home was the outcome of an impulsive decision and prompted by the idea to let Indu know that she, if she wants to, could come that day for study, as it was a school holiday. Shetu, in his inner self, was candidly clear that what he stated was not factual. He very much wanted to meet Indu and made up the story for the sake of social propriety. To give the story a semblance of authenticity, he soon stood up to leave the place.

Indu stopped him. Shetu's unexpected presence made Indu very happy, swayed by a feeling of innate joy beyond decorous description. She said that he just could not leave their house without having anything. She further clarified that first-time guests never go empty mouthed, *"Ate giroster omongol hoy"* (It is tantamount to bad omen for the family). She asked Shetu to wait and ran toward her home. Soon thereafter Indu returned with some *Tiler naru* (small round sweet made of sesame seeed popular among Hindu families) in a big leaf and offered the same to Shetu. The service in a leaf was either due to not having suitable service plate or because of his Muslim identity. Shetu was not at all concerned and leisurely started eating Tiler naru, finishing all before departing.

At its initial phase, Indu unexpectedly acquired noteworthy ability to read and write to the immense pleasure of Shetu. The progression was significant even though gradual. To his dismay, however, Shetu simultaneously observed recent palpable lack of commitment contrary to the early phase of her learning effort. Such visible lack of interest became pronounced with the passage of time, impairing expected level of sustained progression. That was evident too from the occasional gaps in attendance without excuse. The slide in commitment on the part of Indu was perhaps due to two factors: First, regular negative feedback from her family who always told Indu that for the family, being from the lowest caste and poor, education has not much significance in day-to-day life. Rather, she should concentrate acquiring early the art of doing household chores. Second was Indu's progression to early teens of her life with ever-increasing discussions of family focusing on finding a groom for her.

In such a setting contrary to earlier supportive endeavor, Shetu one day tried to reprove Indu but was taken aback equally by her response. In her rejoinder to what Shetu said about her evident lack of earnestness to learn reading and writing, Indu quite firmly said, "These are good and relevant for someone like you but of no practical value for a girl like me. I am a child from the lowest caste. No upper-class Hindu boy will marry me. I am from a very poor family. No well-to-do family will have matrimonial relationship with our family. For that matter, no Muslim boy like you will have relationship with me. People say I am a fair-looking, attractive girl. But that alone will not take me anywhere. Even getting married within my own setup is increasingly becoming difficult for a girl like me due to ongoing migration of Hindu population. So learning, reading, and writing have no practical relevance in my life. That is the reason for my gradual withdrawal. I just could not say these earlier. Your admonition of today opened up the opportunity for me."

Shetu had nothing to say or contest. He realized that what Indu just said was what she was being told by parents and elders in her family environment. He just maintained a solemn silence, looking at her with both the element of sadness and frustration. In his inner self, Shetu revisited all the reasons articulated by or imbedded in Indu's reasoning, and was convinced about the rationale of many of them. In that early phase of life, Shetu had no doubt that to attain something in life, one needs to have both the need and the desire. In the case of Indu, the need was not relevant, and the desire steadily evaporated due to continuous repetition of the same logic by family elders. He also realized that children of depressed setting have tremendous acumen in accepting reality. He thus kept quiet. Indu, after her robust defense, was too sitting in a corner of the *choki* (informal bed) and sometime thereafter quietly left.

Interactions between the two slowly slithered without noticeable emotional backlash. Indu kept on coming for her routine task of filling up the kolshi and carrying that home. She started spending more time talking to Shetu's mother. Shetu, overcoming the earlier frustration with the passage of time, occasionally had friendly discourse with her, more about social niceties, but did not refrain from playing mischief by touching her kolshi. This sort of behavior pattern patently had the element of inner desire encompassing likes and pleasures about which the outward self of Shetu was totally oblivious at that age.

An elderly lady from Indu's home started coming to fetch the needed drinking water. Shetu came to know from his mother that Indu, though not ailing, was not keeping well, and the elderly lady came as a temporary replacement. Shetu shrugged off that information and was preoccupied with his school, study, and games.

Indu showed up after about five days attired in a beautiful red saree with a kolshi (jar) bigger than the earlier one. She nicely wrapped the saree around her body with anchal tugged in the waist and had her long unfastened flowing straight hair gracing the entire back side of her body. The lower end of her saree was a few inches above ankle, something different than the way saree was being entwined by other ladies. The other noticeable thing was that Indu was not carrying the gamcha to make a base for carrying the kolshi on her head. She was evidently very happy. Her blissful conduct and related body language struck Shetu very much.

Shetu encountered Indu near the tube well location while she was filling up that big kolshi and said, "Look, I have not seen you so happy in the recent past. What happened? Why are you so happy? Is there any marriage proposal for you?"

Indu, with all exhilaration in her facial and body expressions, said, "Something happened to me. As a boy, you would not understand. I even can't tell you. Didima knows about it. Whatever that may be, it made every one of our poor family very happy. My father bought this saree especially for me. I was very lovingly given a shower today by my mother and elders of the kinfolk. They cleaned every part of my body and washed my hair with a new soap. Then I was treated with an amazing lunch made of very thin white rice (first time in my life), fish curry, and vegetable *shukto* (a bitter vegetable preparation of Hindu Bengalis coveted for healthy properties). In addition, my *Jethima* (wife of father's elder brother) made three different types of *dal* (lentils). Our neighbor *kakima* (wife of community uncle) brought very tasty *chutney* (pickle). I ate so much that I can't explain to you. I was so full that I went for a nap to the delight of my elders."

Indu finished that long statement literally in one breath and looked at Shetu with amusement. He could not make any sense out of that, as he ordinarily experienced all those good food items as part of ongoing life.

In preparation for departure, Indu lifted the kolshi and placed that on the right side of her waist with her right arm around the neck of the kolshi for keeping that steady. As a departing comment, she said, "I have now grown up and would carry kolshi this way. I do not need gamcha anymore. I will not wear frock too."

Shetu was taken aback. He started wondering as to what happened to her. The only visible change he noticed is the transition from frock to saree. But that can't be a matter of such jubilation. He forgot about all these once he was in the playground.

But Indu did not. Meeting Shetu after her first period was a beguiling encounter. Ignoring the call of her mother, Indu was mesmerized by a feeling of getting lost and started moving around the premise of their ramshackle house. She casually touched the foliage around, reclined against the bending coconut tree, and unknowingly talked to Shetu while caressing the family cow knotted nearby.

Indu impulsively developed a passionate feeling pertaining to previous physical contacts with Shetu. That was neither harbored nor intended. It never happened before. That reactive sweet feeling was unhesitatingly an impetuous one resulting in insuperable happiness in the mind and thought of Indu. She recalled one by one all the three previous such contacts: the holding of her right hand by Shetu in the shadow of the mango tree; sudden but prolonged sucking of the first finger of her right hand by Shetu to finish the residue of tamarind pickle; and her bewildering but equally forceful suction of the first finger of Shetu's left hand to control bleeding. She returned to the inside of their home and slowly positioned her fatigued self in a state of uninitiated posture to relax.

Life of these two teenagers with different mind-sets progressed in the local setting of Anandapur without much to notice. Indu continued her sojourns for drinking water but ostensibly spent more time with Shetu's mother. Her ever-vigilant eyes used to move frequently looking outside to have a glance of Shetu or hear his footsteps. Whenever they met or crossed each other, Indu would focus her eyes on Shetu as if those eyes wanted to convey the most treasured feeling that an early, and equally socially deprived, teen girl could cherish.

Shetu had no idea about the inner feelings of Indu and gaily preoccupied him with other activities after occasionally sparing a few words. The latter definitely was not the preferred position of Shetu. Interactions with Indu were preferable but not necessarily a compulsive desire. He himself was confused about his priorities in the midst of multiple desires of emerging youth. The related attitude was not of thinking about choices but of availing those without focus. In his inner mind, Shetu always wanted proximity with Indu, but his growing-up ego and current frustration because of her lack of commitment to much desired reading and writing would preclude its outward acknowledgement.

Shetu sporadically continued to touch the kolshi and enjoyed occasional side comments during the process of refilling by Indu. There was, however, a marked variation in this mischief playing, as, unlike past time, Shetu would not always wait to witness and enjoy her reaction. Indu remained calm and quiet, and was happy that he occasionally does so even now. She used to look for that, as it provided the rare proximity with him.

It was Shetu's fourteenth birthday evening. Though it was unusual to celebrate birthdays, Shetu's mother prepared *pitahs* (homemade rice powder cakes). Indu was told earlier about the birthday. She brought some *narikel er shondesh* (sweet made of coconut). She came twice to say "*Shuvo Jonmodin*" (Happy Birthday), but he did not look at her. Shetu was preoccupied in making an indigenous kite for his younger brother. Disappointed, she left on both occasions with temporary sadness immersed on her face.

Shetu was preparing to go to the games and did not respond to the repeated calls of his mother to eat pitahs. He was mostly busy combing his hair recurrently, sometimes sidewise or trying to back brush like some youths of the locality. Shetu was visibly spending more than usual time before the hanging mirror, pretending his preoccupation while continuously scouting the surrounding around the kitchen.

Suddenly he noticed that his upper lips had some hair growth. He was both surprised and excited. He also recalled noticing some hair growth under his armpit a few days back. Shetu concluded that these are possibly some signs of his growing up in tandem with changes in some physiological response indicators. He wanted to be sure, but prevailing social dictum precluded discussing the same with anyone.

In the midst of such thinking, he saw Indu stepping in with a tray containing some pitahs made by his mother on the occasion of his birthday and some shondesh she lovingly brought from home. Indu put the tray on the table and said, "Didima asked you to eat prior to leaving." Shetu could not conceal his earlier excitement. He told Indu about the growth of hair in his upper lips and drew her attention. She retorted, saying, "So what! Should I dance?" and then left the room in a rage.

That was an unprompted reaction of Indu without any malice due to earlier perceptible apathy shown by Shetu to many of her friendly overtures. She was observing a marked flout in their recent contacts since they had the cantankerous discussions on matters related to studies. Even then, she mostly tried to ignore the same with the objective of not hurting his feelings in any way and to nurture their present affiliation. Indu reconciled with the discernible slide in their current exchanges and gracefully acquiesced with that, exhibiting most startling balance between expectation and reality. But repeated and visible earlier indifferences shown by Shetu ignoring Indu's presence twice before on the happy occasion of his birthday was too much for the caring, and definitely esoteric loving feelings of a teenager.

Shetu's reaction to that somewhat ignominious remark of Indu was of momentary disenchantment. He did not think much about that either. Shetu consoled himself and parked his dismay with the thought that what else he could expect from one like Indu considering her background and educational attainment. He conveniently forgot his own immediate reaction of flaunt evidenced by throwing off the comb to the side of his bed and marching out too. He did not touch anything that Indu brought earlier.

Those were retracted by Indu later on. Seeing those, Shetu's mother said, "Don't worry. When he comes back, he will eat, as he would be hungry at that time. When he is upset with me, he also does the same thing."

On his part and for reasons ambiguous, Shetu could not concentrate in the games that evening. More than his signs of growing up, he was preoccupied thinking what Indu meant when she said a few days back—"I have grown up." He tried to relate his own growing-up feelings to those earlier words of Indu. Was that the reason she started feeling a new sense of identity? Was that the reason she has been spending increasing time with Mother? He did not have answers to those.

Indu returned home with a sad face. She did not respond to any query of her mother. Indu just spent the time with herself, bearing the burden of ever-agonizing thoughts within. She blamed herself for reacting like that when Shetu excitedly told her about the manifestation of some physical changes in him. She also felt bad, as due to her behavior, Shetu left for the field without taking food his mother prepared and she brought in on the occasion of his birthday. She did not sleep that night and cried most of the time in silence lest her mother was aware of her emotional upshot. Occasionally she fought with herself with distinct effort not to cry but could not check tears rolling from her eyes. She nevertheless decided not to visit Shetu for a few days and slowly went back to her normal life except fetching drinking water. She, to the delight of her mother, devoted more time in helping her in household errands.

The family received a letter from Tripura state of India where Indu's Mama (maternal uncle Ominesh) migrated soon after partition.

Tripura, especially South Tripura bordering Noakhali, was sparsely populated at that time. The land was relatively cheap and available with farming practices more similar to Noakhali. The additional advantage was that Bangla (anglicized word "Bengali") is also the native language of Tripura. Ominesh Mama bought a homestead in a habitation known as Patiya Nagar and focused on establishing a retail business. He simultaneously concentrated in being a part of the surroundings by increasingly getting involved in community matters. Ominesh Mama's focused priority was not to have any blemish in family's resettlement process in his new country due to historic relocation from East Pakistan (now Bangladesh) soon after partition. That much Indu knew about him.

Indu's family and neighbors rarely received letters. When one was received, that was treated with all somberness and seriousness. They needed someone who could not only read but also relate the contents in the context one is written. They thought that it would probably be matters concerning migration. Thus, they needed a trustworthy person too.

A cousin of Indu's mother, Rattan, was called in. All family elders, including ladies, sat around him. Rattan started reading the letter loudly and then, to the surprise of all present, initially lowered his voice to be followed by total silence. After finishing reading the letter, he said it contains a serious matter and that it needs to be kept totally secret. His apprehension was that if the full settlement knows about that, then one could possibly play foul with the information. He then, in a very low voice, told those present, "Dada has a very good marriage proposal for Indu. That family, of the caste similar to us, migrated from Lakshmipur of Noakhali and established a successful grocery store in a small town called Santirbazar. They live further south in an area known as Shukhipur and has a son of about twenty, Kiran by name. The boy is a good one but not family or business oriented. He presently spends most of his time with friends in and around Santirbazar. Thus, the family is looking for a beautiful bride so that his attention can be diverted to home and business."

He took a pause, surveyed the facial expressions of all present, and commented, "I understand the inner thinking all of you are having. I had the same feelings when I read the letter up to this point. But there is further good news in the latter half of the letter." Rattan started rereading the second half of the letter in a low voice still and said, "Dada also wrote, 'We, the immigrant families, have close relations among us. We are almost like brothers to each other. So is the case with Dhireen, father of the boy. Not only that we are from same district, but also he is really a genuine person with golden disposition. Dhireen *Babu* (salutation with respect) enjoys the esteem and trust of the Santirbazar business community. He occasionally discussed with me his earnest desire to get his son married soon.

In one of such follow on discussions, I told him that I have a very beautiful and attractive niece on the other side of the border, but they are financially not well-off. By the time I said so, Dhireen Babu held my right hand with his two hands and said, "If she is your niece and beautiful, I do not need anything else. Who cares about the family's financial status in East Pakistan? My social identity here will be that my son got married with your beautiful niece." He gave me the word specifically mentioning that they do not have any demand.'

Rattan continued reading, as slowly as he could, the remaining part of the letter: "I wanted to give time to Dhireen Babu to think through in consultation with family, and said once he is certain, we will talk about it further. A few days later, Dhireen Babu, accompanied by his younger cousin and eldest brother-in-law, came with the formal proposal to convey full consent of the family, reconfirming all earlier stipulations. I accepted the proposal, and prospect of our relationship was sealed. Everything now depends on your consent and early arrival."

The last part of the letter addresses the most worrying element of the proposition: "I am conscious of the short notice and the predicament it would cause due to that. I have three sons and no daughter. I still remember the sweet and loving face of dear little Indu who at that age even resembled our mother. I will do everything within my means to ensure a good wedding as if it is my own daughter's one. I assure you that I will try to do everything possible so that dear Indu can always keep her head high in the new family. I have a hidden agenda: By doing this, I will possibly be able to pay a part of the enormous debt I owe to Mother for all her love, care, and support in my early life."

Those present were astounded by the tone and content of the letter. Indu's mother started crying, thanking her brother and adding that "finally *Bhogoban* (god) has mercy on us converting our core worry to most happy event-to-be of our life with unexpected facilitation from Dada." All present agreed with her.

A moment of silence permeated the setting with most male elders looking down and female elders gazing at each other. Rattan broke the silence. Emphasizing that the contents of Dada's letter should not be taken lightly and a prompt response would be needed, Rattan suggested that all present meet at the same place after two days around late afternoon, and they could have further discussions on way forward. He further elaborated, "The response is the simplest thing, which ought to be in the affirmative having faith in Bhogoban and trust in Dada's judgment. For that we do not need another meeting." What he had in mind were matters pertaining to preparation for going and other obligations, despite Dada's helping hand, concerning the marriage. To lighten up the somber setting, he said, "Didi, when we meet next time, we all present will have dinner at your place. Since we will not be in the wedding of dear Indu, we will take that as a substitute before we formally bless her." On hearing that, a fickle smile flashed out from otherwise serious faces present, and that was agreed to. Before departing, Rattan reemphasized the need to ensure total confidentiality of the matter.

Indu was sitting under a coconut tree, all throughout maintaining a respectable distance from the gathering of the seniors. Local traditions preclude her presence in such a gathering unless otherwise desired. Seemingly, she was mending a worn-out *katha* (traditional substitute of quilt made of layers of used saree). But she put her full attention and commissioned all her alertness to pick up a few words at least, if not the whole of it. But to her dismay, she could not pick up a thread of what the gathering was immersed with in a very low voice. Indu was certain that there could only be two issues that warrant her mother's presence in such discussions. It is either migration or her marriage. She rebuked herself for suffering unnecessary stress, as she has no say on either issue.

Indu's mother was looking for time and space to talk to Indu and convey the good news, but she was avoiding Mother. The more Mother wanted to be close, the farther Indu moved away. Surprisingly, Mother did not lose temper even if gestures of Indu in maintaining distance were very clear.

Indu crossed her father while going to the kitchen from the main home. He looked at her with all the happiness he could muster and greeted her with a very loving smile. Indu could not recall when her father bestowed such a smile last, as meetings and conversations between the two were limited. He was always preoccupied with sustaining the family with dwindling income as *palki* (traditional means of transport and his source of livelihood) soon got outdated as mode of transport; the ongoing migration issue; and the persistent worry about Indu's wedding. Observing her father, Indu was certain that the previous discussion of elders pertained to her marriage. Indu was least interested to know about it.

At bedtime, Mother came to sleep by the side of Indu, a practice repeated many times in the past. After lying in straight position for some time, her mother turned to her left and started caressing Indu's hair, gently asking, "Are you asleep?" Indu answered in the negative. The mother got the opportunity and detailed the full text of the letter received that day while continuously shuffling her fingers around Indu's hair with all the love and blessings she could bestow.

The mother's last indication cautioning Indu not to let anyone know this at that time including neighbors, and especially Shetu's family, bothered her very much. She understood the reason for not discussing with neighbors but could not understand why it could not be told to Shetu's family, particularly Didima who loves her so much.

The agonizing thought that pervaded Indu's mind pertained to when and how to let Shetu know about this. Indu was clear in her conclusion that not doing that at proper time will reflect badly on her. She argued with herself that it would be a breach of trust and tantamount to bad faith considering the solid mutual understanding, trust, and feeling that permeated their relationship of about the last four years. The decision of elders about confidentiality continued to trouble her. In her mind, she was suffering excruciating pain. She finally decided to let Shetu know about the marriage proposal, simultaneously asking him to keep it within himself.

After taking that final and absolute decision, Indu felt relaxed but still could not sleep. The mother, lying by her side, after relieving herself by off-loading full information mentioned in the letter, was in deep sleep, occasionally snoring rather loudly. That caused annoyance to Indu. She could not do anything or call Mother to stop that, as she was perhaps having a dream of her daughter's future life in a relatively affluent family.

Indu was just tossing in the bed, trying out alternative sleeping positions, neither of which could facilitate her falling asleep. Her hyperactive thinking about her future life was dominated by many unknown and uncertain inquisitiveness: permanent separation from Anandapur; irreversible relocation to another country; unknown surrounding of Shukhipur; scantiness of information about the family setting; and other immediate matters pertaining to the physical features of the groom-to-be, his liking and disliking, and so on.

Suddenly, Shetu issue reemerged in her thought. Her anxiety refocused to Shetu's possible reaction on hearing the news if she divulges that now. What happens if he reacts almost the same way she reacted when Shetu was telling her about some hair growth in his upper lip on his birthday—"So what! Should I dance?"

Any such or similar comment would hurt her with unimaginable as well as impetuous consequences. That would be a frustration and burden that might affect the core foundation of carefully nurtured loving emotions, which unknowingly got ingrained in her mind and thought without preconditions and expectations so far. Any spiteful comment might haunt her throughout life. Even though there were some fleeting strains in their relationship of late, more due to reasoning of elders based on real-life precincts and her follow-on actions, each such happening, after some lapse of time, strengthened the very base element of feelings, at least on her side. She would anchor that in the inner corner of her heart, nevertheless trying to fulfill all obligations of future life. That was the promise she made to herself, representing a contract between her mind and heart. She decided that it would be best not to tell Shetu directly anything about the marriage proposal at that point in time.

In the midst of all these, the proposed marriage involving migration to another country continued to pester her. She was distraught with the thought that immigration to India would permanently close any opportunity of knowing anything about Anandapur, and more particularly about Shetu, and there would be no way to redress that ever.

The other contract she made with herself was to make her parents happy unconditionally. She also decided not to let others know about her real feelings. No one should have any inkling about the sacrifice she is going to make in this regard. Her resolve was strengthened further when she recalled the last few words of Mother before she fell asleep. Mother said, "Ma, since birth, I have had seen only the ugly face of extreme poverty. None of my hopes and desires was materialized except having in you the most beautiful baby. The second time I found meaning in life was when I came to know the contents of today's letter. I am sure similar is the feeling of your baba (father) who always suffered due to his inability to provide even the basic necessities. When he bought that red saree on your having the first period, he was so happy as if he had conquered the world." Her mother slightly raised her head from the pillow, put hands around the stiff body of Indu, and quietly said, "Please, please do not act or say anything that can blemish our happiness."

Sensing Mother's teardrops on her bare back, Indu suddenly loosened her body, relaxed her system, paused for a few minutes, held her mother's right hand, and resolutely told her, "You have my word whatever pain it causes to me."

It was past midnight. Indu continued to struggle within herself, occasionally cursing for having a life with conceivable all-negative attributes but a mind full of emotions. She considered various familiar options including leaving the house or committing suicide. She thought of traditional ways to commit suicide. Absence of a nearby big pond to drown herself quietly was considered an irrelevant option. There was no possibility of hanging herself from the trunk of a big tree, as she did not know how to climb a tree. But what preponderantly influenced her thinking was that none of the options would lead her to have what her emotions and feelings pine for. Moreover, any such action would be contrary to silent contracts she made with herself, and absolutely contrary to the solemn assurance given to Mother earlier. So Indu permanently disassociated herself from that sort of thinking.

Indu always hoped that she would have occasional chances to meet Shetu and know about him even after her marriage, somewhere in the vicinity. But the present proposition is contrary to that. Once in Shukhipur, she will never see or know anything about Shetu and his life. That continued to trouble her very much.

JAHED RAHMAN

The surrounding around Indu's house appeared to be unusually calm that night. It was partly due to the fact that Indu never kept awake so long and had not much idea about midnight tranquility. She could hear periodically the sound emanating from movement of two cows tied together a little distance from the main house. The other little sound she could recognize was the movement of leaves of coconut and tamarind trees in the backyard of the house.

The mild breeze of that night, penetrating through the numerous minute holes of bamboo strap boundary frame of their thatched house, created much helpful conditions for Indu to fall asleep in due course. Mother Nature prevailed in helping to park her worries for that night.

Indu's mother got up from bed early the following morning and quietly left to take a bath in the nearby pond. After taking a bath, she wrapped herself in a relatively clean saree, plucked some ganda flowers, and went straight to *puja* (Hindu prayer) place within the house. She filled up the longish nickel-made container with new dhoop chips (processed aromatic herbal dust with long-lasting combustion, which, when lit, emits thick harmless smoke and is considered to be an essential element of Hindu puja) and lit it up. As the burning chips started emitting the smoke, she carried the container from one corner of the house to the other, spreading the smoke to get rid of possible evil energy. Indu's mother then placed the plucked ganda flowers at the base of effigies of gods and sat before them with a sense of absolute submission and prayed earnestly for everything good to happen in Indu's future life. She then got preoccupied with small preparatory chores for the big feast one day after. But she did not, unlike other days, call Indu to get up.

Indu woke up relatively late, came out, and greeted her mother with a half smile from the midpoint of their small *uttan* (similar to traditional quad between main home and kitchen). She also exchanged glances with her father, who just returned with some fresh vegetables from the market, and was sharing information about prevalent prices compared to earlier periods. Indu came near the entrance of the kitchen and stopped momentarily, looking at the contented faces of both. Once inside the kitchen, she observed that her father was continuously, contrary to what he was noted for, rambling on disjointed matters. In between, he said very coherently that he opted not to buy fish that day for reason of being short of money due to the high price of vegetables. But more importantly, he thought buying on the following day would make the curry more tasty because of the freshness of the fish.

Indu quietly sat by the side of Mother and tried to extend a helping hand in sorting out the vegetables. But her mother's immediate reaction was totally contrary to what Indu was used to. The mother very lovingly said, "Oh no, there is no need for you to work. I can handle it myself. You better freshen up yourself, take some *proshad* (puja offering), and eat some *muri* (puffed rice). You should take rest until your wedding."

Indu's father got up to leave, took steps outside, and then turned back to say, "From today on, Indu would not go to fetch water from Shetu's place. You better request Rolita's ma (mother of Rolita) to help us with some excuses." After saying this, he hurriedly left the place without even looking at either his wife or his daughter. It appeared to be a deliberate act, precluding any further discussion on the issue. The mother kept quiet, looked at the astounded face of Indu, and concentrated on slicing the vegetables.

The gentries of two days back assembled one by one around the appointed time and started discussing the future moves. Mother also participated while Indu was given the responsibility to oversee the cooking of rice.

In the initial phase of discussions, a conclusive understanding was reached concerning agreement with the proposition and moving fast. Indu's father stated that "notwithstanding the assurance of Dada, we need some cash with us, and time is too short for me to arrange that. I am planning to sell some trees at my backyard including a parcel of land. Hence, some time is needed." Indu's mother silently expressed disagreement by moving her head.

Cousin Rattan noted that and, after a careful scouting of various faces, observed, "Indu is not only your daughter. She is our daughter too. We will pull whatever we can to facilitate immediate departure. You can pay us back later on. But if you go to market for selling a parcel of land with some trees, you will not get any price, forget about the time element. The price of remaining property will also be affected. It would send a wrong signal premised on our possible migration. Let us wait for the right time and right price. There is a

JAHED RAHMAN

demand for land in this vicinity. It will be better for all to sell the entire enclave at a time when we get potential and equally influential buyers." Everybody agreed.

Rattan continued that he would write a letter that night to Dada in South Tripura indicating total agreement, conveying unconditional gratefulness, and advising the arrival of the family around noontime of Friday to the following Friday. He further said that he checked the timing of the connecting trains, and if the family leaves by early morning train, then they will be at Belonia border crossing about late noontime. He also said that as an abundant precaution, he would make a copy of that letter and would repost that on the following day to ensure receipt.

Indu's mother was mostly a silent participant except shaking her head when her husband was asking for time to arrange fund. The following discussions and indications overwhelmed her. It reaffirmed the very common social saying that "he who has less can share much than he who has more."

She never expected that close relations and well-wishers would demonstrate such magnanimity at the time of their pressing need. Tears started rolling down the cheeks of Indu's mother even with repeated efforts to wipe that with the tail end of her anchal.

Observing that, Rattan said, "*Didi* (sister), we have not gathered here to see you crying. You would have plenty of time when Indu leaves for her in-law's place. Now, we are all hungry. Have you forgotten that we are here to have food too?"

Indu's mother was slightly embarrassed and hurried toward the kitchen. Rattan called her back and requested, "Please send Indu to us soon."

Indu took slow small steps, keeping her face down, and positioned herself behind Father. Rattan said, "None of us would be present on the happy occasion of your life. We would not have the chance to see you in your wedding dress. Thus, I have bought a red saree with turquoise and golden imprints on behalf of all of us. Please wear this and then serve food to us."

She went inside, put on the new saree, and came to the kitchen to show Mother. Without noticing the mother's reaction, Indu rather took an arcane look at the large and round brass plates, each of which had rice in the middle, different items of vegetables around, having as well a small bowl filled with liquid *dal* (lintel). Those were arranged by Mother with all her love and happiness just before Indu's arrival. Mother asked her to take them carefully to the main room of the house. Indu nicely placed them on a big *pattie* (local spread for sleeping and seating) and respectfully called the elders to come in.

As everyone sat on the pattie spread out on the clay floor with plate in front, Indu started serving big pieces of *ruie* (similar to carp) curry to each of them from a common container. She was certain that there was never a fish of that size in their house as far as she could recall. Everybody relished the food. After the meal was over, the elders present thanked Indu for serving them well. They also congratulated and blessed her, placing their hands individually on Indu's head to the delight and happiness of her parents. Within herself, she was experiencing severe frustration and pain due to permanent separation from her home and surrounding. The certainty of imminent severance of contact with Shetu had always been tormenting her. Each talk and each progression taking the destiny to its ultimate was more agonizing for her, as she was not allowed even to tell Shetu about leaving Anandapur permanently.

Within the days stipulated, time was the only thing in short supply. It suddenly dawned on each of them that there were so many things to be taken care of in such a short time. Among many, Indu was always thinking of the appropriate time and way to talk to Shetu. She passionately discussed that with her mother too in the backdrop of instruction of Father. Mother reluctantly gave her permission but only a day before the departure.

In the afternoon of the day before, Indu put on the new saree received as gift, applied *kajal* (something indigenous but akin to mascara) to her eyes, combed her hair nicely with a loose *koppa* (informal hair updo), and went to Shetu's place at a time when the latter is likely to be back from school. That was the first time she went without her usual kolshi.

As she was approaching the kitchen, Shetu stepped out after finishing his afternoon meal on return from school. They crossed each other. Shetu stopped momentarily and asked her, "How are you?"

In a very low and soft voice with the sense of guilt for not visiting them for quite some time, Indu responded, saying, "I am OK. How are you?"

Shetu quickly replied, "I am carrying on," and then left the place.

While in his room, Shetu started thinking about sudden and noticeable changes in the look and body demeanor of Indu. He positioned himself near the window overlooking the kitchen entrance door and noticed Indu sitting near the main opening, being engrossed with his mother in talking. Indu kept her eyes down mostly with occasional straight glances at Didima while helping her in cleaning and slicing usual vegetable items for cooking. Shetu kept on looking at her. He was amazed to note how Indu changed so vividly within a short span of time. She was looking ever beautiful in her new saree and kajal makeup of eyes. Shetu kept on standing there, slightly hiding himself but looking at Indu. He unknowingly touched a number of times the hair growth in his upper lip with a sense of growing up too.

The feeling that he had for Indu's company was abruptly changing to liking but nothing near to a relationship. That was partly due to not seeing her for quite a while and a recent slide in communication. The other part undeniably had root in his growing-up phase. Shetu was always aware of related impediments and never harbored any desire for a future relationship. But at that point in time, it was difficult for him to take away his eyes from Indu.

In spite of wearing a new saree and putting on kajal, more symbolic of happiness, Indu that afternoon was somewhat sad and unmindful in social exchanges with Shetu's mother, her very dear Didima. Both of them all along had very friendly and open grandma-and-granddaughter relationship. Didima directly asked her about the reason of her long absence and what she was undergoing. Indu, keeping her head down, slowly told her everything including the reason she could not come earlier.

Didima took her time in absorbing the news and related implications. She looked at Indu intensely and said, "Hearty congratulations. You are a wonderful young lady. This is to happen today or tomorrow. While I can understand your agony, you have all my blessings. I wish you a happy and wonderful life." To create a desired level of geniality, she, in a lighter mood, continued, "Do not forget your Didima in the warm embrace of your husband. Do not cry on your wedding day. Whenever that mango tree will bear fruit in future, I will remember you specifically and give at least one mango to someone as if you were having that." Indu looked at her Didima and reciprocated with a half smile.

Didima then touched base with the issue of confidentiality her parents and family elders wanted so much. She said, "I fully understand the premise of keeping the information confidential. I will only tell the family after you leave Anandapur: first by saying that you went to Mama's (maternal uncle's) place in India, as there is a marriage proposal for you. After a few days, I will inform them about your wedding."

As Indu was handing over some sliced vegetables to Didima, she looked at the main house, noticing Shetu looking at her with discernible passion and sadness. They glanced at each other for a few moments, though Shetu was slightly hiding himself.

Indu kept quiet for some time and then said, "Didima, I at least want to tell Shetu that I am going to visit my mama. I want to be honest to that extent respecting our friendship of the last many years."

Didima said, "You go and tell him but do not cross the boundary."

She literally ran to the main house, met Shetu's younger siblings, but did not find him anywhere. She looked around and, being dismayed, returned to kitchen. She stayed for a little longer and had very few words with her dear Didima. After some time, Indu touched the feet of Shetu's mother and took permanent leave from her, wiping tears by the anchal of her saree.

Indu was on her way home and was about to cross the property boundary of Shetu's family at its northwest edge. She suddenly turned back and silently went to the tube well base. Indu stood there for some time, nonchalantly pumped the tube well handle, looked around, and heedlessly resumed her journey back. She again stopped below that particular mango tree where she had her first physical contact with Shetu. She peeped around and took a final look at Shetu's home and started for her home against the setting of the waning sun.

Upon return, she went to each tree of her homestead with which she grew up, touched each one of them, went to the cows, gently caressing them, and then retired inside. Indu did not talk to anyone that night.

On the following day, the family of three, as earlier decided, quietly boarded the morning train on the way to Belonia via railway junctions of Laksham and Feni. None of the close relations and family elders were present to keep the departure a low-key one. Though the ultimate destination for Indu was Shukhipur, the place they were heading presently was Patiya Nagar, southwest of Santirbazar, and the home of Ominesh Mama (uncle). It is relatively close to Belonia border of East Pakistan and Tripura.

As the train started moving, Indu's father was much relieved for having a quiet departure as planned. Crossing the border was a nonissue at that time, as there was no visa requirement. His other worries were concerning unfamiliarity with the setting of his daughter's wedding. In his mind, he prayed to his *Bhogoban* (god) by raising two hands and holding two palms together, touching his forehead with all devotion.

Indu's mother was very happy thinking about a comfortable life her daughter was going to have. Though she had not much information about the groom-to-be and other family members, she found consolation in knowing from the letter of her *Dada* (elder brother) that Dhireen Babu is a nice person. This and that the family is financially well-off were sufficient enough to park safely all other worries that normally bother a mother's mind at the time of the wedding of any daughter.

Indu, dressed in a very ordinary saree not to attract attention of others at the railway station, rested her head against the tail end of the compartment and closed her eyes. Seemingly that was her way to minimize the pain of leaving her own place. Inside, it was a desperate attempt to control all her emotions. To Indu, each vibrating sound of rolling stock was echoing the pain that was pumping her heart. She had no coherent thought within herself. She was in a state of daze.

Shetu, as usual, returned from school and was finishing his afternoon meal. His mother, exercising due diligence, slowly told him about Indu's sudden departure for Patiya Nagar of South Tripura to visit her mama, Ominesh, who has a marriage proposal for her. The groom's family was from a habitation, also of South Tripura, known as Shukhipur. She also advised that Indu went to tell him the same yesterday but could not, as by that time he left home for games. Shetu had a cold look at his mother, left the kitchen, and retired to his room. He then inadvertently went to the sites of the specific mango tree and tube well and, unknowingly, repeated what Indu did the previous late afternoon. He did not go to play that afternoon.

The mutual feelings of the two teens suffered in their respective ways: Indu had intense feelings with the thought of permanent separation; Shetu's was poignantly premised because of the possible loss of someone for whom he was gradually developing an immense liking. One was leaving her birthplace Anandapur (place of merriment) for permanent living in Shukhipur (place of happiness). For the other, Anandapur became, for a time, a place of *bishad* (sorrow).

PROGRESSION

INDU'S PARENTS RETURNED to Anandapur after her wedding. Soon her mother visited Shetu's home and happily detailed everything related to the marriage. She did not fail to describe each and every event including what her Dada and three nephews did to make that small wedding a memorable one. At that stage, she started sobbing, saying, "Ma, all these happened because of blessings of you all. We could never think of such a marriage. Her in-laws brought very nice and likeable gifts for our Indu. She was looking very beautiful in her wedding dress, and more when she, with her groom, was completing *shat pake badha* (performing the religious ritual of completing seven circles around the fire as a sign of permanent bonding). Our *konna-dan* (handing over the girl to the care of the groom) event was likewise a very happy one. That was performed by my Dada." She did not mention anything about Indu except that before leaving for her in-law's home, Indu drew her close and whispered, "Tell Didima I did not cry."

That was gradually told to everyone in the family including Shetu. The family consensus was that though Indu's leaving was sort of sad, it was nice to know that she had been married into a relatively congenial family having the same caste but much desired financial standing.

Shetu was growing up in his known setting without being bothered by changes around. One of them was that many Hindu families gradually sold their properties to Muslims and left for India, mostly Tripura and Assam states. That happened in the case of Bera Bari settlement too at a much later stage.

It was time for Shetu's first parting away from his very dear place. He left for Dhaka, the provincial capital at the time, for higher studies. The move to Dhaka excited him, though the sorority of Anandapur and impending severance from that remained unabashed.

Shetu made it a point to visit Anandapur on every possible occasion ever since his relocation to Dhaka. He nurtured his strong emotional link with his birthplace. Anandapur was his center of the world in early childhood. That continued in his growing-up phase, remained unblemished after his departure for Dhaka to pursue post-high school education, and even in his matured phase of life. The link with and feeling for Anandapur was so intense that Shetu would not spend a single day of his youth in Dhaka during any holiday. He would board the night train after availing a discounted student ticket to enable prestigious travel as an interclass passenger.

Shetu's arrival in and departure from Noakhali Railway Station had an inimitable experience centering on a local unemployed guy by the name Baila. Shetu had no idea about the milieu of Baila or his family. A very common face in Noakhali Railway Station, Baila was omnipresent during arrival and departure of trains.

Baila had the uncanny ability to notice Shetu in a sloweddown moving train approaching the Noakhali Railway Station. He would invariably maneuver actions to board the moving train and would take possession of Shetu's modest luggage and used ticket. Disembarking from the train, Baila would walk past the ticket collector of the station, showing his finger toward Shetu with a lot of pride and element of marked satisfaction. Coming out of the station platform, Baila would select the *rickshaw* to take Shetu home but would invariably wipe the seat first with *gamcha* (handwoven cotton scarf), which he used to keep on his bare left shoulder. The anecdote would come to an end with unnoticed passing of some small changes from Shetu to Baila. The latter never bothered to look at that. He would casually park those little changes in a pouch-type arrangement of the knot that tied his *lungi* (similar to *sarong*) to the waist and happily spin his gamcha to sweep the back side of the body.

Baila was more relevant to Shetu at the time of departure. On being informed earlier, Baila would take early possession of the inner-end portion of the long interclass compartment seat and patiently wait for the arrival of Shetu. Thus, Shetu always had a comfortable seating space for his overnight train journey to Dhaka. This practice continued until Shetu finished his university education, joined government service, bought his personal vehicle, and started traveling to Noakhali by road. Even though Baila was no more relevant, Shetu maintained contact with him and continued to pass on quietly small amounts to Baila's hand.

After successfully completing his master's education, Shetu got a teaching job in the premier community college of Comilla District. While on that job, he appeared in central superior services examination conducted by the Federal Public Service Commission for entry into central government services, a prestigious target for most of the ambitious youth of the time. Based on merit, Shetu, to the delight of his parents, got inducted in All-Pakistan Police Service.

While on his teaching job in Comilla, Shetu came to know a number of young folks of both genders and got involved in staging plays and other cultural activities. Some of them became his close buddies. They were Sanu, a young lawyer; Haseeb, midthirty younger brother of a colleague with full-time commitment in cultural activities and addressed by all as Haseeb *Bhai* (brother); and Himu, a fresh graduate with keen interest in dramatic activities. Another young man, Mikku, only son of a well-to-do Brahmo (followers of Raja Ram Mohan Roy, Hindu religion reformist opposing *sati* [in which Hindu widows were to immolate themselves on their husband's funeral pyre], polygamy, caste system, and child marriage) family, was also close to Shetu. The family owned a huge chunk of property in one of the upscale residential areas of Comilla. The relationship between the two was very warm, as Shetu used to live nearby.

In addition to being a lawyer, Sanu owned a rest house (similar to a motel) by the name Prestige and an upscale restaurant in Downtown Comilla by the same name. One Joyonto Rakhit was the manager of the Prestige restaurant. He was a person of many qualities, and Shetu bonded with him easily through Sanu. All of them addressed Shetu as "Shetu Bhai" with all the fondness and respect.

Joyonto had two teenaged sisters. The family was facing difficulties in marrying them out, with Hindu population gradually dwindling in East Pakistan. Primarily because of this, as Joyonto told, the family decided to immigrate to Agartala, the capital of Tripura state of India. That was a preferred and practical option due to the presence of relations who emigrated earlier.

In sharing this, Joyonto emphasized the confidential nature of that information and requested Shetu to keep that as such. As they were discussing emigration matters, Indu's memory flashed back. Shetu told Joyonto that while he would keep the information shared strictly confidential, he had also a request to make. He then detailed his association with Indu and requested that communicating any update, as feasible, on Indu's life in Shukhipur would be appreciated with thanks and gratitude. Shetu then wrote in a piece of paper a few information in helping Joyonto to locate her: her name, Indu; the name of her mama, Ominesh; Indu's father-in-law's name, Dhireen Babu; with additional information of the place of his living, Shukhipur, and location of his business, Santirbazar. On his part, Shetu then made an additional specific request: Joyonto's possible search for information should be undertaken with total secrecy and that should too be kept confidential. In no way that should make an impact on Indu's life. Joyonto promised but also added, "Shetu Bhai, I love and respect you. My leaving Comilla would not have any bearing on my feelings for you. As long as I am alive, I will look for opportunities to trace Indu, and privacy would always be ensured. If at any stage of my life I can gather related information, I will pass on the same confidentially to Haseeb Bhai, as he is one among us likely to have permanency in address."

Joyonto and family crossed the border soon thereafter. Shetu left Comilla to join All-Pakistan Police Service Academy at a place called Sharda in Rajshahi District of East Pakistan (Bangladesh). Upon completion of one-year training and other police administration–related requirements, he was posted as a subdivision police official. This was followed by both headquarters-based and district-level postings by rotation.

Shetu got married during this period with the bride from a respectable family, and the marriage was an arranged one. Her name was Anjuman, and Shetu lovingly called her Anju. He had the chance to meet Anju once before the marriage only after most of the unofficial formalities were finalized by the elders of the two families with the involvement of a middleman.

The first son of the newlywed couple was born when East Pakistan was in the midst of political turmoil centering on demand for full autonomy, but more specifically focusing on the issue of trial of Sheikh Mujibur Rahman, the president of opposition political party Awami League on ostensible treason charge. The political slogan of *Joiey Bangla*, meaning "Victory for Bengal" in the context of ongoing struggle for autonomy, was very popular. So the couple, in addition to formal name, also nicknamed the newborn as *Joiey* (in pronunciation, the Bangla word *"Joiey"* is very similar to English word "joy," which, when translated, is very close to another Bangla word *"Ananda"*).

The family, like million others, spent a very miserable and challenging time in 1971, the year of Bangladesh war of liberation. Soon after liberation, Shetu was posted once again as police chief of one of the administrative districts to revamp a broken setup jolted by the unmanageable euphoria following liberation. Their second son was born around that time, and, as was the case with the first one, they nicknamed him as Ananda, consistent with the prevalent overall sense of happiness. When the two boys grew up, they used to taunt their parents for the two nicknames meaning the same when translated into Bangla and English, respectively. Shetu's convincing defense was the relevance of the names in the larger context of history, and the specific meaning did not matter in that setting.

Shetu enjoyed contented professional career, and progression was steady even though sometimes slow due to tangential reasons. In family and social life, he enjoyed an affable gratification with support of a very genial spouse. Both Joiey and Ananda grew up as well-rounded young persons. They successively left for Canada for higher studies after their school education in Jhenaidah Cadet College, specialized residential public school (in line with British military boarding schools).

Joiey got admission in the prestigious University of Toronto to study engineering. Ananda, after three years, got into the School of Economics, University of British Columbia (UBC), Vancouver, for his undergrad studies.

Joiey traveled to Vancouver to settle Ananda in his school. Considering overall congenial climate, surrounding and related quality of life, and the likely comfort of living, both the brothers agreed that they would like to settle in Vancouver in the future. The additional justification was it would relatively be more genial a place if their parents ever immigrate to Canada, the preferred option of both brothers.

As the time passed, Ananda did his master's in economics and enrolled in PhD program of UBC. Joiey moved to Vancouver with a new job. By that time, he was also eligible to be a citizen on which he acted promptly. He did another thing. Soon after becoming citizen, he also applied for his parents' immigration. Joiey kept his parents duly informed about this action who took that very casually.

The main priority of Joiey's parents at this point was to get him married. They were pressuring Joiey, as he finished his education and got a job with permanent residency status under Canadian immigration policy. His becoming a citizen later became an additional justification. This was consistent with the prevailing social norm. Getting an established son married on time is the ultimate objective of any upcoming middle-class family of Bangladesh. Indirectly it testifies that the children, even though grown up, are still obedient, and parents enjoy a sort of social kudos for rearing up offspring properly. Shetu's family was no exception.

Joiey was deflecting that pressure on one or the other excuses. But his parents did not give up. They merrily continued looking for a beautiful girl of a respectable family, and the mother was very keen about it. They continued visiting houses of likeable young girls, based on social contacts, and in some cases, at the behest of a third-party matchmaker. Anjuman enjoyed lavish service of food and sweets on every such occasion to the embarrassment of Shetu.

Shetu achieved progression in career and reached the second-highest level of his service even though that headway was always not smooth. There were a number of reasons for that: sweeping changes in evolving social contract, rapid changes in service ethics, and noticeable quick depletion of respect for decency. Professional steadfastness was being considered as a timid attitude. Politicization of bureaucracy gradually was creeping in. High-level positions became vulnerable to political maneuvers and pressures.

Shetu was heading the investigation agency of the department. Political turmoil was at its zenith. At the personal level, Shetu found himself at the crossroad of conflicting indications, both from the authority and the opposition political parties, with respect to a sensitive case. While the authority wanted a report tailored to absolve itself from any wrongdoing, the opposition exerted all influence for a report contrary to that with veil threat of consequences once the party comes to power. But both the indications were contrary to investigation findings and the draft report emanating from that, besides being against all norms of public service and public good. As contents of the draft report leaked out, causing embarrassment to the authority, Shetu was posted to a position much beneath the level of his seniority. Shetu suffered both internalized pressure and annoyance. His own repeated efforts to reconcile with the most recent transfer to a lower-level responsibility as part of public service in evolving administrative arrangement were of no consequences to others.

It troubled him professionally, socially, and even at family level. Many family members and friends would often raise this issue ostensibly to express their sympathy, but Shetu felt embarrassed on every such occasion. The resultant lingering frustration gradually made an impact to his zeal to work anymore. He was certain that it would be of no consequences in ravenous surrounding to represent officially against the decision of the government. Suddenly, Shetu became quite serious in complying with religious practices, saying prayers five times in a day and going to mosque for *Jumma* (Friday communal congregation of Muslims).

Anju could sense fully what Shetu was going through. His sudden emphasis on religious practices, besides being faith related, could be an excuse to seek justice from the divine. She was worried and placed calls in Canada and talked with both their sons when Shetu was in the office. She explained everything, including the mental agony suffered by their father. It was agreed that her sons would call their father during dinnertime in Bangladesh and would direct the discussion to what their mother told, pretending that they do not know anything.

The call came, and discussions proceeded as planned. Not much effort was necessary on the part of their sons. Shetu was in a mentally strained stage needing to release some of his agony. So it was he who opened up and told the sons about his inability to work anymore in the prevailing environment. Joiey got hold of the opportunity and said, "Dad, Ananda is sitting with me and heard all our discussions. It is just a coincidence. We are together to jointly give you both a good news. That is why we called. Processing of my earlier application for both of your immigration to Canada has advanced per website information, and that will be done within months with papers going to you for medical examination. You should not think twice. Since we are not going back to Bangladesh, it is perhaps better for the family to be together in Canada. We also want you to be out of that depressed setting."

Shetu, being a fallen man, had not much mental strength to disagree with what their sons were proposing. They have grown up, and they know it better. In agreeing with what Joiey was proposing, Shetu lamented, saying, "How will I pass time in Canada all alone? I will also be miserable if I can't go to the mosque to say Jumma prayer."

At this stage, Ananda took over. He said, "Baba (father), do not worry about these, please. North America now is not what you saw in the early '70s. Things have radically changed. There are a good number of Bangladeshi families here with their parents. So you, with your gifted social skills, will definitely find a setting to your liking. As is the case of prayers of other religions, Muslims now have many mosques in Vancouver. There is a road in Vancouver that, for fun, has come to be known as Highway to Heaven because of propinquity to churches, temples, gurdwaras, mosques, synagogues, and many others, like Chinese places of worships. We will definitely find a place for both of you close to a mosque. Moreover, once you receive permanent residency status, all your future health-related needs will be taken care of by the government. So please do not worry."

Ananda then handed over the telephone to Joiey, who made few specific suggestions: "Do not share this information with anyone at this stage. You can tell close relatives and friends once health clearance is received, but be very careful not to let anyone in the government know about it. You should now apply for early retirement citing family needs and health as reasons, and take necessary steps to give a power of attorney favoring Mafuz *Mama* (maternal uncle), as your only property (house) is located in Chittagong, and he also lives there."

Things moved as planned. Shetu and Anju arrived in Vancouver as permanent residents. The couple was warmly greeted by both Joiey and Ananda and some of their friends, as the date of arrival was a Sunday. The couple was overwhelmed by such unexpected reception and started feeling at ease in a place they do not know much about. Friends of Joiey and Ananda instantaneously embraced them as *Chacha* (paternal uncle) and *Chachi* (aunt), and took care of their belongings impulsively. They straightway drove in two cars to a very likeable small house in Richmond area.

On their drive, Joiey informed their parents that they had already gotten a house for them, after finalizing the mortgage in the name of the two brothers, for their independent living. Sensing a sign of anxiety on the face of Shetu, Ananda assured the parents that both of them would service the mortgage and all other related expenses of their living. They should not worry about it.

The arrangement of independent living did not surprise either Shetu or Anjuman. Both their sons were living independently in the same city, maintaining, however, very close contacts. Their preferred option, against all parental advice and mother's insistence, is to be on their own enjoying respective comfort zone. So they kept quiet on their way to the new abode.

Vancouver airport, with the acronym of YVR, is located in Richmond. As the vehicle was negotiating the residential section of Richmond, Joiey went on saying a number of related aspects: "We both believe that as new immigrants, you should have your own identity and, hence, should have an independent living arrangement. Living in Richmond area, though predominantly a Chinese habitation, would allow both of you to easily negotiate other settlements like Burnaby and Surrey, where many Bangladeshi families live. Living option in downtown is not to be considered, as the same is relatively more expensive with negative impact on your quality of life against the backdrop of likeable preferences. Richmond is closest to Downtown Vancouver, and the location would facilitate proximity with both of us besides having easy access to YVR. The house we bought is a nice and manageable one, and the price, fortunately, is within affordability." Joiey ended his briefing by finally saying, "The Blundell Road of Richmond has a beautiful mosque by the name *Jamea Mosque*. It is in proximity to the house that we bought."

Their parents were taken aback seeing three spouses of friends of Joiey and Ananda waiting for them in their home-to-be with cooked food. Anjuman was stunned and could not check her tears.

She embraced each one most warmly and started addressing them affectionately as *Ma* (mother).

After the friends left, Joiey and Ananda started arranging things to make the stay of their parents more comfortable. They, among others, explained the surroundings around and the details related to the house, including using the alarm system; cautioned against not opening door in case unknown persons showed up; advised about weekly garbage schedule; and clarified operating systems of cooking range, television, computer, and telephone. They also told their parents that to give them space to adjust with the entirely new setting, both the brothers took leave of the whole week, and hence they could relax.

On the following Friday, the sons, though not ardent practicing Muslims, took their father to Richmond Jamea Mosque. Shetu was both happy and equally impressed by the layout, structure, and overall arrangements pertaining to conducting of prayers. He was pleased to see a gurdwara in a nearby location.

Amalgamation with Vancouver surroundings was much smoother, compared even to posting in a new place in Bangladesh. The latter was, of course, the observation of Anjuman. Social contacts enlarged, somewhat minimizing the pain of leaving relations and friends back home; roads and places of daily needs became slowly familiar; they got to know many of the neighbors of different religions, races, cultures; and they got fully acquainted with medical arrangements. Much-valued driving license, after initial hassle, was in possession too.

Life in Canada for the new immigrant couple was much more happy and rewarding than they ever thought of. Time passed with its related excitement, pleasure, and happiness. As the couple was not away from Canada since arrival, their citizenships were on time, and the process was completed per legal requirements.

During a family dinner on a weekend, Anjuman unexpectedly raised the issue of selling their Chittagong property. She had convincing reasons: their settlement in Canada permanently, problem associated with managing the property as absentee landlord should anything happen to brother (Mahfuz), and prevalent market conditions. What she did not mention was her agony for sons having the burden of servicing mortgage, and, if it could be acted upon, the sale proceeds would go a long way in minimizing that. All of them agreed. Shetu talked to Mahfuz and advised him to look for a buyer.

Within months, a call from Mahfuz informed them about finalization of a sale proposal and asked Shetu to be in Chittagong soon, as the buyer's preferred option was to get the sale deed signed by the owner.

Shetu soon left for Bangladesh on the way to Chittagong with journey break of a few days in Dhaka. Everything was done as planned and within the time, but the trip back to Dhaka, for scheduled return journey to Vancouver, encountered unexpected problems. Raging political agitations all over the country compounded by impromptu strikes, a series of mechanical problems of aircrafts of the national airline, and a major railway accident precluded scheduled return to Dhaka by any of them. The consensus was to go by road, and a bus journey was preferred because of other prevalent limitations.

Shetu was driven to a bus station by Mahfuz around early afternoon. After the ticket was purchased, Mahfuz had a friendly chat with the driver sharing the high-level police background of his brother-in-law. The driver came to meet Shetu in the car and said, "Sir, this is an honor for me that you decided to travel by the bus driven by me. I am a poor man, and I can't offer you anything. But I will be grateful if you would occupy the other front seat by my side." Shetu readily agreed.

The respect for his companion on the front seat and warmth of happiness were manifested when the driver himself stepped out of his bus and personally brought a cup of *garamchai* (hot tea) for Shetu, taking advantage of a short break of journey at Feni. The chai was too hot, and Shetu was having difficulty in sipping that, keeping the break time in mind. The driver said, "Sir, take it easy. I already told the owner that I will return the cup on my journey back." Shetu looked at the driver and smiled to convey a sense of thanks. Internally, his thought was preoccupied by the genuineness of simple people of the land in embracing totally unknown persons as dear ones.

The bus came to a stop at a designated resting place known as *Kakoli*. That was a break of twenty minutes for passengers to freshen up based on needs and to allow time for snacks and tea. The driver positioned Shetu in a table near the first-floor glass window and ordered some snacks and tea. This time the bill was settled by Shetu in spite of repeated objections of the driver. The driver then stepped out of the room of Kakoli for smoking.

Kakoli is located at the beginning point of Comilla-Chandina diversion section of the main highway (a wide road but nowhere near highway as understood) connecting Chittagong with Dhaka. The driver soon returned with ominous news.

There was a sudden strike in and around the growth center of Chandina. The leadership of that strike, though initiated by students, was soon taken over by respective political bases premised on hidden feuds and took a nasty turn with violent clashes and conflicting blames by the supporting and opposing groups. Soon that took an ugly turn, resulting in some looting of shops by rogue elements. The police was called in and had to resort to fire. Police firing caused death of a student of the local college, and the follow-on abrasive protests, in a rapidly changing situation, brought opposing parties together in denouncing police brutality, each claiming the dead student as their supporter. As the news of police killing of a student spread out rapidly, thousands of people converged. The police, being a small unit at *thana* (local police station) level, retreated within its secured compound. This ignited the problem more. Supporters of both groups took control of the road in respective areas of influence and started damaging buses, trucks, and cars within their proximity. The traffic came to a standstill. Even some of the shops were set on fire. Areas in and around Chandina were in a rampage. A gentleman, who was going to Dhaka by car, hurried back to Kakoli to ensure a resting place for the night. The driver of the bus, who heard the full story from the horse's mouth, contacted his offices in Dhaka and Chittagong. The advice was to wait at Kakoli until further instruction. That put the resumption of stalled journey to a total uncertainty.

Shetu, unlike other copassengers, took the unexpected development easily. In fact, he had a sense of happiness, as it would enable him to revisit his old place, having a bundle of past memories. He soon took leave from the driver and slowly walked toward a waiting rickshaw with his carry-on. His destination was a rest house in the town, and he asked the rickshaw puller whether he knows the

Prestige Rest House. The rickshaw puller said that "Prestige is no more a rest house. It is a big hotel."

After a while, the rickshaw stopped in front of the Prestige Hotel. Shetu had no problem recognizing that, as the façade of the old structure was maintained, and a new four-storied reverse E-shaped structure was built behind that.

Soon after setting his foot on the stairs of the old Prestige, negotiating the reception desk located at the entrance of new structure, Shetu encountered an impressive portrait of the owner with big flowing white beard. He had no problem identifying the owner as Sanu, the transformed flamboyant young man he knew while teaching in the local college. On inquiry, the staff advised that the owner, addressed as Sanu Sir, was presently at Makkah to perform *Umra* (little Haj).

Standing before the reception desk, Shetu somehow became very emotional. He instantaneously developed an inner urge to spend the night in the old structure with the setting prevalent at that time.

As precursor of making his inner feeling public, Shetu voluntarily started a friendly discourse with the reception staff and introduced himself as a close senior friend of Sanu Sir when he was teaching in the local college around the midsixties. He also availed the chance of mentioning his many stays in the same hotel when it was known as Prestige Rest House with the setting dominated by hurricane lantern and mosquito net. To ensure that he gets what he is looking for, Shetu deliberately referred to his job in the police service.

In requesting a room for the night, he expressed preference for one in the old structure. As the room was allotted per preference, Shetu made the treasured proposition, which appeared to be most weird and awkward to hotel staffs present. They started looking at each other as Shetu made additional requests to have a hurricane lantern and a mosquito net in the room, as he had in the past.

Observing their sense of uneasiness, Shetu reacted by saying that if they had a problem with his requests, and since Sanu was away, he would like to talk to any of his younger siblings. He would also pay for any additional expenses that would be incurred to provide him with what had been requested. After such exchanges, Shetu, with the temporary arrogance of a senior police official engulfing his persona, walked into the assigned room, placed his carry-on, and went to the mini restaurant for a cup of tea.

As he was sipping his tea after the ordeal of the day, the manager of the hotel stepped in, introduced himself, and politely told Shetu that he was sorry for the delay by his staff in acceding to his desires, and he would be provided with what he requested at no additional cost.

Shetu thanked the manager and observed that Sanu had always the exceptional ability of having good staff in managing his business establishments. In this regard, he recalled Joyonto Rakhit, manager of the Prestige Restaurant of Downtown Comilla around the midsixties. The manager happily confirmed that he too heard his name from Sanu Sir and had no doubt in mind that what the guest said so far were all factual and genuine. He volunteered to say that when Sir returns, he would definitely inform him about the visit of Shetu.

Since it was early evening, Shetu wanted to venture out rediscovering his place of youth. He was certain that things around have changed and so are the surroundings. It would be of no use to roam around. But in his inner thought, he was sure that probably the family of Mikku is still in the same upscale residential place, as they had huge properties there. He hired a rickshaw and proceeded to Mikku's place.

As Shetu was approaching the properties of Mikku, he was happy to see the known setting with obvious changes in the shapes and shades of properties. Shetu stopped the rickshaw to inquire from bystanders about Mikku's presence in the same house as his parents used to live. Upon confirmation, he got down from the rickshaw and took slow steps toward the veranda of the house to find a bareheaded Mikku with bulging belly reading a newspaper under an electric light with his eyeglass on the tip of his nose.

Shetu softly tried to draw Mikku's attention. As Mikku removed his glasses and looked outside with the element of askance, Shetu politely said, "Mikku, this is Shetu Bhai. Do you remember me?" Mikku jumped out instantaneously and embraced Shetu for quite a long time. He then shouted with excitement for Roma, his wife, conveying to her the unexpected arrival of Shetu Bhai.

The warmth of old relationship was all pervading in their discourses with unending supply of tea and snacks by Roma. Shetu explained the background of his Comilla presence without any plan. When he checked in to the Prestige Hotel of Sanu, he had the urge to revisit the old places. That brought him to Mikku's abode. During such discussions, the updates and whereabouts of other common friends were foremost.

Mikku suddenly remembered that a few months back, Haseeb Bhai, who is under the weather presently mostly because of age factor, inquired about the current address of Shetu Bhai. He was having a letter from Joyonto Rakhit of Agartala. In his separate cover letter, Joyonto mentioned that the accompanying envelope contained a letter from one known and dear to Shetu Bhai. Joyonto specifically requested all efforts to deliver that to Shetu Bhai, but that should not land to anyone else's hand. Mikku could not help Haseeb Bhai, as, like him, he had no communication with Shetu for a long time.

Mikku referred to that discussion with Haseeb Bhai and suggested that both of them should visit Haseeb Bhai forthwith to see whether he still has that letter. That was agreed to; the family driver of Mikku was called in; and they started their about two-mile drive in the midst of unfettered maneuvering of innumerable rickshaws and unregulated crisscrossing of roads by pedestrians due to both overfull nature as well as inadequacy of walkways. Shetu was lost within himself. Could that be a letter from Joyonto himself giving some update on his parting request to look for Indu? Could that either be a letter from Indu herself? He immediately wrote off the second possibility, as Indu would not be able to write a letter to express herself. In the midst of all these thoughts, he was very aloof and kept to himself, not particularly responding to Mikku's running commentary about physical changes since Shetu was last in Comilla prior to joining the police academy of Sharda in the midsixties.

Haseeb just finished his night prayer known as *Asher* (the last one of the five daily prayers mandated for a Muslim) and was about to retire to bed. On being advised that Mikku had come to meet him with a visitor, Haseeb Bhai changed *lungi* (sarong) and *punjabi* (long traditional outfit of Muslim gentry), and put on his white *tupi* (cap made of cotton material). He then slowly walked into his modest living area with the support of a very elegant walking stick.

Both Haseeb Bhai and Shetu had their respective surprises and were overwhelmed by that. Haseeb Bhai, wearing a flowing white beard and a tupi on with physical posture even with medium-height stooping, was totally different than what Shetu saw him last. His present self stands out in perceptible contradiction with what he was about forty years back with full-time commitment to art and culture, and a sweet smile always adoring his self.

The sudden and equally unexpected presence of Shetu, having not much physical changes except salt-and-pepper hair, was what took Haseeb Bhai by total surprise. As he entered the living area and after seeing Shetu, he stood standstill for a few seconds, released the support walking stick, and rushed toward and embraced Shetu warmly to the delight of Mikku.

After initial sharing of emotions and exchange of pleasantries most concerning health and family, Haseeb Bhai excused himself and returned with a relatively large envelope, surprisingly having no visible postal mark. A houseboy followed him after a while with tea and biscuits.

In offering tea, Haseeb Bhai stated that about nine months back, he received this envelope from Joyonto of Agartala. That was hand-delivered by one of Joyonto's nephews who occasionally visits Comilla for business purpose. Inside the big envelope, there were two other closed envelopes besides a cover letter from Joyonto addressed to him. That separate cover letter addressed to Haseeb Bhai explained the background of the other letters in the separate sealed envelopes. Joyonto wrote that during the parting meeting between them, Shetu Bhai requested Joyonto to locate a particular lady residing in an area known as Shukhipur of South Tripura. The accompanying thick envelope contains a letter from that lady sent to Joyonto with request to deliver that to Shetu Bhai. Joyonto had also a letter from him to Shetu Bhai and placed that in a separate closed envelope. In his communication to Haseeb Bhai, Joyonto specifically requested that Shetu Bhai first read his letter and then open the letter of the lady.

Haseeb Bhai was both happy and relieved to be able to hand over the letters to Shetu Bhai in person. He said that with uncertain health conditions, he had been under pressure during the last so many months as how to handle the same and what one could do with these letters in the event he succumbs to the dictates of nature.

Haseeb Bhai had no choice within the realm of his control and decision, as his movements were restricted within four walls of the house due to health reasons and prevailing medical conditions. He thus requested his both sons to locate Shetu Bhai in Dhaka. The children assured every time and then, perhaps due to pressure of life, forgot to act on that. After following two to three times with same result, Haseeb Bhai stopped making the request. The children were just not in a position to appreciate the depth of the relationship.

But the endgame of that frustration could not be more happy and rewarding than what in reality happened. Haseeb Bhai, demonstrating his unqualified contentment, went on saying that perhaps it is the will of Allah that the uncertainty that hinged around the delivery of the letters would come to a conclusion in a way that was beyond expectation. He observed that all irritants that shrouded Shetu Bhai's travel back to Dhaka were perhaps a prelude to direct handing over of the letters.

Both Mikku and Haseeb Bhai were in the mind-set to prolong the meeting and discourse, but Shetu had the pressure of internal feeling to open the envelopes and decipher the intent and contents of the letters. So maintaining a sense of propriety, Shetu, with reluctant sanction of Mikku, took leave of Haseeb Bhai. But Shetu had to promise to have lunch on the following day in Haseeb Bhai's place in the company of Mikku. Haseeb Bhai took the chance to recall Shetu's liking of *kochur shag* (leaves) or *kochu pata* (tropical plant taro is popularly called kochu in Bangladesh, and the leaves of taro are meshed in the process of cooking), and said that among others that favorite item would also be there.

During the journey back to Prestige Hotel, which literally took a few minutes in view of visible slide in traffic due to relative late hours of the night, Shetu, at the insistence of Mikku, agreed to stay the following day in Comilla with concurrent commitment for dinner at Mikku's place. While parting away, Mikku, observing a rather emotional Shetu, called him from behind and said, "Please take things easy, but before you do anything, inform Vancouver and Chittagong about the change in your travel plan." Shetu agreed to act accordingly.

STEPPING

A S HE STEPPED in, Shetu was pleasantly surprised to see both hurricane lantern and mosquito net embellishing his hotel room. He, however, could not insinuate for the presence of a third pillow in the bed put horizontally. Shetu just concluded that perhaps that is one of the acts to recognize his close association with Sanu. He ordered tea; had routine cleansing of face, neck, and forearms; changed to night outfit of *paijama* and *punjabi* (traditional long shirt); said his prayers including those missed during the day; called Vancouver and Chittagong; placed pillows against the headboard to ensure sort of reclined position enabling comfortable reading of much-awaited letters; and poured tea in the cup.

Keeping in mind the request relayed through Haseeb Bhai, Shetu carefully kept the other letter under the additional pillow gracing the bed and opened the one written to him by Joyonto.

In his letter, Joyonto, alluding to the last discussion that he had with Shetu prior to emigrating, pithily dealt with his life, living and way forward as under:

"Life of family in the new setting of Agartala was unimaginably exigent initially causing both disarray and frustration. It was more so as our liquidity became a constrained one due to purchase of a modest home and the money kept apart for probable weddings of my two sisters. We struggled but overcame the bleak visage of that with total commitment and sustained efforts of all in the family. My father got a professional opening in a school and started private coaching. I joined a job and also tutored students in the evening. Both my sisters, after sporadic induction in employment opportunities while pursuing education, got married within a reasonable time frame. Both were coincidentally married in the periphery of Agartala, but in opposite direction. Their in-laws were also emigrants from Bangladesh. Thus, the usual irritant of a Hindu marriage pertaining to dowry was trivial. They understood our position, and we also tried to do whatever we could. In the process, both Father and myself incurred unforeseen debt. We grappled a lot over a number of years in liquidating the same. The situation took a dismal turn due to successive prolonged illness of my parents before they respectively succumbed to the dictates of nature.

"When I look back, our immigration to Tripura is reminiscent of being the event of the other day. In reality, many years passed by; many events impinged on our respective lives; and many unanticipated bends took us to unsigned destinations with outcomes of divergent magnitudes.

"The same applies to our emotional parting-away meeting when you suddenly opened up concerning your childhood association with Indu. Your handwritten details pertaining to Indu in South Tripura were lodged in the drawer of the only wooden *almirah* (akin to a wardrobe, cabinet) that graced our modest living. Except parents, when they were alive, and myself, no one would normally open that. The information was thus parked in the most secured area of our home, and, when needed, I could easily locate that to recall details even though many, many years passed by.

"The request for possible update on Indu's life that you so emotionally made at your full youth during our last brief encounter prior to emigration would possibly be not relevant in the present phase of your life. Nor would that matter to Indu except plausible flashback in her memory tunnel.

"I feel embarrassed to write to you about Indu after so many years. I am unsure about the relevance of what I am going to share against the settings of present realities of your life. But circumstances are such that I can't avoid that too. Both my commitment to you and since meeting Indu after so many years at her abode of Shukhipur, I started having a compelling pressure to act on your request even though unsure as to whether that information would reach you at all or in time.

"This communication, even though it may fail in terms of all its immediate objectives, would definitely succeed in two fronts: first, in my own self, it would be a solid testimony of my effort to act on your request after inordinate number of years and even at the far end of my life; and second, I will be doing justice to physical and emotional syndromes I observed in lady Indu. Her attached letter to you might reflect on some of those, but I would not like to fail in conveying to you what I observed peripherally. That is the background of my letter.

"In the midst of responding to emerging needs and obligations surrounding the family, my own life floated in a very uncharted way, and I remained a bachelor. With the demise of our parents, I had the pleasant burden of playing the dual role embedded in a relationship premised on 'fatherlike big brother.'

"Consequently, I became very close to my two sisters' evolving families being the only dear *Mama* (maternal uncle) to scores of nephews and nieces. They are my life. They are my world. Though I do not expect anything from any of them, I find solace in being relevant to their life. I was engrossed, quite unusually, though, with matters related to the weddings of two *bhagnees* (nieces) through first sister and the educational pursuits of all the three *bhageenas* (nephews), sons of second sister.

"First bhagnee was married in a mediocre family of Agartala. Second bhagnee Laboni was married in an enlightened and educated family of Bhatipara with her husband teaching in a local college. Though relatively at a distance from Agartala, Laboni could frequent the parental place because of very tolerant and supportive in-law family attitude. That enabled not only sustaining but also strengthening culturally valued *mama-bhagnee* relationship even periods following Laboni's marriage.

"During one of such visits about two years back, Laboni, in the presence of family elders including me, was describing in detail all events and experiences of the marriage of her *debar* (younger brother-in-law) about a year back. She also said that the in-laws of her debar are also an immigrant family and very well settled. The bride is fairly attractive and from a very well-to-do family of a neighboring habitation known as Shukhipur.

"Laboni's utterance of 'Shukhipur' instantaneously worked as a flashback to discussions that we had in Comilla prior to my emigration. I had the compulsive instinct to inquire more about the family trying to trace Indu per your request, but restrained myself. I quickly thought that it would be both inappropriate and cause unnecessary inquisitiveness in the mind of all present about my specific interest concerning that family. In the midst of follow-on queries, it would have been difficult to keep confidential the identity of Indu and your request. I kept my cool, preserving the nobility of my relationship with Laboni and simultaneously upholding the naturalness inherent in your request.

"In the process, I was bothered by my suppressed inquisitiveness to know instantly about the family of Shukhipur in general and Indu in particular. With that sort of excruciating intensity, I reappeared in my sister's place after two days at around noontime. That was a working day, and most of the male family members were out. Though not warranted by any prevalent social dictum to explain reasons of a visit so soon by a brother to his sister's home, I told my sister that as I was in the neighborhood to attend to an urgent business, I took the opportunity to drop by. My sister called Laboni and complained that her 'only brother is becoming so formal that he is justifying his visit to our place as if we belong to different families.' Laboni reacted politely to her mother's complaint, brought a *tal pakha* (hand fans made of palm leaves), and started rotating that to make her dear Mama at ease against the backdrop of prevalent warm weather. Everyone was very happy having me back so soon.

"As a very dear one, Laboni was mostly giving me company during my stay in my sister's place that afternoon. As my sister went to the kitchen to prepare *jol khabar* (serving of snacks with water) for me, I, exercising all care and with all the pretense premised on casual query, asked Laboni as to the distance of Shukhipur from her in-law's place of Bhatipara.

"Laboni laughed loudly and said, '*Ma, dheko-to, Mamar hoey-che-ta ki?* (Mother, see what happened to Uncle?) I just told you all present two days before that Shukhipur is adjacent habitation next to Bhatipara. So it is a very close one.'

"That was my turn to have a soothing laugh within myself. Laboni had no idea that I was laying the setting with a specific follow-up in mind on the matter of extreme personal interest avoiding any possible other inferences. I thus steered follow-up discussions in as unfussy a manner as was practical.

"Though a mama to my nephews and nieces, a relationship of reverence in our culture, I was very friendly, easy, and open to them, particularly to two dear nieces. They repeatedly expressed their surprise for me not getting married. Being fully familiar with my obsession for Comilla and Bangladesh, they occasionally teased me, saying, 'Shombo botto, tumi kau-ke Bangladesher kono jaiga rekhey ashocho (Possibly you left your heartthrob in some place of Bangladesh) and that is why you are a bachelor.' On every such occasion, I used to laugh it away. They had some ideas but did not have any direct experience of our struggle and afflictions in life following years after migration—that we sustained to ensure that the next generation has a better footing in life.

"With that sort of milieu, I willfully laid out the premise of my following query to give that a more plausible reason. I told Laboni, 'When I was emigrating and about to leave Comilla, a dear friend, almost like an elder brother, from Noakhali District of Bangladesh, mentioned about a girl of his locality known as Anandapur. She was Indu and was married in a family of a habitation known as Shukhipur of South Tripura. I remember the name of Shukhipur after so many years, as my brother had a mischievous physical expression saying Indu left Anandapur (place of merriment) for a place known as Shukhipur (place of happiness), and I hope she found happiness there. So when you mentioned Shukhipur, it instantaneously rang a bell in my ears even after so many years.' After a pause, and without pretention, I directly asked her whether she knows anyone by that name from Shukhipur. I also added that when that name was told to me, she would have been very young, but no more so. She ought to be an elderly lady by now if she is alive.

"Laboni thought for a while and said that 'she does not know anyone by the name Indu; however, her *debrani*'s (wife of younger brother-in-law) mami-ma (mama's wife is known as mami, and 'ma' is added to reflect additional warmth in that relationship) is one who is an immigrant, but her name is Indrani. Even at this age, she is very elegant and attractive, which testify about her beauty in youth.

'Debrani's mother died when she was a toddler. Her mami-ma brought her up and discharged all responsibilities like a mother. That is why every time debrani refers to her, she is meticulous in addressing her as Indrani Ma, and occasionally as Indrani-Mami-ma.'

"When sister returned with jol khabar, I changed the subject but maintained some link with previous discourse. I started inquiring about Bhatipara: how it looks like, what the general setting is, the demographic features, and so on. As the discussion progressed, the sister raised another issue stating that no one from the family ever visited Laboni's in-law's place, and someone should visit. They are a very nice family, and they will be happy.

"Laboni became emotional at this stage and said that 'relatives of my debrani regularly visit her and even occasionally stay one or two days notwithstanding the proximity of respective habitations. But no one from my side ever visited me since my marriage. I feel sad about it but never said anything.' She further said, 'I just expressed my frustration as the matter came up in discussion.'

"First sister said that she considered this a number of times in the recent past but could not find a solution. She stated, '*Tomader Jamai* (husband of younger sister) is under serious pressure in his office for a considerable period of time. It is almost impossible to apply for leave. *Bhogoban* (god) has not blessed me with a son who could possibly go and spend some time with that family strengthening the bond of our relationship.' Then suddenly she suggested that '*Dada* (brother), why can't you go and represent the family? After all, you played a primary role in the wedding of my both daughters, especially in Laboni's one. They know you so well.' Laboni enthusiastically supported the idea and said, 'Mama, you have all the flexibility. Please don't say no. Please visit us.'

Joyonto wrote that "I was more than happy with the turn of events, which would possibly help to trace Indu and finally enable me to fulfill the promise I made a long time back. But outwardly, I expressed some hesitation highlighting longtime Hindu tradition that one even does not take water in the house of in-laws of one's daughter and sister. Laboni brushed aside that apprehension, further emphasizing ongoing changes in scripture, entrenched practices, and cultures." She was even blunt in saying, 'Mama, all these are excuses. I won't listen to anything. When I return to Bhatipara this time, I will tell everyone that my mama is coming to visit us. Your negation after that on any pretext would only embarrass me.'

Joyonto was evidently happy in communicating, "Finally, it was agreed that I would visit Laboni's place around the festivity time of *chaitra shon-kranti* (last day of the last month of Bangla calendar), which is celebrated in Bhatipara with special flare."

Joyonto went to Bhatipara per earlier understanding with ostensible objective to trace out Indu of Shukhipur. Initially he was overwhelmed by the warmth of welcome and genuineness of hospitality extended by the in-law's family of Laboni. He started enjoying his stay at Bhatipara but never was sidetracked from his principal objective.

With that sort of mind-set, Joyonto concentrated in spending more time and having discussions with Anjali, the debrani of Laboni. The designed focus of Joyonto's discourse centered on his life in Bangladesh and Comilla with occasional reference to challenges and frustrations associated with immigration. Listening to Joyonto Mama's (per prevalent and more acceptable framework of relationship, Bou-di's [wife of elder brother-in-law] mama [uncle] is also mama of all younger siblings in the family) repeated references to Bangladesh and Comilla, Anjali quickly surmised about evident commonality in thoughts and words between her Indrani-Ma and Joyonto Mama. She opined that her Indrani-Ma would be delighted to meet Joyonto Mama having the same background and would enjoy reminiscing and sharing the shimmer of their lives beyond Tripura.

The idea was presented to the male family elders during dinnertime by Laboni with subtle presentation in a setting and manner that could only have an affirmative outcome. And that happened. It was decided that both Laboni and Anjali would accompany Joyonto Mama in a daylong visit to Anjali's parental home following the day of *pohela boishak* (first day of the first month of Bangla year known as Boishak). Considering that the visit would be a casual one, as well as to minimize pressure on Indrani-Ma, it was decided that there was no need to send any advance information to Anjali's home.

Both Laboni and Anjali decided to limit the proposed visit within a time slot of about three hours excluding both ways' total travel time of about two hours. So the plan was to leave at around 10:00 a.m. and return by 4:00 p.m. with no serious dislocation to household chores. Joyonto Mama was told accordingly.

Joyonto Mama, Laboni, and Anjali started that particular morning with varied intensity concerning respective areas of duty and concern. Laboni and Anjali, with the support of household helps, quickly prepared *prato-rush* (breakfast) and the lunch for the family, and made all preparatory arrangements to cook dinner upon return.

Joyonto was very clear that since it was going to be his first and the only visit to the home of his niece's debrani, he should not fail to observe the embedded social dicta. Thus, he bought a nice *tanter share* (handwoven saree) and sent male household help to the *bazaar* (market) that particular morning to bring untarnished *paan* (betel leaf), shupari (betel nut), and freshly made sweets to take along with him.

As planned, the party arrived at Anjali's grandparents' home. The excitement and pleasure were all pervading in the body language of the three, though Joyonto had internal tension concerning the end result. If the same is a negative one, he would have all the reasons to be frustrated, as all recent moves of his regarding visiting Bhatipara and Shukhipur were predicated on the honest hope of a positive outcome.

As they were walking in and Anjali excitedly calling, "Ma, Ma" (Mother, Mother), Indrani, attired in an ordinary white *tater* (handloom) saree, was taking steps out of *ranna ghar* (kitchen) toward the main house. She turned toward the entry/exit location of the *uttan* (quad of the house) with a welcoming big smile full of surprise. But that was for a few seconds only, as she, noticing an unknown elderly person behind Anjali walking with some parcels in his hand, turned her face around, increased the length of the portion of saree on her head (known as *ghomta* [veil]), and hurried away to the main house.

Anjali, observing the reaction of her Indrani-Ma, gently held the hand of Joyonto and said, "Mama, it is all right. She was just not prepared to see us with one she does not know." Anjali then conducted Joyonto to the relatively spacious front entry room of the semibungalow-type main house. By all counts, the house was a distinguishable one with cement-concrete floor and half-concrete wall, upper portion having framed bamboo spread, and CI sheet roofing. Laboni took possession of the parcels and went inside. The sitting arrangements were very nice and cushy to look at with a fairly large bed placed at the deep end of the room.

Positioning himself comfortably in a chair while both Laboni and Anjali went inside to meet Indrani-Ma, Joyonto, revisiting the glimmer of oomph he observed in Indrani-Ma's face in the first few seconds, had almost no doubt that the lady is Indu. Sitting alone for some time, he planned his moves so that he could have relatively frank exchanges within the available windows, protecting her dignity and the privacy of Shetu Bhai.

Sometime later, Indrani-ma, after changing her saree, entered the sitting room in the company of Anjali and Laboni. Indrani slowly raised her both hands and softly said, "Nomoshkar." Then Indrani, to make the unexpected meeting a casual one and taking liberty that the relationship embodies, continued, saying, "We are so lucky. A special guest from Agartala has come to visit us. It is almost like *goriber uttane hatir para* (footsteps of elephant in the courtyard of a poor homestead). But it so happened that I have none at home to extend proper hospitality to the venerated guest. My husband is physically disabled due to an accident and is confined to bed. Our son, Dhrub, just left for Santirbazar, as our family business is located there. Our daughter Shetupa is in Agartala studying as well as preparing for a big examination to get into government service."

Laboni interrupted, saying, "Indrani Mami, our mama is not like that. Though somewhat aged, he is a man of open mind, and we are all brought up by him. You see, he has come to visit you, being a relation of son–in–law's family, without looking for formality."

Indrani smiled and said, "It is so gracious of him."

Joyonto was very composed and quiet during the initial discourse, conscious of the fact that not only is he in this house as a guest of Anjali's in-laws, but symbolically he also represents the prestige and nobility of Laboni's family. He therefore very carefully opened up and discursively started explaining the backdrop of his unannounced visit.

Could hardly say anything, Laboni interjected by saying, "Mama, you have seen Anjali for the last few days. She is a perpetual talker, and the few minutes we were inside with Indrani Mami, Anjali told her everything about you and your coming nonstop." She jokingly continued that possibly "I do not know that much about my mama."

It was the turn for Anjali to defend her conduct. She said, "Indrani Ma, you tell what I could do. During the last few days, Joyonto Mama continuously was telling me about Bangladesh and Comilla— how wonderful his growing up was, how he enjoyed living there in spite of communal tension, and how he misses those still. As the discourse is familiar to me since childhood, I proposed to introduce him to someone who would appreciate what he had to say. That is the reason why Joyonto Mama is here today. I just told you that."

Indrani commented, "Laboni is right in what she said, but you have not done anything wrong. In fact, your talking enabled me to be at ease in Joyonto Babu's presence." Then she continued, "With sudden death of Anjali's mother, she landed in my lap with Dhrub, about five years old. Soon thereafter, our daughter Shetupa was born after one miscarriage. Though I looked after both equally, I had to give more attention to Shetupa because of age difference, and special dispensation had to be accorded to Anjali for being an orphan. From early childhood, she loves to talk, and I encouraged that, as experience taught me that it works as a great reliever, and everyone needs that sort of relief in life. Within the limits of my own knowledge and upbringing, I tried my best to shape them up to be better people. In my childhood and growing-up phase, I was told many good things by a person I adore. One of them I repeatedly told my son and daughters is to be sympathetic to other people's feelings, as each of that has its own rationale. That is why Anjali always tries to find the comfort zone in other person's mind. Precisely because of that trait perhaps, Anjali made today's visit possible."

Joyonto, in an effort to change the subject, started talking about Comilla and his family's immigration to Agartala. As he was narrating congeniality of his experiences pertaining to interacting with fellow immigrants, highlighting instantaneous bonding with the most as sort of a member of larger family, Nandita, wife of Dhrub, stepped in with jol khabar. Indrani introduced her, and Nandita, bending herself, touched the feet of Joyonto, showing respect to and seeking blessings from a senior. This is commonly called *podo-dhuli* in Hindu culture.

At Laboni's suggestion to have some interesting talk with the new bou-di (sister-in-law Nandita), all three left the front sitting room. Indrani got engaged in serving jol khabar to Joyonto. Considering that to be the most opportune time to pursue his objective, Joyonto, with ubiquitous uncertainty engulfing the words he was going to utter, said, "I am told by Anjali that you are from Noakhali. I too have a friend, almost like a brother, from that district. When I was immigrating to Tripura a long time back, he requested me to trace, whenever feasible, a Hindu girl of his locality married in Shukhipur of Tripura. That is why I am in your place." Then he looked straight at Indrani and point-blank asked her, "Do you know anyone by the name Indu?"

Indrani was picking up *rosgolla* (traditional sweet) from a big bowl to place that in a serving plate when Shetu asked the question. Rosgolla fell from the spoon, and Indrani stood up impulsively. She remained in a standstill position for a few seconds. Then something dawned on her. Indrani repositioned the relevant section of her saree on her head, sat down, and looked directly at Joyonto, asking him, "Who are you?"

Joyonto had no doubt about the "Indu" identity of Indrani and did not like to lose any more time. He narrated the whole background related to bonding with Shetu Bhai, discussions between the two prior to Joyonto's immigration, commitment he gave to Shetu Bhai to trace out Indu, loss of time due to family responsibilities, and coming to Bhatipara at the earliest once he came to know that it is located next to Shukhipur and the in-laws of Laboni have relatives there.

Joyonto then continued, "As Laboni mentioned your Indrani name and your root, and from the family descriptions as well as your attachment to Noakhali that I came to know from Anjali, there was no doubt in my mind that you are the Indu I am looking for. Because of that, I have written my contact address in a piece of paper and leaving that with you. If at any time you feel like to send any message or communication to Shetu Bhai, you may contact me or send that to me. I have my contact in Comilla who too loves Shetu Bhai equally. Shetu Bhai's current position is not known to me, but I am certain that he ought to be someone important in the administrative structure of Bangladesh. My contact in Comilla is most likely to know about that. Even in the worst situation, he will do everything to locate him and ensure delivery of any communication from me. Your privacy and Shetu Bhai's prestige will always be my responsibility. This is my promise. Rest assured about it."

An overwhelming shush prevailed. Indu was speechless. Her physical self was in a state of frigidity with exquisite set of eyes fixated on the floor. Emotionally, perhaps, she was lost in the time tunnel taking her back to early teen period and the surroundings of Anandapur. A total silence permeated the setting in contrast to thinly traveled loud words and laughter of the young ladies, and the occasional coughing bout of Indrani's ailing husband from the northwestern-most room of the house.

Joyonto opted not to disturb her. He concentrated in helping himself slowly with jol khabar. In the process, Joyonto intentionally tried to make some noise by handling the spoons rather stridently. But that was of no impact. Since one of the coughing bouts was a riotous one, Indrani looked at Joyonto and said, "It is my ailing husband, Kiran Babu (salutation showing respect). He has to be confined in bed with limited access to others, as many of his actions are uncontrollable."

Joyonto did not pursue that discussion. From her words and body language, he got the message that Indrani would not like to share any more details about her husband's ailment or be responsive to any request for meeting him in person. Within himself, Joyonto marveled in observing the transformation of poor and deprived half-lettered Indu, as told briefly by Shetu Bhai, into an elegant and elderly lady of a well-to-do house with a lot of social standing, as Anjali told earlier. She speaks softly, she takes time in responding to queries, she chooses her words with care, she communicates by maintaining eye contact, and she is full of self-confidence.

Indrani, to overcome prolonged stillness as well as sensing that all the three young ladies were on their way to the front sitting room, started talking very loudly, profusely thanking Joyonto Babu for taking the trouble of visiting her, a fellow emigrant from Bangladesh. By this time, Nandita, assisted by Laboni and Anjali, placed trays full of delicious food preparations for lunch. Joyonto was very happy to see *puree* (flour-based and hand-pressed flat small *roti* deep-fried in hot oil) instead of rice and thanked Nandita profusely. All of them, except Indrani, who, following the practice of many widows of Hindu faith, opted to eat once in a day before sunset, sat together and started enjoying the food.

Joyonto observed that as the food prepared by Nandita is so delicious, probably he would come back soon once more. Indrani said, "Why only once? Take it as your home. Come whenever you feel like. Nandita will always be happy to see you." Innocent indirect messages were exchanged between the two with the nuance known to them only. Others just enjoyed the congeniality of conversation.

All the three returned to Bhatipara by the time they had in mind. Laboni and Anjali soon got involved with the preparations of jol khabar and dinner for the afternoon and evening. During jol khabar time, Joyonto extensively narrated his appreciation to male family elders as to the ambiance of Anjali's home and the dignified welcome he was accorded even though the visit was an unplanned and unannounced one.

In the midst of such warm discourse, Joyonto conveyed to all present his deep appreciation for hospitality of this house that he enjoyed during the last few days and said, "I will be honored if any of you visit me at your convenience. I do not have a full home like you, but I have a warm heart. I will do everything to make any visitor at ease in my small abode."

The father-in-law of Laboni, the eldest of the family, responded, saying, "You have come by your choice without looking for formalities. We are happy to have you. You are not a special guest but a family member. During the last few days, we have treated you as such, equally enjoying your company. If you want to go, it is your choice, but we would be happy if you stay two more days at least."

Joyonto responded by thanking all once again and said, "I will take a rain check and would like to encash the suggested two days in the near future." Everybody laughed.

Joyonto returned to Agartala and was thinking about the future course of action. In his letter, Joyonto continued reflecting that mental syndrome, "Having returned from Bhatipara, I am agonized by the pervading thought as what to communicate to you. Mere information that I found out Indu and she is alive would not be in any way an adequate status that you would like to have after so many years. On the other hand, I vividly recount observing in the body language of Indu an invasive expression of emotion whose impending course was equally unclear to her. She continuously struggled to convey something but ostensibly withdrew from the process suddenly. The more I thought about her pertinent reactions, the more certain I was that she would soon communicate with me with some sort of message. Thus, I kept on waiting willingly.

"After about a year, my premonition proved to be right. I got hand delivery of the attached letter for you from Indu. That was very safely and securely handled by Laboni during latest visit to her parents' home. Laboni had something else to tell me that eventually explained the delay: being sort of half-lettered lady, Indu was not in a position to convey to you her life episode and feelings in any expressive way. She had to wait for the return of daughter Shetupa from Agartala after finishing her all-India based competitive examination for superior services. Shetupa visited Shukhipur after her examination, and had reasonable time between completion of the examination process and her formal joining for training, if successful. Taking advantage of that, Indu unhesitatingly opened up before the daughter, and it is Shetupa who wrote the letter conveying the words and feelings of Indu."

In concluding, Joyonto wrote, "Notwithstanding my infrequent communication with Haseeb Bhai, I decided to give him the responsibility to ensure that you get the letter. One of my nephews goes to Comilla frequently on business trip. He knows Haseeb Bhai and his address. That made me comfortable as to the safe delivery of the letter to him. I will be happy and will be fulfilling my promise to Indu, hopefully through the effort of Haseeb Bhai, ensuring delivery of her message to you, maintaining all privacy. I only pray that it eventuates."

Shetu folded the letter of Joyonto and was lost within himself in thoughts about the time and events that elapsed since the last interactions with the latter. In his inner self, Shetu was overwhelmed by the sincerity and commitment of Joyonto notwithstanding migration, passage of time, divergent challenges and circumstances of life, and a total absence of communication. He was so thankful that Joyonto not only remembered that departing request but also took time and made efforts to locate Indu after so many years. Joyonto's action gave human feeling and relationship a new face and a unique dimension, which are in conflict with present values, beliefs, and priority based on parameters focusing on faiths, territorial identities, self-interest, and other analogous attributes. To Shetu, it proved beyond doubt that bonding of youth as that of longing for land remains generally strong and solid notwithstanding other compulsions. Shetu felt happy for having friendship with a person of Joyonto's excellence. He just closed his eyes and revisited the gamut of their relationship.

RECOUNT

C OMING OUT OF such a trance, Shetu got up from the bed, washed his face again, and took a few steps outside in a rather quiet surrounding of the hotel around late midnight. He returned to the room, switched off electric room lights, increased the inner wick (woven strip of cotton) of the hurricane lantern to enhance the light, and looked at the cold pot of tea ordered earlier but did not have the mind-set to drink it fully before finishing Joyonto's letter. By the time he finished the letter, the tea became cold, and his urge for remaining tea in the pot evaporated.

Shetu decided to recline in the bed once again as a preferred setting for reading the much-cherished letter of Indu. He also repositioned the table lamp for still clear reading. Before opening the envelope, Shetu tossed the same a number of times with embedded surprises due to evident thickness and weight of the envelope. Based on Shetu's intimate involvement and exposure to Indu's level of learning, and forgetting for the time being what was elucidated by Joyonto with regard to writing of the letter, he was pondering about the content of the same. The weight of the envelope concurrently bothered Shetu very much, and he increasingly started feeling gawky. Both the silent hours of the night and his loneliness, with palpable likeliness to make an impact on his ability to handle anything baffling, were his other constraints. Notwithstanding lack of craving for cold tea in the pot, he poured some in the cup and sipped once. Shetu then slowly opened the envelope with quivering physical symptoms quite contrary to his personality, training, and professional background.

As he unfolded, it became instantaneously clear to Shetu, both due to visible smoothness of the writing as well as the length in pages, that the letter was written by someone else having a beautiful hand in writing and equally enjoying the confidence of Indu. Shetu immediately started reading the letter containing the words and sentiments of Indu:

"I do not recall ever addressing you by name or any other form of socially acceptable salutation during the span of growing up and the time that we shared in Anandapur. Thus, it is my choice to start writing this letter keeping that 'bare.' If you like, you can put anything to fill up that blank if it is considered de rigueur for complete appreciation of the content of the letter.

"But before embarking on the core of this writing, I would like to clarify some background of the person I have entrusted with the most private part of my life and exposed my inner feelings nurtured over so many years, which is difficult for me to count.

"She is Shetupa, my dearest daughter, my friend, and my soul mate ever since she has been growing up. As is with me, privacy of your person too is safe in her hand. Rest assured about that.

"Before leaving Anandapur for Shukhipur, I tried to talk to you and to take leave from you in the absence of options I and my family had. You were one person who was deeply aware of this limitation in our nascent relationship, and you discussed that with me in many ways and on numerous occasions. But just the same you did everything to deprive me in taking leave from you. Perhaps it was your sudden arrogance, your startling apathy, your embryonic frustration, or the outcome of your subdued feeling. But that was very disappointing for me. That did hurt me very much. When I boarded the morning train for Belonia via Laksham, I, because of sheer anger at that emotionally erratic phase of growing up, promised not to remember you at all in my subsequent life. I wanted to have a permanent break with Anandapur, erasing you out totally. Thus I crossed the border on one condition that my parents had to agree with. I told them, 'As I cross the border, no one—not for a single time, not even by mistake—should address me as Indu. The consequences would be irreversible. Remember that Indu is dead. I want to be known to all here and everywhere by my *poshaki* (formal) name of Indrani.' That promise was strictly adhered to even though my desire to have permanent break with you never materialized.

"After many long years and a life satiated with relative affluence—for a girl coming from a very poor setting—but devoid of love faced most unanticipated joggle when first-time visiting distant relation,

Joyonto-*da* (brother), uttered the name 'Indu' in a surrounding of privacy. The sweets fell from my serving spoon, and I instinctively got up from my chair. Feeling totally at a loss and apparent amalgam of confusion, I immediately plunged back to my chair, focusing my eyes on the floor. Resultant elaborative words of Joyonto-da facilitated my calming down fleetingly. I struggled to put up a happy face when Laboni (niece of Joyonto-da) and Anjali (daughter of my deceased sister-in-law Aparna and wife of Laboni's younger brother-in-law), in the company of Nandita (my daughter-in-law), came to take leave from me, as the visiting two would like to be back home on time. Joyonto-da readily supported their proposal while expressing profound thanks for receiving him so graciously and spending time with him reminiscing the days and settings prior to migration. In uttering the last few words, Joyonto-da had an encumbered look at me, the inherent inference of which was known only to both of us. To others, that was a social decency and politeness.

"Much after Anjali and guests left, I continued sitting in my same chair, mostly positioning my eyes outside with a bemused look. Nandita got seemingly preoccupied in preparation for Dhrub's (my son) return from daylong business engagements. A series of very loutish coughs of Kiran (my husband) unsettled me. I got up and took small but reluctant steps toward the room at the northwest side of the house, which Kiran and I share in two separate beds.

"As I was passing the hallway, some eerie thought drew me close to a fairly large mirror with wooden frames affixed on a solid post. This mirror was regularly used by Kiran in his mature life for the final ritual of checking his hairdo prior to leaving for evening outings with friends. That mirror has been there now more as a decorative piece since Kiran got debilitated. I approached the mirror and wiped that with the *anchal* (tail end) of my saree. I stood in front of the mirror looking at my still unblemished face with salt-and-pepper hairline divider riveting with the glow of regularly applied *sindoor* (vermilion).

"Unknowingly, and with the coarse coughing by Kiran having abated, I positioned myself very close to the framed mirror and started having an intense look at myself for the first time in many years. I fleetingly was in a state of awe and happiness, noting lack of wrinkles in the face and absence of sagging skin tone in spite of my age. Suddenly I had the feeling of seeing different profiles of myself at a number of vertically separate mirrors within the frame of the one. In the last one, I identified myself as a teenaged girl putting on a red saree when visiting your place the first time after my first period. All the events prior to and subsequent of that visit flashed in my memory. I instantaneously started feeling good.

"In that sort of situation, and parking away all past promises, emotions, frustrations, and anger, I decided to write to you. The unanticipated discourse with Joyonto-da and his voluntary promise to ensure delivery of any message to you through his Comilla connection were very reassuring to me.

"The real problem was to have someone who knows me, understands me, and can reflect my words, emotions, and feelings properly in the form of a letter. I immediately concluded that daughter Shetupa would definitely be the person. The congeniality of mother-daughter relationship, the depth of understanding and competence Shetupa confidently displayed in handling delicate family matters, and her persistent efforts of the past to open the window of my early life were reassuring. But for that, I had no option but to wait for the return of Shetupa from Agartala after finishing her big examination for entry into high level civil services under the government.

"That is the premise of this communication. The facts detailed in this communication unequivocally relate to and reflect my life, thoughts, and actions. Most of the words are that of mine with variations made for clarity and consistency by my dearest daughter in whose world of social and family interactions both of us will remain safe at all times.

"In the company of parents, I crossed the Belonia border with the help of an agent deputed by Ominesh Mama (uncle) and went for a short stay in a rest house–type accommodation. Soon Ominesh Mama arrived with a bag dangling from his left shoulder and a folded umbrella in his right hand. His all-embracing happiness was discernible in his body language, particularly in facial expressions overshadowed by the visible loss of some tooth of the upper jaw. That definitely amused me. For a brief moment, I forgot my promise not to remember you at all made so boldly about an hour back. Unwittingly, I succumbed and had a laugh, internally recalling your oft-repeated reference to my Krishna *Kaku* (uncle) as *Fokla Buro* (toothless old man). I am more than certain that had you been present, you would have said the same thing about my Ominesh Mama, of course in privacy.

"I promptly commissioned needed restraint, stepped forward, and bent myself to take *podo-dhuli* by touching his feet. As he put his hand on my head, saying, '*Shoda shukhe thako*' (Be blessed with happiness always), I slowly raised myself and softly said, 'Mama, I am Indrani.' By this time, Ma (mother) appeared with all the expression of her emotions in the form of sniveling and was almost shivering when she placed her head on the chest of Ominesh Mama. *Baba* (father) just was in a standstill position with no noticeable outburst.

"To lighten up the sudden heavy undertone causing apparent strains to the otherwise happy ambiance, Ominesh Mama brought out a very nice saree of light orange color tone from his bag, presented that to me, and asked me to wear that before we start for his home at Patiya Nagar.

"The family, consisted of *Mami-ma* (maternal aunt) and her three sons—Obhi, Omio, and Opu—received us very warmly and cordially. I soon started feeling a special position in this house, as my cousins had no sister. Everyone was busy in making me happy, in pampering me—something I never experienced in Anandapur except some limited time with you. There was perhaps another reason for such extraordinary care shown to me: everyone was conscious of my deracinated status together that I am a guest of few days only. I did not think much about that and enjoyed what I was experiencing.

"You may not recall that in our regular but short interactions, you always used to tell or convey to me loaded advices or words. I listened intently, though I did not understand many of them. I am not sure how much you did either. Each one of them has since been embedded in my thoughts and in my mind. I continuously tried to understand them. The process was facilitated as Shetupa grew up, and I often would ask her what particular advice or word meant.

"When everyone started behaving with visible social niceties that I never experienced before, I was sort of both nervous and intrigued. Then one of your golden advice came to my rescue: '*Ja pao, sheta shabavik bhabe grohon koro. Shab kichu te totta khuj te jeo na*' (Accept in good grace whatever you get. Don't try to unearth what is innate).

"The crevice between my arrival at Patiya Nagar and the wedding was seventeen days. I enjoyed every moment of that with dogged endeavor to obliterate your memory. Family members were markedly engaged with marriage-related arrangements. Every time Ominesh Mama would be back from his routine outdoor chores, the ritual was for him to take off his shirt, or *fatua* (relatively short man's wear without neck band), and wipe his bare body with a *gamcha* (handwoven cotton scarf), while Mami-ma would soothe his sweat-laden empty body with gentle move of *tal pakha* (hand fan made of palm leaves). The noticeable attention of Ominesh Mama with little variation was his updating all, particularly focusing on my parents, about progress made and what needed to be done concerning various details of the wedding.

"Surprisingly, my parents, mostly because of unfamiliarity with the place and the people, had only a passive role in such briefings. On one such occasions, Baba (father) took out a small packet containing some money and quietly handed over that to Ma. The recurring emotional scene since our arrival was repeated. Ma started sobbing with simultaneous efforts to wipe her dripping tears. For a moment, the whole setting was very calm. Ma managed to regain her compose. She respectfully approached Ominesh Mama, put the envelope in his lap, and said, 'Dada, this envelope contains little money that we, including close relations and well wishers, as symbolic of their *ashirbad* (blessings), could arrange before coming. We are fully conscious that it is trivial compared to whatever you and *Bou-di* (sister-in-law) are doing for us, and especially for Indrani. But please respect our feelings by accepting this as manifestation of our ashirbad.'

"Ominesh Mama kept looking at my mother as if he traveled years back, picked up the envelope from his lap, held it between the two palms of his hand, and slowly said, 'Before I wrote the letter to you, we as a family discussed the matter in detail, and the concurrence was that we would get Indrani married out befittingly as we would have done for our own daughter if we had one. That was not an imposed decision. We prepared ourselves accordingly. But I also acknowledge that as parents, you must have your role and participation. Because of that, I am accepting this envelope. The added significance is that it also reflects the love and best wishes of people she grew up with.' Ma, instead of saying anything, took steps forward and graced her forehead with the dust on the feet of Ominesh Mama (taking of his podo-dhuli).

"Mami-ma took me under her wings and bestowed me with love and care full of emotions and feelings that I never received from my own mother even. Both Obhi and Omio-das (brothers), being elder than me and per social ordain of the time, were somewhat reticent in their interactions with me, though their affection was paramount. Opu, slightly younger than me, was very open and friendly. He once told me, 'Didi, before your arrival, Dhireen Babu was in our place almost every day revisiting various rituals and formalities as well as associated responsibilities. His prime focus was to avoid slippage of any sort. He emphasized time and again that this is going to be the wedding of his only son, and there should not be any lack of effort to make that perfect in terms of time, arrangements, rituals, and other formalities. Even I had to go to the *purohit's* (priest's) house three times to remind him about his timely arrival on the wedding day.' After finishing his long narration, Opu had a big laugh. He said that '*Jamai Babu* (brother-in-law) will have to pay for all these.'

"That was the first direct reference to my would-be husband in any discourse since our arrival, and I was visibly blushing and radiant. Observing my lustrous facial reaction, Opu said, 'Didi, you are too beautiful. Had you not been my sister, I would have eloped with you, and Jamai Babu would have spent the rest of his life with a deep sense of impassiveness.' Hearing this, I picked up a small canelike thing and mockingly said, '*Ta be re dushto! Onek boro hoya gachesh. Kache ai, toa ke pitabo'* (Hi, naughty one! You have grown up big! Come near, I will spank you). Both of us laughed, and Opu left the place.

"By the time you grew up, Hindu weddings strictly adhering to traditional rituals in and around Anandapur were perhaps very rare. So I need to elaborate on that. Unlike the contractual nature of wedding in your faith, as you explained to me a long time back against the backdrop of marriage of your neighbor's daughter, ours is more based on rituals. And the rituals are many with some local variations pertaining to details. For example, these vary significantly even among Hindu population of West Bengal and Bangladesh. These are acerbically termed as '*Ghotty Bibaho'* (related to West Bengal Hindu weddings) and '*Bangal Bie'* (those of Bangladesh), respectively.

"The traditional rituals with local variations are: *prewedding ones*—*Ashirbad* (separate or joint blessings of the bride and groom by family elders sprinkling husked rice and presenting jewelry), *Gaye Holud* (separate or joint application of grind turmeric), and *Dodhi Mongol* (presenting traditional pair of white Shakha bangles, and feeding of the bride a meal of curd and rice by seven married ladies); *wedding ones*—*Potto Bastra* (offering of new clothes to the groom preferably by the eldest male member of the bride's family once the groom takes his seat at the *chadnatolla* [wedding altar and canopy]. The groom needs to wear this set of clothing known as *Jora* ['Shawl,' 'Dhoti,' and 'Topor,' a Hindu headdress] during the entire wedding rituals), *Shaat Paak* (the bride, seated in a low wooden peera, is carried by her brothers [and their friends] to encircle the groom seven times while covering her face and eyes with betel leaves), *Shubho Dristi* (after shaat paak, the bride puts down the betel leaves, and exchange of looks takes place in public. This is celebrated by blowing of conch shells and ululation), *Mala Badal* (still seated on peera, an exchange of garlands of fragrant flowers takes place between the bride and the groom), *Konna Shamprodaan* (the bride is taken to the chadnatolla and is seated by the side of the groom while the senior male member of the family, who earlier presented potto bastra, formally hands her over to the groom), *Yagna* (both bride and groom chants Vedic mantras after the purohit, keeping fire god, *Agni*, as divine witness), *Saptapadi* (both bride and groom undertake seven circles around the fire), and *Sindoor Daan and Ghomta* (in seated positions at chadnatolla, the groom puts sindoor [vermilion] on the bride's hair parting. The bride then puts a new saree offered by the groom on her head as ghomta. In most parts of Bengal, this saree is called *lojja bostro*. The couple is officially treated as married when sindoor daan and ghomta rituals are complied with); and *postwedding ones*—*Kaal Ratri* (the couple lives separately the first night in the groom's house), *Bou Bhaat* (the serving of rice with *ghee* (similar to butter oil) to all her in-laws at lunch following kaal ratri; and *Phul Shojja* (the first official night of conjugal bliss after long wedding rituals).

"Hidden in these rituals are some specific features of Hindu wedding where mothers are given special role and specific responsibility. Some of these are receiving Bor Jatri (bridal party) by the mother of the bride; the groom needs to seek the permission of his mother before leaving for the wedding, and is to be blessed by her; and groom's mother is not to attend the son's wedding. Rather, she stays back home to receive son and new daughter-in-law.

"There are three other specifics of Hindu wedding that need to be mentioned: first, it is arranged at bride's place; second, the first night following wedding, also commonly called *Bashor Ghor,* is spent in bride's home (it is not a night for conjugal bliss; rather, it is meant for familiarization and initial bonding between two unknown persons in the presence and participation of young relations and friends); and, third, the presence and participation of two purohits from two sides conducting the wedding through dialogue between them in the form of reciting Sanskrit *mantras.*

"These details are not my sayings. When I opened up and suggested that Shetupa writes a letter to you on my behalf, the only suggestion she made was to elaborate Hindu marriage rituals so that you could have proper perspective and appreciation of what Shetupa's Thakurda (grandfather Ominesh and the family) did for her mother.

"In my wedding, each of the above rituals was timely and meticulously complied with. It was difficult for anyone to think that it was not the wedding of the daughter of the house. My mami-ma (aunt) and Ma jointly received the Bor Jatri. Ominesh Mama did the konna shamprodaan. My cousins and their friends took me, seated in a peera, around Kiran seven times to complete saat paak. My father-in-law, Dhireen Babu, was very happy in the process as Opu reported to me from time to time.

"My Bashor Ghor night, in coherence with prevailing traditions, was in Ominesh Mama's house with the presence and participation of close young relatives and friends. Most of the night, they talked and laughed, with the loose ends of our respective dresses still tied together. This, otherwise known as *Jor Bandha* (tying loose ends of the dresses of the bride and the groom is symbolic of permanent bond) was done after our Mala Badal ritual. Kiran appeared to be happy and contented, except for occasional ostensible advances to touch me in the presence of all. Initially, I accepted that. But that became obvious and quite unpleasant when he tried to grab my hand with noticeable smugness as I was offering him water because of obvious dryness of his mouth. As the boisterous reaction of his friends bear witness, and notwithstanding the presence of his younger sister and her friends, Kiran was replicating the type of advances he is used to, as I came to know later, most of the nights in the *para* (restricted area) of Santirbazar.

"By early afternoon of the following day, I started from Ominesh Mama's home for my new identity as *bou-ma* (daughter-in-law) of Dhireen Babu. While Patiya Nagar, after many days of hectic activities, suddenly became quiet with all-round tranquility, added preparations were in full swing in Shukhipur for gracing the new bou-ma. Dhireen Babu got up early morning to supervise preparatory activities even though he detailed each of those to respective individuals days and nights before.

"Bou boron is the first and the most significant family ritual performed in the house of the groom when he, accompanied by his newlywed spouse (Bou), arrives. My *shashuri-ma* (mother of Kiran) led the ritual process by bestowing her blessings on me, the *nutun bou* (new daughter-in-law), in the midst of intensive ululation accompanied by blowing of conch shells by female relatives and community ladies. Then I was ushered in the home as a nutun bou. This ushering has a process too to be followed by nutun bou. So I did.

"One platelike brass utensil with plenty of milk and *Alta* (known as rose Bengal and is a red dye) is placed just following the lower frame of the main entrance door of the house. I had to step into my new home by dipping my both feet in that platelike brass utensil, complying with the requirements. But more importantly, I was needed, under the careful watch of my shashuri-ma, to step in with right foot first, leaving behind visible red footprints.

"Relative affluence of the family I was to move in was always at the center of all discussions with regard to my marriage. Perhaps it was so by design. It could be a calculative move to build a refuge in my very poor parents' mind against all possible anxieties for marrying out their only daughter in a totally anonymous surrounding and among unfamiliar people. The other reason could be to remind everyone about the most staggering favor that Ominesh Mama and his family had done to us without interest. So I had an idea about possible freedom in life from the persistent cynicism that poverty, by connotation, is associated with, and my familiarity with that since early childhood.

"As I stepped in, I was bemused by the relative affluence of the family. Perhaps, due to my background, everything, from the layout of the house to ordinary décor, appeared so unique, so special, and remarkably noteworthy. Seeing household support personnel in action reminded me of the setting of your house in Anandapur.

"The first night in groom's house is traditionally called *Kaal Ratri* (more akin to ill-omened night), and the groom and the bride are to sleep separately. My knowledge about kaal ratri was premised on what I heard in early childhood at the time of the wedding of our neighbor's son, Laxman. As I was told, this ritual is the byproduct of epical legacy based on the medieval story of *Behula* and *Lakhindar.* I had no occasion either to get the story reconfirmed or to think through its relevance and implications in real-life situation. People of your time and age are expected to have some idea about this epic as I know that there was a popular Bangla movie made in Dhaka depicting the same epic.

"Hinduism embodies narratives dating back to 10,000–7,000 BCE. The most valued ones are *Vedas, Upanishads,* and the *Puranas,* supplemented by epics: *Ramayana, Mahabharata,* and the *Bhagavad Gita.* These narratives reflect divergent traditions evolved and developed at different times, by different people, and in different social conditions but still esteemed and practiced in most Hindu society notwithstanding their being oldest in terms of origin. The epic pertaining to Behula is one such that had, I am told, roots in Bengal.

"For me, this night was a very germane one. I had the unfettered opportunity to know and bond with my only *nanadini* (younger sister of Kiran), laying the foundation of a relationship based on openness, trust, and goodwill. She is Aparna, a midteen young girl with all the attributes of grace and sublime beauty. We talked through most of the night. To my utter approbation, Aparna was very frank, straightforward, and friendly, and did most of the talking, occasionally amusing me. She explained at length how, most of the days prior to wedding, my *shoshur moshai* (father-in-law) would happily report to the family the progression in every step, or repeat his instructions to household helps pertaining to pending preparations at this end. He would even talk about infinitesimal matters like ensuring availability of *kula* (bamboo winnow), mix of milk and *alta* for *Bou boron.*

"While detailing these, Aparna, perhaps unwittingly or may be due to the open nature of her persona, traveled back to the family's initial struggle soon after emigration. She continued, 'Baba moved into Shukhipur, a totally unknown place and equally inhospitable surrounding, with his immediate family consisting of Ma, Kiran Dada (brother) in his early teens, and myself being about seven years old. The local inhabitants, in spite of commonality of language, did have reservations and difficulty in embracing ever-increasing inflow of refugees. There were palpable social tensions making settling process both arduous and exigent at the initial phase of migration.'

"Aparna continued, 'The rest of his family stayed back in the new country called Pakistan. Some close ones mocked at Baba's such quick decision even before political fallout of partition could settle in. Baba, otherwise a very calm and quiet person, never looked back. Negative comments of relations and adverse environment of settlement in a totally new place did not deter Baba's focus and determination. He used to tell Ma that "I have left Lakshmipur (place of goddess Lakshmi [wealth]) for Shukhipur (place of happiness) not to be deprived of either. I will make sure that goddess Lakshmi smiles at me to ensure gargantuan happiness for my family."

Referring to previous statement of her Baba, Aparna resumed her avowal, saying, "Baba soon established a grocery store in Santirbazar and earned a name and fame for his business acumen, honesty of his dealing, politeness of his behavior, and eagerness to help anyone in need, whether local or an emigrant. Goddess Lakshmi literally was extra kind to Baba. The business flourished at startling alacrity. The items and stock of things in the store went on increasing with Baba remaining fully engaged in business from early morning to late evening. His other acquisitions soon multiplied side by side with the business growing in size. The house was redesigned and reconstructed; new furniture items were brought in; and farm lands were acquired. Baba soon carved out a niche for him in the immediate social setting but always kept himself away from politics. He definitely succeeded in attaining the favor of goddess Lakshmi but plausibly paid dearly in his equal endeavor to have 'happiness.'

"The immediate effect of that was visible in the ever-changing mood and behavior pattern of my Ma's ordinary interactions. Depressed by being away from large numbers of close relations and familial links, and engorged by Baba's continuous and long business-related preoccupations, Ma soon developed eccentric traits in communication. While Ma enjoyed every bit of Baba's economic and social success, she gradually mastered the art of commenting on everything, whether it concerns her or not. She steadily developed an opinionated discourse pattern to the dismay of all of us. But no one dared to tell her anything. I, Aparna, was a silent and obedient observer, always looked at as the youngest in the family who is not to have an opinion of herself. Kiran Dada never bothered about it, as most of the time he was away from home and with his friends. Baba ignored that, as coming back after daylong work, he would much prefer to have peace with himself instead of picking up something upsetting with his wife. So literally Ma did not have much of interactions with anyone close to her, but her monologue rattled inexorably throughout the day in one form or another. Mostly the defenseless household helps have to sustain those.

"But possibly Baba paid most dearly for his unrelenting pursuit of goddess Lakshmi. He neither had time nor made the effort to develop a bond with his only son. They are just opposite of each other. Baba is a calm, levelheaded, determined person with amiable disposition and open mind to help others. He was not greedy but very much wanted to settle his family in unknown settings so that they do not ever regret his prompt decision to migrate soon after partition of India. Enhanced social standing that he started to enjoy with each economic success made him happy otherwise.'

"Without any dithering or reservation, Aparna then detailed to me so far hidden elements of Kiran's approach and attitude toward the family, and his very discernible and atypical personal lifestyle. She frankly said, 'Kiran Dada was just the opposite of my Baba in every respect. Ever since our emigration, with Baba being preoccupied with business and the absence of extended family framework, as was in Lakshmipur, Kiran Dada grew up as a slapdash and egotistical young person with no sense of responsibility. He was enamored by despicable words and activities of his close friends who mostly circled around him due to his affluence. Baba initially ascribed this to the fault of age and was mostly certain that Kiran Dada would come out of this with maturity. It never happened. It was not to happen either.

Kiran Dada's behavior was premised on his understanding of Baba's apparent priority in life.'

Being agonized, Aparna once most courteously suggested to her Kiran Dada the imperative need for him, as the only son, to have better relations with Baba and his responsibility to help Baba in his ever-increasing business activities. The response astounded Aparna when Kiran quietly stated, 'Look, Baba neither needs me nor can tolerate me. He is at peace when I am away from him. If I show up in his *gadi* (his place in the store) and ask him for small amount of money, he would prefer to give that without questioning, as in his mind that is a waste of time. That is Baba. I know him very well.'

Aparna soon became very worried about that sort of mind-set of the son of a noble person like Baba. She then decided to talk to Baba with regard to Kiran Dada even being fully aware of challenges she had, that was goaded by the isolated location of the family and the absence of opportunity in terms of time and convenience against the setting of the house.

Aparna took efforts to explain those limitations. She said, "We did not have many relations around Shukhipur. Most of our subsequent emigrant relatives settled around Agartala, and other places like Shipahijala, Bishalgarh, and Teliamura. So community elders are the friends that Baba has, but that friendship has its own limitations. In the house, Baba's discussions with Ma mostly centered on household needs. With Dada spending most of his time with friends, I was the only one with a support shoulder for him. From childhood, I observed him intently. As I grew up, I developed a very sweet and cordial relationship with Baba. He likewise demonstrated unrestrained love for me, showed gargantuan confidence in my judgment, felt at ease in sharing his concerns, and often sought my opinions. Baba is the first one to treat me as an individual, tried to nourish in me a sense of self-confidence, and encouraged me to think independently instead of mastering the art of total obedience. That had its side effects too. Ma was apparently jealous of the time Baba spent with me. Often she would loudly comment, 'What is going on in this world that father and daughter are trying to solve? There is no time for me.' I made efforts to have intimacy with Ma, but on most occasions she would snap off the discussions in two words: '*yes* and *no*.' We both exchanged looks and smiled.

Aparna thought it relevant to touch base more intimately the extent of friendly access that she enjoys with her Baba. So Aparna continued saying, "In all my interactions with Baba, I always discovered a person totally unfamiliar outside. Compared to attributes for which he is socially adored, viz., his chic persona, cautious approach, and focused responses, Baba has always been totally at ease with me with refreshing simplicity and an innocent facial expression. More than his own comfort level, which has all the elements of spontaneity, he always made me comfortable in his presence. It has always been such a magnanimous gesture that it is well neigh impossible to forget that ever. It fostered the growth of confidence within, enabling me to discuss delicate family matters even. Baba always gave me a patient hearing and most of the time respected my opinions.

"The principal impediment was the absence of opportunity for discussing any sensitive and delicate matter with enough time in hand. Any incomplete discussion not only would be useless but also might generate unpredictable misinterpretation of the intent and content of discourse. Soon the needed opportunity was there. That was an occasion of one of the many festive *pujas* (Hindu religious prayers) related holiday. Its special relevance was that Bhallab *Kaku* (uncle, as father's friends are always addressed) of nearby Gobindapara village made that particular puja an annual event of his family. As most of the locals were expected to join that puja, Ma went there too with our neighbors. Baba normally distanced himself from such gatherings and was therefore resting at home. Aparna had the opportunity.

"In spite of that, Aparna admitted having her dithering in raising the issue of Kiran Dada, as he, being the elder brother, is to be respected like a father figure per cultural norms. In standard family mores, any observation about a senior brother's conduct and behavior by his younger siblings is not only odious but also to be equally abhorred. But the special facet of the family setting and the warmth of cordiality that Aparna enjoyed in interactions with Baba gave her the needed confidence to raise the issue of Kiran Dada in otherwise casual discussions.

"Aparna told Baba all that she wanted to, that she had in her mind, and that she thought she should say to create an outrage in his thinking, propelling in him the imperative need for quick recourse.

Baba listened intently, kept eye contact always while Aparna was talking, and made efforts to absorb the inferences Aparna was trying to draw.

"A total silence descended as soon as Aparna finished narrating her concerns. Her ever-loving Baba (Dhireen Babu) appeared to get lost in a setting of emptiness. A ubiquitous silence permeated the setting, which normally used to be a joyful one during any discourse between the two. With his head down and eyes fixated on the floor, that silence was unbearable to Aparna. She started to blame herself for what she brought up in the discussion. Aparna suddenly had the feeling that perhaps she touched upon the weak and vulnerable point of otherwise a socially successful and contented person.

"Baba slowly got back his equanimity, raised his head, and greeted Aparna with a comatose half smile. He slowly but cogently said, '*Ma* (for mother as daughters are often affectionately addressed), I am thankful to you for raising an issue that continuously made me nervy in the recent past. I was always looking for time and opening to discuss that with you. Though manifestly a delicate issue, I do not have anyone to share my burden with the objective of redressing it, as possible. I can't even raise the issue with your Ma, as she would find faults at my end only. Her blind love and unreserved indulgence accentuated the problem that we have. She possibly lacks mental frame to comprehend the magnitude and related implications of her endorsing all that Kiran is doing. But let us focus on the issue you raised. Before doing that and reverting to all that I thought through in the recent past, it is my position that before we get involved with options, you need to understand who I am and also know how I grew up.'

"Aparna was amazed observing Baba's composure and steadfastness in handling the most sensitive quandary of his life that she raised. Simultaneously, she was thankful to him for taking her to confidence in sharing his own thought about that. Baba continued, 'In pre-partition social system of Bengal, most of the low caste Hindu population were landless, unlettered, derelict in all senses, and logically very poor. I was born in one of such families of our locality with two elder sisters and one brother preceding me. Both your *pishi*s (sisters of father) were married out in their early teens. Our very scanty financial position suffered enormously in the process, as *konna dan* (handing over the daughter and synonyms to marriage) is always an expensive compulsion in Hindu religion and culture. The pain of poverty and helplessness at that phase of life were excruciating ones. That impact embroidered manifold with the sudden death of your dadu (grandfather) sometime after the marriage of your second pishi. The magnified nature of impetuous pressure was a horrendous one. My mother struggled on a daily basis to ensure that we had something to eat—the type, the quantity, and the taste of food never mattered.'

"In unfolding his early life, Baba became not only emotional but also almost in a state of being sodden, especially when he was referring to my *Didima* (grandmother). After a pause, he continued, 'I still remember that Ma had to go door-to-door, with the grief of losing the most important man of her life parked temporarily, seeking help of others for his cremation. I had seen the ugliest face of poverty, both in its atrocious and sinister forms. We saw our dear Ma struggling daily in moving from house to house to perform part-time contractual works to sustain the family. We thus grew up in the midst of absolute poverty.

'That agonizing family position slowly took a relative compassionate turn with my elder brother getting married in a comparatively well-heeled family. That was the upshot of a number of propitious support factors,' as Baba explained.

'Your *Jettha Moshai* (elder brother of father) was a student of class nine when Father died. My brother did not have much option but leave his study to support Ma and to ensure that I could pursue my education. He had always been a calm, quite, responsible, hardworking son with devotion to family, and thus earned a very good name in and around our habitation. Two villages southwest of our place, there was a family of same caste as ours having an unmarried daughter. Her marriage was delayed for no other reason except lack of a suitable proposition from the same caste. By all prevalent standards, she could be a likeable bride for any family, but the requisite quintessence of caste system stood on the way. She was definitely senior to my brother.

'A family well-wisher, our dear Prodip Kaku, saw this as a "win-win" possibility. If a relationship could be worked out between these two families of the same caste, then the family of the groom may be able to escape from the persistent burden of their financial constraints, and the family of the bride could get relief from social stigma of having an unmarried daughter first approaching the borderline of socially acceptable age of marriage.

'Prodip Kaku took the idea quite seriously after having initial exchanges with some other family elders. He started shuttling between two families with his umbrella under the armpit and all-pervading smile on his face. His only demand was a delicately prepared *paan* (betel leaf) from Ma. He soon was able to mitigate all sorts of concerns and reservations of both the parties. It was not considered necessary at all to discuss the proposition with my brother or his wife-to-be, the principal characters involved in the proposed relationship. They were to behave; they were to act—that was what expected of them.'

"Baba continued, 'My bou-di (sister-in-law) was a blessing to our family beyond all expectations. She stepped in our humble house with the fineness of both Goddesses *Lakshmi* (wealth) and *Saraswati* (knowledge). When she arrived first in our home in the company of *Bor Jatri* (bridal party), her accompanying goods, symbolic of *Ashirbad* (blessings), were so overwhelming that we had difficulties in placing and storing them. That sort of support from Bou-di's family continued informally all through ensuring due decency and dignity. But the most noticeable one was Dada's commitment to still work harder to make a difference in our family life. Ma never defaulted in maintaining her self-esteem. She continued working but on a selective basis.

'Bou-di's depth of knowledge and understanding were manifested in her prudence concerning family and social deftness. Though from a relatively well-placed family setup, she never exhibited that by words and deeds. She focused on embracing all of us as her own notwithstanding our multifarious inherent limitations so evident. After the night of phul shojja, she got up early, took her bath, performed morning *puja*, and went to Ma to take her *podo-dhuli* (seeking blessings by touching feet). She then said, 'Ma, I am your daughter.' From that day onward, she took care of all of us as her own, guiding us with her profound sense of astuteness. While the family benefited at large, Dada slowly lost his own identity and became dependent on Bou-di for every minor decision. But being youngest in the family and due to absence of father in my life, I grew up with a carefree mind-set in spite of initial conditions of deprivation, hunger, dismay, and frustration.'

Baba continued assiduously his life story, stating, 'That initial conditions of life disturbed me a lot during both growing-up phase and my early youth. I developed a trait of talking to all creations of God around, as I saw God in each one of them. I talked to water, I talked to trees, and I talked to cows, and so on, asking literally, "Why am I destined to be deprived of all that is good in life?" In other words, "Why me?" Engulfed with such thought and resultant agitated mental setup, I struggled but nevertheless finished my intermediate education in our local college. With Ma, Dada, and Bou-di looking after the family and two sisters living in their own places far away, I had no pressure to do something tangible. A slender physique, reasonable height, and a skin tone between black and fair made me a conspicuous young man of the local surrounding. I was very popular among youngsters of the locality. That gave me occasional relief from the pervasive trotting around limitations of my life, more particularly the earlier one. But one thing persisted within me even though our financial condition improved as I grew up. I could never forget going from house to house accompanying Ma seeking help for the cremation of my Baba (father). Lack of support from Baba's close relatives distressed me most.

'An elder uncle of my late father visited us for a short period. I never saw him, but Ma eloquently talked about him when information trickled about his upcoming visit. Ma also did not forget to mention how much our late father was to revere him.'

So Baba continued, "He was our Borun Dadu (grandfather, being uncle of father), a slim, fit, and alert gentleman with straight posture betraying all negativity associated with aging. Borun Dadu, a strict vegetarian and committed to *jog ashan* focused physical postures of Hindu faith and Indian culture, was an amiable and friendly person with wide-ranging knowledge and great communication skills. He was at ease in talking to each one of us from a different pedestal. As I was not meaningfully engaged in any work, I spent a lot of time with him and soon bonded very intimately. Borun Dadu noticed something in the way I talked and responded. Possibly, he could read my mind. He took me aback when he said, "I do not know what, but something is bothering you definitely. Whatever that may be, and I do not have interest in knowing that, I would like to leave with you a piece of advice: never torture yourself by thinking about a position that is past or a situation you can neither alter or have control over it. One can sustain oneself in a static position by belonging to the present and accepting life as it unfolds. But if one is to achieve something in life, one must look forward; if needed, take risk and plunge into uncertainties, try the best but more importantly in a timely manner, and carve out a destiny of your making. Irrespective of outcome, the solace will always be that you tried your best and on time. In that journey of life, always be guided by *Shuvo Chinta* (good thought) and *Shuvo Asha* (positive expectation)."

Baba had no inkling of other subjects that Borun Dadu discussed with his Ma, Dada, and Bou-di. But Borun Dadu's visit definitely was the presage concerning Baba's marriage with our Ma. "Like Bou-di, your Ma also came from a comparatively well-to-do family, but there was an important distinction: she came from a huge joint family. I still remember that I spent most of our bashor ghor night listening to incessant rendering of niceties concerning her forty-one cousins."

"Baba then stated that 'during our phul shojja night, I decided on two objectives of my married life. First, unlike Dada, I would not have a life subservient to her family's wealth and the pressure of innumerable cousins. Second, I purposely will act and behave in a way to embed in her mind my perceived superiority. The second one was necessary, not to belittle her but to ensure that I could have recourse in the future life according to my ambition and preference. I started talking to her about prevalent political issues, faith-related tensions, and social impediments, occasionally reciting poems and talking about various poets. On all these, I had upper hand, and your Ma was just a listener with awe.

'Kiran was born within one year of our marriage. I was mentally unprepared, but everyone else was naturally happy. I started exercising due caution. You were born five and a half years after Kiran, around the time of the Second World War.

'With the war raging at various parts of the world, Quit India Movement was at its peak. The last damaging ploy was played by the

British government dividing Mother India into Bharat and Pakistan, befooling both Hindus and Muslims in a single stroke.

'People suddenly faced the veracity of partition, a much-debated political option but never thought to be a reality. For many people, it took time to assess the real implication of the fallout of division of India. I was debating within me the preferred recourse in the context of my immediate family even before partition happened. Considering across the board Hindu-Muslim animosity and observing its ugly face of 1946 communal riot in neighboring Ramganj *thana* (a police station) of Noakhali and its aftermath in Bihar province of India, I had no doubt about the emerging cold reality and the crucial need for immigration. I recalled every piece of advice that Borun Dadu passed on me. I did not like to see myself continue to struggle along with family at the tail end of the long train of immigrants. I decided that if I am to be an immigrant and to be on that train, I must be at the front so that I can avail of and convert possible opportunities into probable success. I started exploring alternatives for emigration and considered Tripura as the best one due to linguistic, cultural, and social similarities.

'I had my disagreements with Ma, Dada, and family elders but decided to migrate at the earliest. Thus, in late 1947, I arrived along with your Ma, Kiran, and you in a totally new surrounding of Shukhipur and settled here, as I found the location to be a very enticing from business opportunity point of view. The place demonstratively has had business prospect with the possibility of rapid increase in population due to its natural factors, communication facilities, and specific location adjacent to the commercially important Santirbazar. I missed the broader family, especially Ma and Bou-di, left behind but never looked back. I devoted myself fully in establishing my trading business in Shukhipur initially and soon relocated that in the prime location of Santirbazar itself. I soon established myself as a prominent businessman of Santirbazar. Mother Lakshmi (goddess of wealth) smiled at me finally.'

"Baba not only paused this time but also kept quiet for long. He opened up very cagily and, to Aparna's utter surprise, very frankly. He said, 'The concern raised by you today has had been bothering me too of late. But the fact is I am responsible for the way Kiran is currently behaving, and hence at a loss as to remedial measure. Ma (as daughters are affectionately addressed), I do not recall any happiness in childhood, not even at an expense of one poisha (hundred poisha make a rupee). All I remember of childhood was deprivation, hunger, and frustration. Thus, I have had atypical pleasure seeing Kiran spending some money and enjoying himself. My preoccupation with business became an addiction. My penchant for social recognition multiplied. And my focus for landed property as a safety bulb sharpened day by day. I always had the hope that Kiran, with maturity and seeing me working hard, would be by my side with his helping hand. By the time I could recognize the reality, Kiran lamentably molded himself in atypical personality totally oblivious of his obligations and sensitivity toward the family. He took his way of life as being routine. Overindulgence on the part of your Ma unknowingly goaded the position. This has been agitating me for some time, but I do not have anyone in the vicinity, except you, to share this agony. Though our relationship has the pedestal of frankness, openness, and trust, necessary confidence was definitely deficient within me, and both opportunity and time were other constricting factors. I am grateful to you, Ma, for raising the issue today. That enabled me to open up before you without any rider, including the depressing part of my childhood. Besides the glitch we are presently discussing, my only other concern is with whom I will share my future concerns once you leave after your marriage.' After finishing this emotionally imbued trepidation, Baba asked for a glass of jol (water).

"Aparna promptly served the jol but was equally taken aback by the startling reference to her own marriage. That, in the prevalent culture, is generally not mentioned in any discussion between a father and a daughter. She suddenly felt bashful and kept her face down. Baba took the glass of *jol* with a queer but palpable expression of sound, and sipped quite a bit of that with unusual whoosh.

"Seated in that position, Aparna suddenly had the kick of ecstasy. Baba's fortuitous reference to her marriage suddenly propelled a brilliant reflection within herself. She was swamped with impetuous happiness. Armed with renewed confidence, she raised her face to find Baba looking at her with all the calmness that he could possibly muster but still holding the empty glass in his right hand. Aparna did no more shy away. She said, 'Baba, I have a brilliant idea to solve both your problems by one stroke.'

"Reaction of Baba to those few words had the discernible mix of uncertainty, expectation, and relief. He repositioned himself on the *choki* (wooden flatbed with slightly raised headboard), placed his upper body in a sort of reclining pose against the room separator, picked up a side pillow and put that on his lap, and animatedly looked at Aparna as if he would not like to miss any more moment. Aparna quickly but very persuasively formulated her thoughts and presented those by saying, 'Baba, before we discuss options in vacuum, we must have a proper diagnosis of the problem. I have your life background, which you very honestly shared with me. Based on that and the nature of problem, I hope you would agree that we have four specific wedges in this regard. These are Kiran-da's life and living attitude including attraction for outside amusement in dirty places, lack of attachment for home, perceptible absence of sense of responsibility, and influence of his so-called friends. To my mind, there is a quick solution for all these: get Dada married soon with an attractive girl. This is likely to work as a miracle. I have come across such situations in many novels, and in most cases things changed positively after marriage. Well, you could as well contest this assertion of mine as a sort of erudite one, but it actually happened in the case of the brother of my friend Shilla. Both the cases are very similar. Shilla's brother changed dramatically after marriage.'

"They were once again in a silent mode as if someone is orchestrating that. After some time, Baba commented, 'I do not have any difference with what you articulated and suggested, but my real worry is whether, in the process, I will knowingly be playing with the life of another loving soul.' He once again went to a state of extrication with all discomfiture engulfing Aparna. Her instantaneous comprehension was that it would be disastrous for the family to have inconclusive discussion on this matter. She was also certain that the two (father and daughter) may not have another opportunity in the near future to have one-on-one frank discussions on a subject of such sensitivity. So the issue needed to be discussed in its totality today culminating to a realistic resolution. There was no time to waste.

"Aparna slowly said, 'Baba, if we premise our thought on a negative stance to begin with, the resultant outcome is bound to be negative. You taught me that in the past on many occasions. Your advice of *Shuvo Chinta* (good thought) and *Shuvo Asha* (positive expectation) always guided me. The reality of life is that one can never foretell what is in store. So we need to avoid that mind-set. Let us assess the articulated options from positive points of view. First, an attractive and hopefully supportive life partner may impel a sense of inward attraction in the mind of Dada. That happened in vast majority of cases. So it is most likely that it may happen in his case too. We will have to keep our fingers crossed. Second, as and when the couple is blessed with children, a sense of responsibility is certain to enmesh his thoughts and actions. Third, with Dada expectantly getting involved in family matters and with the passage of time, the extent of present peer pressure will diminish. Fourth, if you can find such a girl, then I may have time and opportunity to mold her, without any imposition, as my replica so that you do not miss me after my marriage.'

"At this, Aparna's edgy Baba, with serene smile engulfing his entire facial expression, commented, 'Ma, do you think so? Do you believe that once you are married and leave for your place, I will not miss you, or someone else can take your place, how much loving she may be? A daughter is a daughter. A daughter-in-law is a daughter-in-law. One may love them equally, and a daughter-in-law can be loved as a daughter too. But in all practical and emotional sense, a daughter-in-law will always remain so. She can never be a daughter. That by itself is a conflict in relationship constricting innate emotional balance. So you will always be where you are now, but I may have the advantage of additionality if am blessed with a good daughter-in-law. I will value and enjoy the additionality from that perspective.'

"Both of them felt relaxed and contented, noting emerging commonality in thought and approach that steadily surfaced. Baba then said, 'My real problem is how your Ma would take the proposition. She was not of the type that you have had observed her while growing up. She was a carefree young girl from a huge joint family. After our marriage, she had been under the shadow of your

Didima *(grandmother)* and *Jetti* (wife of elder uncle). So her carefree lifestyle had no negative smudge.

But my decision to portray my persona with artificial superior aura permanently made an impact on our relationship. That reduced her to be just a wife. And my second and quick decision for migration, much ahead of, and to the exclusion of people around, deracinated her totally with momentous impact. Thus, once in Shukhipur all by herself, she started showing signs of crabbiness. I had no time to either give her company or be bothered by it. I settled in a lifestyle with clear focus that I carved out in attaining financial well-being and relative social recognition. Both these were ingrained in my mind, as I was deprived of both when growing up. Once I had the feeling of relative success on both counts and the time to browse, I realized it to be increasingly difficult to communicate with her. She developed an eccentric attitude and started having opinion on all matters, whether they concern her or not. Her increased quirkiness has had been all invasive.

'Though some segments of both the families migrated later on, each one of them settled in different and mostly faraway places. We have had communications, but those were neither regular nor of intimate nature. So I had no scope to share this very personal verge of life with anyone in the family or locally. I emotionally became vulnerable and spent a good amount of time thinking about divine recourse.

'Gurudashpur Moharaja, a person of exceptional holiness, used to visit Santirbazar annually. He had many disciples among the bazaar community and adjacent areas, but few knew his real name. Gurudashpur is a place in western India from where he came, and Moharaja is a title his followers bestowed with love and respect. As a bazaar community member, I had to participate in arrangements related to his visits but initially did so with reluctance. But he had startling attributes to attract people toward him. His very soft, thoughtful, and measured communication style; fair complexion; and slender tall built with long white hair and flowing amorphous similar beard used to have deep impression in the mind of most who came into contact with him. He readily resembled some of the popular Indian saints as they are depicted in portraits. I was no exception. That was perhaps aggravated by the emotional stress within me due to concerns about your Ma's behavioral pattern. Once I requested a one-on-one session with him and paid a *pronami* (sort of donation having more element of devotion and respect). That was granted but for a brief period, as he always preferred to have open sessions for people seeking *ashirbad* (blessings) to heal their agonies.

'Gurudashpur Moharaja intently listened to what I had to say, closed his eyes, took a few deep breaths, and softly said a few words preceded by short statements. Perhaps you would recall my patchy efforts to convey or teach you some of those in the past or may refer to some just narrated in discussing the problem pertaining to your Ma. None of those are my words or derived from genetic astuteness. Those were the words and statements of Gurudashpur Moharaja. But the most striking phenomena was that the words he voiced were almost a reiteration of what Borun Dadu told me many years back in Lakshmipur. For a moment, I felt like that angel philosopher guardian, Borun Dadu, was talking to me. I was so overwhelmed that I instantaneously went to the posture of *Shashtanga Pronam* (most reverential form of Hindu greeting where six limbs or parts of the body [feet, knees, stomach, chest, forehead, and arms] touch the ground as the whole body lies flat).

'I can't relay to you exactly what happened to me at that point in time. I was in a static position during the posture of Shashtanga Pronam and that too for quite a while. My return to normalcy was ushered by soft peddling of Gurudashpur Moharaja's blessed hand on my head. As I left the audience, I suddenly felt relieved and at ease with myself. Since that time, I started seeing things around me from a different angle. I was visibly impressed when Gurudashpur Moharaja advised me, "Do not try to correct your wife or confront her now. It will aggravate the problem for which you have your share of blame. Your effort should be to seek improvement within the current limitations, and sustain present inconveniences." That is the reason you all see me tolerating her occasional awkward behavior. That is not the sign of my weakness. That testifies my sense of judiciousness.

'I would like to pass on to you something on which I believably attained enlightenment, even though partial, during my audience with Gurudashpur Moharaja. As his words and statements seem analogous to those of Borun Dadu in setting and situation markedly different, I became increasingly convinced of the fact that good words, good thoughts, good deeds have no frame of time, place, and personality. They are universal, augmenting life in its journey. It is up to an individual to avail them to boost happiness of life. I also realized that best response to such advice and words is to practice those first by thyself rather than just pass on the same advice to others.'

"Aparna was certain at this point that her dear Baba was traversing in the higher plain of life philosophy. There was thus the need to bring him back to reality with which they were confronted with. She thought through quickly and decided to do so but respecting his thoughts and yearning. So she said, 'Baba, I have always valued whatever you told me and tried my best to adhere to what you taught me. There were obviously things that did not register in my ears when I was told initially. I, however, did not write them off. I carefully stored them in my mind. Gradually, and with growing up, I slowly assimilated those in their proper context. I never failed to revisit with all earnestness what you told me and to get to the bottom of those through acquired knowledge, social interactions, and observing human behavior. But we need to converse this afternoon as to strategy for responding to the problem relating to Dada.'

"Baba agreed but kept quiet. Aparna was certain that following the trait of his growing-up phase, Baba was mapping out the canvas in terms of options. And precisely that was so. He said, 'There are three imperatives involved in any decision pertaining to the problem. First, we need to have an attractive girl. Second, she should be from a family with relative marginal economic status. Third, she should preferably be from an emigrant family so that your Ma can relate to her easily.'

"Aparna was taken by surprise due to Baba's quick framing of very germane criterion for future course of action in the context of the problem being discussed. The first one was aimed at Dada. The second one was meant for the new daughter-in-law's overall adjustment with the family. The third one was to ensure Ma's sympathy for the girl from the other side of the border. Aparna readily agreed. The subsequent steps were taken in quick succession, and both of them piloted the proposition without any inhibition on the part of anyone. 'That is how, my dear, you have become my bou-di (sister-in-law).' I looked at her and slid away my eye focus with a giggling facial expression.

"Aparna, referring to my very visible physical attributes and quite likeable complexion, taunted me by saying, 'Bou-di, are you a victim of your inherent beauty? Did you create any problem for your parents? I am asking this, as most attractive girls in every social setting have common handicap of being imprudently influenced by partisan maneuverings of goaded individuals around her. Even if your response is a negative one, I am the last person to accept that. I am at a loss to think that why a beautiful girl like you would be married out in a totally unknown setting and in a different country. If that was my case, I would have been the last person to agree to such a proposition.'

"A glimmer of my association with you in Anandapur, even if devoid of any explicit attachment, flashed back. I had a half-concealed smile in response to what Nanadini Aparna just said. She also confided to me that she neither has any liking so far nor is she averse to marriage proposition. But she made one point very clear: 'I would never agree to get married in a totally unknown setting.'

"As her only, though new, Bou-di (sister-in-law), I, that very first night, made an irrevocable promise to do everything to ensure that Aparna's specific position is honored in the future matrimonial arrangements. Our brief formal relationship of bou-di–nanadini unexpectedly got rooted in a bond of firm friendship between two young persons of totally different background.

"Around midnight of kaal ratri, our edifying discussion suddenly turned to matters that were of significance in the context of my induction to the family and future conjugal life. Aparna, who so far was initiating me to their family settings as a careful, conscious, and considerate guide, suddenly deviated. That possibly was the upshot of emotional burden she had been harboring since preceding late afternoon. That sad feeling was premised on seeing her brother misbehaving with their father on a trifling issue. On being informed that Kiran was planning to spend the kaal ratri outside with his friends, Baba politely advised him not to do so, as that is against norms and practices of holy rituals pertaining to a Hindu wedding. At this, Kiran became agitated, and his outburst crossed all sense of propriety, embarrassing every one of the family, including his ardent supporter, Ma. Though it was decided to keep the incident as a secret, Aparna could not hide it anymore from me. Before doing that, Aparna argued with herself and decided to be frank and candid so that I became aware upfront of the challenges I had. According to Aparna's considered assessment, such a course would only enable a new bride like me to prepare well without just recourse to crying silently. It was bound to help me prepare emotionally to handle future unpleasant situations, about the recurrence of which Aparna had little doubt based on experience and maturity.

"Aparna's depth of understanding, sense of aptitude, and enormity of poise overwhelmed me right from the beginning of our impromptu one-on-one discourse, but I was really taken aback by the radiant positive note with which she premised the most delicate part of our discussion. Aparna averred, 'Bou-di, you are singularly lucky to have Baba as your *shoshur moshai* (father-in-law). Not only will he love you as a daughter, but you will soon find in him a friend, a well-wisher, a guide, and much-needed shoulder. I am saying this based on my own life experience and recent discussions that I had with him. You would encounter some difficulties with Ma, your *shashuri* (mother-in-law). But if you are smart and have patience, then you would soon be able to convert those innate negativities as something positive, and to your advantage. Ma has developed a habit of commenting on everything that comes to her attention or she observes. Most of her comments have not much relevance. She generally forgets them after a few minutes. So if you can have patience for those few minutes even if you don't like the comments, then you can do whatever you want, and she would not bother you at all. In that sense, living with Ma will not be that challenging. But you are certain to encounter gargantuan difficulties in handling the eccentric overtures of my loving *Dada* (brother). He is also not a bad person, but his whims and temperaments are totally impetuous. I do not have any opinion or suggestion pertaining to the relationship that you would be having with him. To me, he is a mixed person of conflicting ideas, and plausibly he himself does not know what he wants from life. His good side is ephemeral but sufficient to create erroneous expectations, and his bad side is scandalous, mostly triggering extreme frustrations. But more significantly, his vulnerability to peer pressure, even at this age, worries me most. I can only say that you must show extreme patience in handling him so that you can protect your own dignity. Baba has a lot of expectation in your ability to handle Dada, and you can always seek his guidance. It is immaterial whether I am here or not.'

"During the entire process of such discourse, I was constantly preoccupied internally thanking my luck to have a nanadini having such an open way of thinking with very organized communication skill. She did just not hint something. She did not try to hide anything. She presented before me facts as they were even though that was my first night in their house. Possibly Aparna had the objective of molding me adequately right from day one so that once she leaves the house after eventual marriage, I could smoothly fill up her position with full understanding of related background. Also probably she narrated most pertinent facts upfront to take care of Shoshur Moshai's concern of spoiling another life by getting Kiran married.

"But whatever Aparna had in her mind, I was definitely benefitted by her open and contemplative narratives in many ways just when I was about to begin my own married life. The base concerning my new family and possible challenges in scouting through connubial life were crystal clear to me. Unlike most newly wedded brides, I consciously narrowed down my expectation level. I conditioned myself to have a rough start in my conjugal life, taking each small happy experience as additionality to find exhilaration in Shukhipur. I also decided to manage my future relationship with Shashuri-ma with understanding, patience, and abstemiousness while focusing on developing an enduring affiliation with my shoshur moshai. Following prevalent tradition, a common feature of both Hindus and Muslims of the subcontinent except variation in related addresses, and to get fully inducted in my new family, I also decided to address my shashuri-ma as *Ma,* and my shoshur moshai as *Baba.*

"I experienced on the *phul shojja* night what Aparna alluded during our late night tête-à-tête of *kaal ratri* about connubial relationship. Aparna, other female relations of about the same age, and friends spent the afternoon of the day following kaal ratri in preparing me and embellishing the setting for much-cherished conjugal bliss. The time was just before sunset. Kiran, dressed up elegantly in a cream-colored silk *punjabi* (traditional knee-length man wear) and a very white *dhutti* (about four-and-a-half-meter-long fabric worn by Hindu male to cover the lower part of the body) with noticeable border, entered the room. He was seemingly in a good mood, smiled at young girls present, and combed his well laid out thick black hair a number of times. Some of the girls noted that in the pretext of combing hair, Kiran was trying to have a full look at me through the fairly large mirror that was procured as one of the many items to decorate the bedroom for our wedding. At the friendly behest of Aparna and others, I too looked at the mirror, and we had our first informal pithy look at each other. On his way out, Kiran suddenly approached the side of the bed I was occupying. As an instantaneous reaction to that sort of advance, girls around me sprawled out; Kiran positioned himself just opposite me; and without any shilly-shallying took out the small fragrance container from his pocket, opened it, and put the same on both sides of my elongated neckline, and left the place with the side comment, 'See you at night.' He demonstrated no coyness in acting like that either due to social dictum or the presence of other girls. Within myself, I really enjoyed that first touch by him and liked that brashness too. I had no time to be nostalgic about that sudden but equally elevated experience, as Aparna and girls continued to giggle centering on that act of Kiran and joshed me about what to expect at night. I had no idea that the said brief experience would be the only such one in my entire life.

"That was past standard dinnertime as I observed the night before. Monitoring the overall mood around, an art in which girls like me from poor families excel just to survive, I could sense that a situation of stress was being built up. That was accentuated by repeated restless gesticulation of my shoshur moshai—seating on the chair of the veranda and leaving that too soon to take a few steps around and then once again reclining in the chair. Aparna's visit to our room became infrequent and shorter. Those visits were just for basics: no loose talk, no laughter as was in the afternoon. The young damsels, who were preparing me for the night with light talk and dirty jokes, were not to be found anywhere. Even Ma, my shashuri, was very quiet. Everything around appeared to be frozen in inexplicable uncertainty. Everyone was waiting for something to happen.

"In that situation, and as I could see through the narrow opening of the door, *Gokul*, the senior household help and trusted person, approached Shoshur Moshai with his head down and two palms clasped together, whispered something, and turned back to retreat.

Most unbecomingly, Baba (my shoshur moshai) thunderously called back Gokul and loudly and firmly said that 'all present in the family will have dinner together tonight in the veranda, and Indrani would sit between Aparna and me.' He also said, 'Both Gokul and *Bishnur-ma* (mother of Bishnu, the cook) will serve the food tonight welcoming *Bou-ma* (daughter-in-law).'

"I could discern the inexorableness of the most creepy situation I was going to face on the night that for a bride is the most cherished one. I did not exhibit any reaction. I was still enamored by the first and most loving touch of Kiran the preceding afternoon. I was mostly alone when others were preparing dinner service or sharing the stress. I earnestly prayed to Bhogoban (the Lord) not to deprive me from the golden night experience of my life. Simultaneously, I prepared myself for all eventualities and promised to myself to remain calm and dignified under all adverse situations, both during dinner and afterward. Though not wanted to, I remembered you and your utterances every moment of that solitary hiatus. Your golden advice, 'Patience and less words are often the best defense,' ricocheted within me.

"Dinner arrangements were made as desired by Baba. *Patties* (homemade bedspreads of local vegetation) were laid out covering most of the veranda. Family members sat in two opposite rows facing each other. A mortified and sad Aparna entered our room and very softly said, 'Bou-di, Ma and Baba are waiting for you to have dinner together. Please come.' I had no chimera about what I was going to face. By this time, I was certain about the absence of my illustrious husband and had the feel of stress that it caused to all. But what bothered me most was how I would handle the resultant anger of Baba. I slowly stepped in. Aparna escorted me from near the exit door, and Ma graciously put her right hand on my shoulder, helping me to sit by the side of Baba.

"All my internalized coerce evaporated as soon as I took my designated place of seating. Baba, to my surprise, looked toward me, wore a full smile on his face, and with a loud happy enunciation said, '*Bishnur-ma, ar deri keno* (why the delay anymore). My new mother is here. Now start serving the food.' Everyone in that assembly appeared to enjoy the food and the occasion, and the absence of Kiran was neither felt nor had any impact on the joyous mood, at least outwardly. It was difficult for me to be oblivious. My discomfiture and resultant pain in munching food and ingesting the same were not noticed by many. Aparna was the exception. She continuously whispered in my ear words of care and diversion to ensure that I was at ease.

"As the dinner ended, Gokul-da placed two chairs at one end of the veranda. Baba and Ma sat on those. All others casually occupied spaces, facing Baba and Ma, of their choice on the patties. Aparna and I were part of that assembly too. Gokul-da slowly approached Baba's chair with a *hookah*, a simple form of locally made single-stemmed instrument in which smoke passes through water, causing a bubbling sound (hubble-bubble).

"Hookah's shape and size vary from area to area. Originating in India, it perhaps reached its zenith during Ottoman Empire. Upscale hookah is generally made of a number of components based on design. Its topmost part contains a bowl (vessel) made of clay or marble to hold tobacco. This is a special tobacco normally made of fresh tobacco leaves, pulp of semidried fruits, and honey. I was told that puffing hookah was a favorite pastime of Baba, and he would always have that after meals.

"Gokul-da moved with care and caution, occasionally blowing the burning tobacco put earlier on the bowl of hookah, and placed that on the right side of Baba's chair. Observing the timing of doing this and the manner in which that was carried out, I had no doubt in my mind that it is a regular postdinner ritual of the house. Baba, so it appeared, really enjoyed his hookah with intermittent long inhaling and casual emitting of smoke, keeping his eyes closed occasionally. That assembly was all fun embellished with hilarious recall of old family incidents and stories. Not for a moment was there any rumination of what was experienced in the early evening when Baba detailed very loudly the setting of the dinner. The more I thought about the variance in two reactions, the more I was convinced that Baba's early evening loud reaction was reflective of frustration at his own end rather than the anger at hearing of what Gokul-da had to whisper. I always felt bad for Baba, as he desperately tried in his life to shelve his dismay, frustration, and scantiness in putting up a face of calmness and compassion.

"Aparna and other young relatives and friends accompanied me back to our room at the end of the assembly. Most others retired to their respective places. A sense of total stillness was all pervasive in our room. That was a very unnerving situation, but I had one advantage. Persons, particularly girls, from lower stratum of social setting grow up with immense mental power to face adverse situations. That was germane in my case too. In addition, I had the blessings of your company and constant guidance in my growing-up phase. You would remember that my reading sessions in your place had always been less of reading and a lot of heavy statements, many of which I did not understand at that point. But most of them I remembered and got clarified from different sources at different times.

"Because of that background and my resolve before going for dinner to conduct myself with dignity, I took the initiative. I said, 'Why are you all so quiet? Do I not look beautiful in this red saree and the way you made me up?' All present were taken aback, and then laughter broke out. One of the cousins of Kiran tried to dupe me by saying, 'Bou-di, you are looking fantastic! But where is our prince charming to admire that? The night is not getting younger.' She thought that I would be mortified by the tenor of the comment, which was a reality and undeniably to the discomfiture of any bride. I, based on what you had always advised me, prepared myself before unleashing the earlier light comment. I responded by saying, 'my dear *nanadini* (younger sisters of husband and their friends are addressed such), the admiration of beauty is always an impulsive, and equally personal, feeling. It is often a captive of a wink. The comportment of its rapt is never measured in terms of time. It does not matter at what time my prince charming shows up. I will adore his presence whenever he is here.' The reaction was just what I thought. Some of the girls were surprised. Some others were happy. Aparna took quick steps to be by my side. She hugged me and very slowly said, 'Bou-di, you have done very well. I am proud of you.' I responded by saying, 'Credit goes to you too.'

"But as the time rolled by, every minute, which was to be the witness of pleasant moments of our maiden conjugal night, appeared to be too long, creating suppressed stress on my thought, on my nerve, and on my physical bearing. My outer posture was contrary to my inner paroxysm, though I did preserve a calm continuance. In my internal self, I continuously prayed for face-saving finale of the night. My eyes were interacting with the girls giving me company, but my senses were parked outside, and my ears were tweaked to capture any remote movement.

"The time was around twinkling hours of early midnight. I could sense a commotion in the *uttan* (quad) surrounding. The girls around me suddenly disappeared. Gokul-da and two others clenched Kiran from both sides, helping him to take steps into the room. Kiran was at the height of wobbly physical condition. He, though in a state of unstableness, resorted to brazen verbal gesticulation attempting to free him from the clutch of individuals accompanying him. I positioned myself near the headboard side of our bed decorated with varied and multicolor flowers. In my eyes, they suddenly lost their glow and color. I had no illusion about what was in store for me with respect to much-cherished phul shojja night of a bride. I was just construing the situation as 'what to expect next.'

"Aided Kiran took few jagged steps, vomited copiously as he stepped into our room, and passed out to the embarrassment of all accompanying, and to my total degradation and consternation. Aparna rushed in but refrained from having eye contact with me. Keeping her head down, she instructed others taking him to the bed. They managed to drag and place him on the bed with one hand and one leg still dangling. Their predicament was where to put him in a bed arranged for phul shojja.

"I quietly told Gokul-da to leave him there as he was and requested him to bring a pail full of water, an empty container, and a few cleaning and dusting pieces. Aparna turned around to leave the room. I politely called her back and requested for a cotton saree. She opened the *almirah* (wooden closet) and brought out one. I whispered to her, 'When you all were putting this red saree on me, I prayed to Bhogoban to give me the opportunity to bless my would-be daughter-in-law with the same. So I do not like to spoil it. You go and take rest. Please also advise Gokul-da to do that. I will take care of him. Rest assured I will not create any scene either at night or in the morning.' Aparna just left the room after softly saying, 'Thank you.'

"The phul shojja night of the poor and deprived girl of Anandapur had its initiation in a relatively well-off family setting of Shukhipur by cleaning the face and hands of the drunken husband. I had no special feeling as I first touched him. That was quite contrary to the earlier experience of the afternoon when Kiran put his fingers on my neck to titivate me with his perfume. I straightened him, properly aligned his head on the pillow, placed a light comforter to cover the lower half of his body, cleaned the floor, and put the bucket with stinking water outside the room. I then looked for odd bedspreads, placed them on the floor by the side of the bed, lifted my earmarked pillow from its original placement, and lay down with unexplainable prostrate feeling.

"I had no inkling for sleep initially. In that tattered condition, my stymied emotion suddenly focused on my parents. It was true that they could not provide me with any tangible thing, but it was equally true that they protected me at all costs from all conceivable outward impediments, and always focused on decisions that likely would augur well for me. Their decision to readily agree to what Ominesh Mama proposed was an obvious manifestation of that mind-set. I had my somber laugh within myself when their supposed happiness, in the backdrop of phul shojja night, for getting me married in a well-to-do family traversed me. It pained me inside for being where I was instead of where I was supposed to be. It was just difficult for me to bear that demeaning posture in the august night of my conjugal life.

"In that milieu, you resurfaced in my thought against all my promise and intents. Your oft-repeated assertion that 'it is sheer foolishness to seek happiness in everything and in its entirety' started clinching my thinking. I also started recalling your advice 'to enjoy smidgen of happiness as it occurs and use each of that to build blocks for greater one.' I did not know whether you said all those understanding their content and intent, or you just used them to unleash on me what you heard your elders were saying in social discourse. Whatever that was, those few words came to my rescue at the most exasperating situation of my life. I overviewed probable upshot of life and relationships emanating from my wedding. Instead of harboring negative stances, I looked at probable positive bare bones. They were quite pervasive: love, care, and affection of Baba (shoshur moshai); a simple but somewhat opinionated shashuri-ma (mother-in-law) -- as told by Aparna night before--; very understanding nanadini (sister-in-law); the affable family setup; and financial affluence beyond my imagination. I remained inconclusive about the most important connubial relationship that eventuates in wedding. My determination not to allow Kiran to snap me out from other positive facets of my future life became stronger.

"The moments passed by. The night grew older. Kiran was sleeping in a static position with occasional deep breathing. I was tossing on the floor bed trying a restful posture for myself in the midst of excruciating mental pressure. Slowly and unknowingly, I fell asleep.

"Presumably, it was early following morning. I sensed that someone was sitting by my side, lovingly moving his finger between the side of my forehead and neckline. I had no doubt that it was Kiran. But in a state of procrastination triggered by both frustration and internalized anger, I did neither open my eyes nor move my body. I was in a traumatic situation, hating his touch, nevertheless having a sensation within me, for which my corpus was waiting for so long. After a while and perhaps observing me in a stale state, Kiran put his left hand below my hips and right one under my shoulder and softly lifted me. Placing me on the bed where I was to be, he sat by my side and started playing with my jumbled uncombed hair, picking up a few of them in between thumb, index, and middle fingers of his right hand and amused himself with their unsynchronized move. Kiran then, in a state of self-talking, murmured, 'I am sorry for last night. I had no intention to get drunk. My friends offered one to toast your beauty and pressed me. I could not say no. Then there was the second one congratulating me for having a very beautiful wife. I could not say no. The third one followed for having a successful wedding. I joyously had that one too. In the process, I gradually lost my senses and had a few more. That was the reason for the most undesirable outcome of last night. I am aware that it caused a lot of pain in you. I am just sorry for that. It was not intended to be such. Please trust me.' After saying those words, Kiran went to a state of curious silence. I was unsure how to react. Thus, I preferred to remain as a motionless body bag with eyes closed as before.

"In an engrossed mind–set assessing the nuance of words Kiran just muttered, I did feel a heavy and cheek inhalation engulfing my face. I was certain that it was of Kiran. Soon he adorned my two lips with a deepening kiss. I just did not know how to react but enjoyed that initiation to our conjugal link. I slowly opened my eyes to have a full look at my dubious life partner but closed those quickly as reactive shyness related to the kiss. I then reopened my eyes and fixated them on his face, trying to convey many unspoken words pertaining to feeling and frustration. Kiran did not utter a single word. He looked at me avidly, placed his two hands on the back of my body, suddenly lifted my upper body, and continued pressing me against his chest with all the passion he possibly could muster as the sleek sunrays of early morning were penetrating through window slides.

"Kiran released me after a while and went to take a bath in the family-owned outer *pukur* (pond). Fortunately, I could escape that sort of traditional bathing. Baba, as he always acted with prudence, thought through this ordeal as Aparna grew up and built a bathroom near the house located in a pastoral setting. I was to be the eventual beneficiary of that.

"I finished my shower; came out dressed in a bright pink saree, as shown by Aparna the previous evening, and performed *pronam* (also known as *charan-sporsha*) by touching the feet of Kiran (a Hindu cultural practice that makes one an integral part of religion-related darshan [vision of the divine]). I had no idea about Tripura-based requirement; so following what I knew, I folded the *anchal* (tail end of a saree) around my neck and performed the pronam. Kiran palpably was oblivious of those requirements and only laughed at me for doing that. I then rearranged the said anchal to cover part of my head and told Kiran that I am going to join Ma (*shashuri-ma*) in the *puja ghar* (prayer room) for morning *prarthana* (prayer). He was sitting on the bed with an impish smile and said, 'I am waiting for you. Both of us would step out of the room together once you return from prarthana.'

"I went to the adjacent puja ghar and quietly sat behind my shashuri-ma. She had an askance look and nodded her head slightly, conveying both approval and pleasure. Hindu family starts their day with morning prarthana normally conducted by the mother. Though called a puja, it is possibly not one by strict interpretation. Prarthana is a normal prayer. Puja, on the other hand, is a formal one with elaborate rituals. Pujas are performed by reciting different chants in Sanskrit. One thing, however, is common in both prarthana and puja: the burning of incense powder, commonly called *dhoop*. Dhoop is burned in a container called *dhoopdan*. The circling of dhoopdan after prarthana or puja with emitting smoke is called *aarti,* a primary constituent of prescribed rituals. After each such prayer, the said dhoopdan is normally taken to each corner and setting of the entire house with the belief that the emitting smoke removes all negative energies that sheathed the house.

"In such solemn setting, the ordained focus is on seeking mercy of and blessings from god with total devotion. I continuously struggled within myself to have that devotion, but my thoughts were preoccupied by the acts and words of Kiran in the preceding night and that early morning. While my overall agony loomed large, making an impact on my ardor, I somehow derived happiness from discrete other realizations. I felt happy that though my phul shojja night was marred by startling happenings, I had a nice and pleasurable follow-on morning. But the uncertainty that hinged around Kiran's conduct and his penchant to repeat misdemeanor without remorse continued to batter me. In such discomforting situation, I decided to give my new bond an unabashed try. I prayed to Bhogoban earnestly to help me.

"As both of us stepped out of our room together with normal countenance, all present in and around the kitchen were bemused with instantaneous exhilaration overflowing in actions and words. Baba was very expressive, while Aparna unremittingly teased me through eye contacts. The family had *prato rush* (breakfast) together. That was an exception for the family and made everyone happy, particularly my shashuri-ma. She just could not help herself but gleefully prodded Baba by saying, 'You always had negative views about my son. See today. He is so changed a person. Did not I tell you about this before?' Baba nodded his head and kept quiet. Shashuri-ma's ecstasy knew no bounds. That made me happy too, erasing all the immediate abysmal experiences.

"I never expected that the said ubiquitous happiness would be an ephemeral one with enduring smudge on my conjugal relationship in years to follow. Initial few days after phul shojja night had my surprises coupled with enragement. Kiran would hug me, kiss me, and play with sensitive engorged sexual tissues such as nipples, buttocks, and vulva, and then would retreat at the time my sexual arousal was picking up. I consoled myself as that being primarily lack of confidence on the part of someone being angst with thinking about performance. After a few days, and being aroused by his cuddles, I forced myself into the act and started the maiden conjugal ecstasy. Like all other happiness of mine since the wedding, this was also a short-lived one, as Kiran ejected much sooner. That was much earlier than the plausible normal duration to experience orgasm. I reconciled with that, always hoping that time would heal that. In the process, and totally unwittingly, I was harboring a discontented self within me.

"This pattern of experience and disdain depicted the motif of the portrait of my follow-on married life. I continuously tried to manage my frustration tranquilly. I parked my frequent irritations in the canvas of Baba's love and affection; occasional good words of Shashuri-ma; care, concern, and congeniality of Aparna; increased devolution of responsibility in managing the house; and the authority and influence I was exercising on even senior household helps like Gokul-da and Bishnur-ma. For a girl coming from a very poor stratum of social and economic setting, all these are phenomenal augmentation in life. I always hoped positively for the other part of my life so far typified by occasional connubial engagement of short duration.

Kiran never discussed about or expressed interest with respect to children. I too was insensitive due to perceived frustration. Occasionally, I shared a part of my disconcertment with Aparna, but my relationship and her maiden status were prominent impediments in sharing that in totality. Shashuri-ma articulated her anxiety periodically and occasionally lamented, saying, '*Amar ki shay kopal hobey je acta nati natnir mook deheky morbo*' (Will I have that luck to die seeing a grandchild?).

"As the time passed, I charily observed a trend in Kiran's behavior. Kiran was always very nice, gentle, and supportive as the day dawns. But he would change notably as the day used to get older, the more culpable one at bedtime. Taking cover of any excuse, real or phony, Kiran would swiftly turn to a different side with pretentious anger and go to sleep soon. With my limited sense of understanding and exposure, I came to the conclusion that the challenge of performing at night haunted him incessantly and bigoted his thinking and behavior as the day progressed. That very often culminated in rough and apathetic responses.

"As Aparna advised, I gaily overlooked the lamenting words of Shashuri-ma. But I had a definite snag in handling ever-flowing comments and recourse suggestions of all and sundry, from among both relations and neighbors. They not only happily elevated themselves as well-wishers but also thought it to be an obligation to tell the family elders and me to do what they considered to be right. In the process, my life was miserable. Even in a sort of open social system of Tripura, it was difficult to share one's private agonies with anyone else. Worst of it was that female relatives and neighbors were the most unsympathetic ones in the type of situation where I was. I realized that women were the most contemptible barrier to women's poise. Many of them had ideas about the vagaries of matrimonial relationships, but they would prefer to place those under the rug. All deficiencies and blames are directed against the *bou* (daughter-in-law).

"Even Bishnur-ma came up with a golden suggestion. In my presence, she told Shashuri-ma to arrange a special prayer called Aagneya Snanam. I later asked the *purohit moshai* (priest) of local *mondir* (temple) about that special prayer. According to him, as I understood and recalled, that was a prayer that entails praising the name of Lord Shiva, after every normal bath, as '*Om Namashivava Namaha*,' continuously applying holy ash all over the body.

"Snanam is the Sanskrit word for 'bathing.' It is an integral element of Hindu faith and its ordained daily ritual. There are fifteen different kinds of snanam, each having its own benefits. Snanam can be done individually or as a group. One, *kamya snanam* can only be done in the River Ganga (anglicized word is 'Ganges') and at a point near Allahabad of India, while others can be performed after normal bathing. Each such prayer is accompanied by reciting and repeating *slokas* (anglicized word "shloka") for solving various problems.

"I was edgy and unnerving the more I thought about it. I knew full well that the reason was an emotional one having bearing on physical feat. That has nothing to do with faith. Things were not expected to change with prayers alone. But resultant frustration would be good enough to put all blames on my shoulder. The prime need, as I gathered from side discussions of some ladies and once from the narration of Aparna detailing the story of a novel she just finished reading, was counseling with associated medical intervention. But who could talk about it? In our society, men do not have any imperfection. If a wife is not conceiving, it is the problem of the lady. If the wife can't deliver a son, it is her fault. Thus, any word from my mouth to the contrary, or expression otherwise, would certainly put me out of the house of Dhireen Babu, and out of Shukhipur with likely hostile cousins and Ominesh Mama in Patiya Nagar. I passed many tensed nights thinking all these and eventually came to the same conclusion based on your oft-repeated words in my early teens. I decided to hold back, enjoy what I have, and try to build blocks one way or the other.

"Fortunately, and perhaps due to her inability to pursue any matter for a long time, Shashuri-ma did not react on diverse advices of relations and well-wishers. She neither acted on the specific suggestion of Bishnur-ma. But I concentrated on getting involved at night. I tried to make him easy as night gets older with happy words and light societal talk. I refrained from conveying to him any sense of expectations. I never said any negative word. Neither did I accuse him for any shortcoming. I took a definite decision to support him in whatever he loved to do without reward or return. Perhaps my inner sense of insecurity because of lack of fallback position influenced such a decision. I opted for it without reservations.

"Sudden developments related to my cousin Obhi-da's (eldest son of Ominesh Mama) marriage took both of us to Patiya Nagar for a few days. The mirthful reunion with cousins, the presence and participation of Kiran, and all-round preparations for the upcoming wedding made the whole visit a wonderful one. As usual, and like all previous happiness, this had its hiccup too.

"Opu, who was marginally younger than me, heaved me to a side of the house at the tail end of our visit for some confidential discussions. First, he asked me whether I had knowledge that Kiran drinks regularly. I paused for a minute, smiled, and said, 'Yeah, Kiran drinks but not regularly. I have told him that if he likes or gets bored in Patiya Nagar, he can do so more often. That would be fine with me.' But his second query totally baffled me, as I did not expect Kiran to discuss such matter with his young brother-in-law. Opu said, 'Two days back, I was in the company of Kiran Jamai Babu (brother-in-law) while he was having a drink, sitting on the wooden bench adjacent to our guest house. My presence was at Jamai Babu's behest to keep watch so that he could be assured of necessary cover against unexpected traffic of elders.

Opu continued, 'During casual discussions, Jamai Babu asked me whether I have had visited kotha (a respectable reference to brothel). As I answered negatively, Jamai Babu derided me as a useless guy. He then explained that this has had been a supportive social institution from time immemorial. In ancient times, the rich would ask *nagarvadhu* (brides of the town) to sing and dance. Examples are like those of *Amrapali,* who was state courtesan. Subsequent Muslim rulers added novelty by classifying "courtesan" as *"tawaif"* and developing institutions like *mafhil, mujra, musaara, etc.*—all related to public face of performing arts (dance, singing, poetry recitals) with covert agenda of sex. Partly following that tradition and mostly to take care of natural corporeal craving, brothels are allowed in most areas having floating people (men living without family and in distant place for work). This has had been a societal response to meet the innate physical need of people. In such brothels, there are a few, especially young newcomers, who would pretend to behave like Amrapali and her descendants. Such exceptional young ones are also prostitutes with a difference. They provide recreation in the form of drinks, rendering of songs, dance performance, and recital of poetry. The chosen one from among attendees, obviously having more money, is taken inside for intimate recreation. Kiran Jamai Babu, to my surprise, then told me that he still goes to such kotha.'

"I was dazed for a few seconds but recouped from that soonest. I immediately focused to articulate a brief and to-the-point response based on what I learned from you earlier. My quick response to his concern, based on very convincing but equally sham validation, was 'Opu, you have grown up but are still very simple in thinking and attitude. Your Kiran Jamai Babu was mocking with you taking advantage of relationship. You know, he has always been very outgoing type. He went to kothas a number of times with his friends prior to our marriage for occasional indulgence in drinking. But neither he nor his friends ever had that sort of money to get an entry into the inner setting. I am certain that he just told you to portray himself before you as someone special. Moreover, in our social setting, Jamai

Babus do indulge themselves in loose talks with younger brother-in-laws more to test them.' I do not recall how I had conjunct thoughts and words in a situation of unmitigated cacophony. But observing Opu's facial expressions, I was certain that my handling of the situation was able to garner his confidence back about the congeniality of his dear sister's married life. I deliberately did not lengthen that discussion but took care in emphasizing that this matter should not be discussed with anyone else. Opu assured me about it. I refrained from discussing this with Kiran either being conscious of the fact that it could infuriate him. That was also reflective of my earlier understanding with myself to enjoy what I have without any expectation. That could sound funny to you, but that was the simple route I charted for myself in my delicate journey of life.

"Time passed by. My decision pertaining to self-containment and our short visit to Patiya Nagar without any unpleasant incident started having a positive impact on our relationship. Somehow a miracle mirrored. Kiran started to be much more easy and joyful with the advent and progression of night. We started experiencing occasional engagements even though for a short duration. I had an early miscarriage some time after returning from Patiya nagar. That was a frustration for all. That discontent, however, did not last long, as I conceived again soon. We were blessed with a fine-looking baby boy. The impulsive joy was plausible, as a baby boy is the most venerated present that a daughter-in-law could give to her in-law's family. As mother of succeeding generation, my position and status in the family suddenly skyrocketed. Baba gaily named him *Dhruva*. I started calling him Dhrub.

"In naming his grandson, Baba himself read Hindu epics afresh and consulted the local purohit. He had chosen the name Dhruva who, per Hindu mythology, was blessed by Lord Vishnu with eternal glory and life as the pole star. Baba's happiness knew no bounds, though Shashuri-ma's one was more sublime. I spent my time and energy in rearing up Dhrub. Bishnur-ma and Aparna joyously supported me.

"In the midst of such joy and happiness, I observed two negations. One was related to the marriage of Aparna as she was first approaching the upper limit of what the society termed as 'marriageable age.' Baba was very concerned, always looking for an agreeable proposition.

He occasionally shared his anxiety with me and discussed various propositions, more to ascertain the reaction of Aparna in a very subtle manner. In relation to time and level of upbringing, that was a remarkable phenomenon of his personality trait. He never imposed anything on his family members. He always tried to cultivate a more understanding and supportive relationship with his offspring. His rather poignant experience in rearing up Kiran did not derail him from that approach. Baba was able to make me totally comfortable in his company in no time. It taught me a lot with respect to nurturing children and developing relationships. I was guided by that all my life.

"It was around the second birthday of Dhrub that the lingering disquiet of Baba suddenly came to an end. One of his business acquaintances brought a proposal for the second son of a well-known *arathder* (wholesaler) of adjacent Dhalai District. The arath (business place) of the gentleman, a widower, was located in Ambassa, the district headquarters, and he was fairly well known. His married eldest son was a government functionary and residing in Agartala with his immediate family. His two daughters were married out prior to the demise of his wife. The gentleman was living with his two other sons of which Proshanto, the proposed groom, is the second one. Proshanto abandoned his bachelor of arts in education when his father fell sick after the sudden death of wife and joined hands in helping the father in running the business. The youngest son was a senior in the high school.

"By all consideration, the proposal was an ideal one. The caste was compatible. The family locale could not be better. By being the only female member of relevance to be, Aparna would have full control over the affairs of the family soon after the wedding. She, on her own right, fitted in very well in that sort of situation being supported by her upbringing, personal attributes, temperament, and ability to see things in broader perspective. Most importantly, Aparna gaily consented when I floated the proposition.

"The wedding took place soon with all merriment and fanfare. Baba went out of his way in discharging his obligations as ordained by Hindu rituals and Indian cultures. As Hindu rituals, being spread out on a huge geographical area, have many variances, so is Hindu wedding. But three features are generally common. These are known as *Kanyadaan*, *Panigrahana*, and *Saptapadi*. The first one denotes the giving away of daughter by father (also called 'gift of a virgin' or 'gift of a maiden'); the second one relates to holding hands by the groom and the bride in the presence of fire to signify union; and the third one is a demonstration of promise to each other before the fire by taking seven steps, each step embodying a vow. In Bangla-speaking areas of prepartition eastern India (i.e., Bengal, Assam, Tripura, and adjacent areas), the *vivaha* (wedding) of daughter in a Hindu family is etymologically related to Kanyadaan.

"Kiran's involvement was a rather peripheral one in that gala event of the family. That was partly due to his behavioral precedent and partly Baba's lack of confidence in his only son and elder brother of Aparna. I was embarrassed sometimes having more than my share of responsibility, even bypassing shashuri-ma. Baba would call me in the presence of all and direct me about some actions, which were generally in the domain of Shashuri-ma. I had a tightrope walking and never allowed that sort of recognition to derail me. I made it a point to discuss any such issue with Shashuri-ma before acting so that she had her mental satisfaction of being involved. I was an uneducated girl from a very underprivileged family, but my association with you and the love and guidance that I constantly received from Baba allowed me to broaden my sense of understanding. A very cordial postmarriage relationship with Nanadini Aparna hastened the process. I somehow developed a great sense of perspicacity for which I often received kudos from Baba.

"As expected, Aparna settled well in her new place Ambassa to the happiness of husband's family. Baba's fondness for Aparna was known to all, and her in-law's family not only recognized but was also sympathetic to that. She thus had periodical visits to Shukhipur. The one most memorable was on the occasion of her pregnancy. In Indian Hindu culture, a mother-to-be is honored and blessed by all in the family and from among friends. The related ceremony, and in some cases puja, is scheduled with the completion of seven months of pregnancy. This is generally called *godh bharai* (fill the lap), but in Bengal it is known as *shaad*. Originally 'shaad' was a 'women only' gathering; however, male presence is gradually being accepted. The essence of the ceremony was to fill up the lap of mother-to-be with gifts, fruits, sweets, and arranging a grand feast for, and in, her honor. Previously, it was a strict religion-based cultural ritual, but now singing, dancing, and guessing games pertaining to gender of the baby based on the shape and size of the belly are slowly creeping in. Very commonly, elder female relatives or community ladies play an active role in such guessing game, making the event a joyful one for all present.

"Aparna gave birth to a beautiful baby girl about two and a half months of her 'shaad.' As custom dictated, the delivery took place at our home of Shukhipur. The baby girl just looked like a doll. Everyone was happy with the arrival of the new baby. Her father-in-law, accompanied by his eldest son and two married daughters, traveled from Ambassa to bless the new granddaughter, and to take new mother and baby to their home with full affability and decorum. Baba, showing due reverence, requested Aparna's father-in-law to name the baby girl before she leaves for Ambassa. It so appeared that the father-in-law and the family came prepared for it by consulting their 'purohit' prior to leaving for Shukhipur. Instead of naming the granddaughter, he took a rather uncommon step of proposing a name to Baba. That was *'Anjali,'* meaning offering to a Hindu deity at the time of puja (prayer). Aparna's baby was named accordingly. The related puja was performed with all devotion and gratitude. A grand feast followed the puja. Baba was particularly very happy. After a few months, he and Shashuri-ma even traveled to Ambassa to see Anjali.

"Aparna's full assimilation with the family of her husband, and the very affable relationship she soon established with both father- and younger brother-in-laws earned a social recognition beyond the boundary of Ambassa, and traveled to Shukhipur even. That made everyone happy, particularly Baba. He made effort to find solace in that against the backdrop of irritation concerning social behavior and deranged personal life of Kiran.

"The second negation related to visible changes in the behavioral pattern of Kiran and the isolated nature of his role and responsibility concerning the family. While I was enjoying a fulfilling life, beyond my wildest dream and compared to what I had in Anandapur, the inner cloaked frustration had always been all pervading with inescapable bearing on my thinking and peace of mind. But I never allowed that to overpower my happy public face pertaining to state of mind and life. I was always very careful in upholding the unqualified love Baba bestowed on me, the unreserved understanding he had shown toward me, the unrestrained vigilance with which he protected me, and more significantly, the incomparable zeal with which he established me in the family.

"My initial strategy of being nice to Kiran in all situations undoubtedly yielded some results. But most of them were the outcome of his decisions and desires, and the product of his impulse, though limited in terms of contents and impact, and reflective of features of his actions lacking malleability in all respects. I still hoped for the best and conditioned myself with patience. His occasional spending of more time in home, sporadic slack in contacts with friends, and visible interest in matters related to Aparna's marriage process were some of the encouraging signs. But none of these were a substitute for the very normal conjugal expectation of any spouse. Most poignant internalized feeling had its roots in not being able to boast of a relationship based on pride in having him as a husband. Still, in my surreptitious mind, I was always hoping for some change, looking for some signal. The more I looked for that, the more frustration engulfed me with excruciating pain.

"With the passage of time, and after the wedding of Aparna, Kiran started bringing some of his close friends to home and spent a good amount of time with them. That was a derailing change. Perhaps having a grown-up sister created a sense of insecurity within Kiran, more so as he knew himself well and was aware of the attitude and fickleness of his friends, particularly pertaining to young girls. So he deliberately avoided that sort of idea. Things radically changed after Aparna's wedding. Both spending time with friends in home and late evening outings, occasionally in para, became a norm of Kiran's daily routine, totally neglecting me, my presence, and my desire.

"Most distracting aspect of this episode was the attitude and harsh comments of Shashuri-ma. She started directly and loudly reproving me for not being capable of satisfying the physical need of her beloved son, and opined that he had every right to go outside for what he was not getting in his bed. Her words of filth crossed all limits of tolerance, affecting the solid fence that Aparna tried to build as a shield against some of her often unintended brutal annotations.

"By connotation, many of such remarks were premised on wrong perceptions. With Dhrub as evidence of physical ability of Kiran, my shashuri-ma loudly proclaimed a certification about the emotional zeal and physical capability of her son. She occasionally taunted me in the presence of others by saying, '*Ruper bhadhuri kore ki hobey; shorirer tagat thakte chai*' (The pride about beauty is of no value; the body should be able to perform). I was often publicly accused whenever Shashuri-ma had some ostensible grievances against me in her mind. During her periodical outbursts, she would reroute all unrelated issues to this one, her apparent comfort zone, to blister at me by repeatedly saying, '*Dhekey shuney kono dabi daoa chara cheleky bia koralam, hi Bhogoban, amar cheller ki kopal*' (Got the son married after detail scouting and without any demand, but, oh Bhogoban, what a bad luck of my son). Most of the time, I used to have silent stern look at Shashuri-ma, and occasionally a few teardrops would roll down my cheeks unknowingly. Bishnur-ma would often drag me to a side of *ranna ghar* (kitchen) and would try to console me by saying, '*Oner shorir ta bhalo na; mathar tik nie; ki na ki bolan*' (She is not keeping well; her health is not good; she doesn't know what she is saying). I would look at Bishnur-ma with all the anguish one could muster but did never react verbally.

"Life's cruelty has its unique attributes, and these are mostly beyond human ingenuity as long as one does not face them in real-life situation. Smaller problems often unnerve individuals beyond comprehension. Many such persons lack grasp about the extent and upshot of other unknown problems. They often lament for problems they have oblivious of what worse could have happened in a given situation, or what other people are going through. I was one such individual. Kiran's nonresponsive and equally eccentric conducts and Shashuri-ma's frequent antagonistic commentaries were my major problems in life, and I just could not think of anything that could shatter the family's locale and my own life. Soon that happened precisely and most unpredictably but still worse pertaining to dear Aparna.

"Aparna, in the absence of any grown-up female elders in her in-law's home, successfully assumed full responsibility of managing the family. In doing so efficiently, she had the close support of her very amiable husband and guidance of father-in-law. The young debar (brother-in-law) soon became Aparna's best friend. His love, care, and consideration overwhelmed Aparna, as she never got that from her own brother. Anjali, the daughter, became a sweet baby girl of eighteen months old, taking small steps with some confidence and uttering a few half sentences. She kept everyone in the family busy. The abode of Ambassa came to full life with the presence of Aparna and after the arrival of Anjali, leaving behind the period of desolation caused by the death of the mother-in-law prior to Aparna's wedding.

"In the midst of such adorable background, Aparna suddenly fell ill. That became serious in a few hours, and she succumbed within a short time. The diagnostic findings remained inconclusive during the few hours she was ill, and the after-death findings concluded that the cause of her death was *meningococcal meningitis* (affecting protective membranes of brain and spinal cord). News of her illness and death reached Shukhipur concurrently.

"In a moment, Shukhipur (place of happiness) of Dhireen Babu became a surrounding of sadness. Speediness of shock and sorrow engulfed the setting. The homestead was full of people from the community, each taking positions and role according to age and depth of social relationship. Baba, seated in his usual chair located at the veranda, was both speechless and calm, and had occasional impassive look at the sky. This mold of his reaction caused silent but staid reaction among the assembled gentries. Efforts were made by some good friends of Baba to trigger a physical outburst of the massive grief he was internalizing. But those did not yield any immediate result. Shashuri-ma was grieving at the top of her voice. Generally nonresponsive Kiran even stood standstill aligning against a post of veranda. While I was pouring water on the head of exhausted Shashuri-ma with the help of Bishnur-ma, Gokul-da quietly took Dhrub and placed him on the lap of Baba. He placed his hand on the head of Dhrub and, to the relief of all, started sniveling.

"As Baba slowly started unburdening himself of his grief, Shashuri-ma's continuous and loud expression of appall and glumness took a startling turn to the surprise of all. All of a sudden, she transitioned from a stage of loud acquisitions against everyone including the Lord to a stage of total calmness and silence. Soon she became impassive to all sorts of indications. Ladies present tried to bring her back to original self for which she was noted. But nothing worked instantly. Baba's slow response to unleash grief was suddenly overtaken by intense anxiety concerning Shashuri-ma's well-being. Kiran restlessly moved around wooden posts of the veranda and close assembled elders, but amazingly not to any of his friends. The suddenness of his only sister's death and the resultant shock were unsurprisingly irksome even for someone like him whose world so far gyrated in spending time and money with friends, and frequently in paras, without encountering any financial or disciplinary duress. He had never faced a situation like this and was in a state of absolute disarray.

"With the help of some elder ladies of the community, I moved Shashuri-ma and took her inside the home. Bishnur-ma cleansed her body, and then Shashuri-ma was attired in a fresh saree. She slowly took steps toward her bed and positioned herself in a reclined posture with blank looks. The local licensed medical practitioner from Santirbazar was rushed in and started attending her. The doctor administered an injection and put a needle in one of her veins to ensure drip flow of needed fluid. Shashuri-ma fell asleep soon.

"As the night evolved, community presence emaciated, and eventually the core family was left to itself to bear and handle the tragedy. Baba came a number of times to monitor Shashuri-ma's condition. Kiran was in the company of two of his closest friends and was sitting under a huge jackfruit tree, which was a special feature of their inner courtyard. The presence of two friends was more for any emergency support.

"In spite of repeated requests, neither Gokul-da nor Bishnur-ma went to sleep. While Bishnur-ma was sitting in the steps of the kitchen stairs, Gokul-da surprised me by overtly holding his *hookah* (hubble-bubble) and having his puff, sitting near the entrance of the kitchen. Neither of these he did ever before. Being a person of traditional values, he never publicly smoked in front of Baba and Shashuri-ma, and even in front of juniors like us. That was the way he showed respect to all of us. This particular action made me worried. I soon came to the conclusion that perhaps that was his way of expressing anger for what happened to the family of which he was an integral part.

"In spite of the request from Ambassa, Baba did not agree to attend the *shraddha,* Hindu religion's prayer event at home intended to liberate the soul of the deceased. This takes place around the tenth (in some places on the eleventh) day and food is served to people attending shraddha. Shashuri-ma was neither physically and mentally fit to travel. It was decided that Kiran and I would travel to Ambassa to attend the shraddha.

"Time passed after shraddha. Members of the family, including household helps, got involved in their own world bit by bit. Life was never as before, but it sustained itself with normalcy overtaking grief. In the process, I had a unique realization. I have, as you know, marginal attainment in education, and that was nothing compared to others. But I believe that Bhogoban has bestowed his choicest blessings on me by giving me a frame of mind to assess and comprehend matters and issues of life in their greater perspectives. That significantly shored up by your presence in my life while growing up; Aparna's frankness with a sense of care and understanding; and Baba's candid love and support with the blend of amiable temperament and specific focus on approach and attitude in handling challenging issues of life. All these unknowingly shaped my inner ability. I developed a keen sense to think about various opinions and statements, which are generally taken for granted by our social system.

"One Joti Kaku (uncle) was a friend of Baba and a regular visitor to our place. His presence increased significantly both in terms of numbers and duration of stay since the death of Aparna. We welcomed that too as a diversion for Baba. Among others, his most oft-repeated philosophical statement was 'Time is a great healer.' Every time I heard that, I had difficulty in absorbing. To my mind, time does not heal the wound. It minimizes the pain. The wound just does not disappear with the passage of time. It enables people to sustain life inclusive of that wound.

"That was very much evident in Baba's subsequent decision. After some days of our return from shraddha, Baba called all in the family, including Gokul-da and Bishnur-ma, for a meeting. With Dhrub on his lap, and calm and quiet Shashuri-ma sitting by his side, Baba said that he had decided to go to Ambassa. He also said that 'it is my desire, and hope that to be of you all, that Anjali should grow up in our place, as that family has no grown-up female members to take care of her. Aparna's father-in-law's family will have full access to Anjali and participation in decisions pertaining to her future life always.' Baba further said, 'I have written a letter in this respect to the father-in-law of Aparna.' He further said, 'I thought of this earlier too. That is the reason I did not go to shraddha. I am now going to bring back Anjali, who will grow up in our home as our daughter under the care of Indrani-Ma.' Baba also opined that 'Anjali's presence will help the process of healing of your ma.' That whole statement was a surprise but delighted everyone. I was very happy with the decision. Anjali soon landed in my lap.

"While handling the grief of losing dear Aparna and adjusting with Shashuri-ma's health status, Kiran, contrary to all expectation and emblematic response that normally is expected in such a situation, started behaving quite bizarrely. That was being manifested in his relationships with all in the family including myself: erratic in behavior, aggressive in posture, unpredictable in temperament, and an evolving tendency to shout. All these pained everyone, more particularly Baba. But Kiran was oblivious of all these. He started spending more time with his few friends and visiting frequently the paras.

There were three of his friends who had easy access to our home. Among them, one Bijoy stood out for being less boisterous and relatively sober in articulation. He impressed me from the beginning. I always enjoyed his company. He slowly became more a regular visitor to our home, developing and maintaining congeniality with all in the family, from Shashuri-ma to Gokul-da. Bijoy-da's (meaning Bijoy brother) initial visits had always been to meet Kiran. Over a period of time, it took the turn of visit by a family friend, and Kiran was comfortable with that. Everyone else was at ease with his presence. That allowed me to be close to him too. I started spending more time with him, mostly in the company of others but sometimes alone. As our one-on-one discourses became informal, friendlier, and more personal, I carefully articulated our discourse to get authentic information about Kiran's outings, his behavior, his inner likings, and reasons for his continued attraction to kothas.

"By all standards, Bijoy-da proved to be a very loyal friend. Many of his responses to my specific and encumbered queries were framed in a way that it was mostly difficult for me to reach a conclusion. He somehow maintained the warmth of our communication and contact notwithstanding my frustration. I even started feeling sad whenever there was a gap in his visits. Every day I looked forward to spend some time with him. Bijoy-da gradually carved out a space of emotional dominance in my world of thought, filling up a vacuum that remained unfilled so far.

"That was the day of *Saraswati Puja* (Hindu prayer for the goddess of knowledge, music, and culture). All elders of our home, like others, went to local *puja mondop* (venue of puja, which normally is the temple). Baba particularly desired Dhrub's participation, and, for the first time, to my knowledge, he decided to go. Hence, Bishnur-ma was asked to accompany them along with toddler Anjali. Kiran went to visit friends on the pretext of attending a larger puja slightly far away. I and Gokul-da were only two in the home. A feeling of loneliness jaded me. Unexpectedly Bijoy-da appeared. My containment disappeared suddenly, and happiness escalated. I did not vacillate in conveying the same through all sorts of expressions except words. For a moment, I felt at ease with myself.

"In the midst of affable and guileless discourse, I unexpectedly put a straight question to Bijoy-da, saying, 'Bijoy-da, I have asked you many a times in the past about enticements or compulsions that motivate Kiran to visit paras, but you never answered them explicitly. You always bypassed my queries. Today, there is nobody at home. There will be no interruption. No one will know that we discussed anything like that. Can you or will you be frank and honest with me? This is a burden that I can't endure anymore. Please help me out.'

"Bijoy-da looked at me straight without any blink as if he was seeing something astounding never stumbled upon before. I had every reason to be embarrassed, but I was not. Bijoy-da said, '*Bou-di* (sister-in-law), you have put me in a very delicate position. In the past, I refrained from answering to your allusive inquiries directly, as I always believed that the answer is known to you. I considered it impolite to tell that to you. If you really want to know in the setting of life that you have to live with, then I need to step back so that my answer can be assessed in the relevant context.'

"Bijoy-da poised for some time, looked outside intensely, and continued his recount in a self-talking fashion by stating, 'Most close friends of Kiran, like me, are natives of Tripura and from a lower middle-class society. We the local fellows, unlike emigrant friends like Kiran, have two commonalities. First, our world was limited to our immediate surroundings, and we never had expectations except mundane ones like growing up, getting married, and doing something nominal to sustain life based on ancestral properties. The second one was that none of us had liquidity to indulge in things for which most young men have fantasies and expectations. Our financial limitations made those more special and pounding, compounded by social restrictions and impositions. Fortunately for us, Kiran has been an exception. He never was short of money, and we, close ones, always pampered him with superlative attributes about his family, himself, how every young damsel of the community is crazy about him, how a young person of his background should behave and do to be more prominent in the society.

'In response to our occasional query as to magic wands he has in getting money from his father, Kiran always had the same answer: "Father considers it to be a waste of time in having discussions with me concerning money. His mind-set is that instead of talking and arguing with me, he would possibly make more money by trading during the time. Thus, he is always comfortable in giving me some money and getting me out of his way. But one thing I have observed sometimes. In handing over the money, Baba would occasionally give a very drab look at me and breathe quite heavily. But I do not care."

"Bijoy-da continued saying that 'general discussions among friends were regarding local politics in terms of influence peddling, games, social and religious events, local incidents, and so on. But when we four, Rajesh, Barun, Rohit, and myself, were together in the company of Kiran, we would indulge ourselves in discussing matters and issues that are prohibited by the societal aphorism. We always got immense pleasure out of that sort of exchanges, and our bonds and loyalty strengthened immensely. We started spending more time together. People of our area referred to us as *Pancha Pandava* (jokingly relating us with five sons of King *Pandu* who, among others, fought their cousins, the *Kauravas*, in the famous battle of *Kurukshetra*, the premise of Hindu epic *Mahabharata*).

'We were all in our late teens at this time. One fine evening, Rohit informed us about a specific development in the para located in Santirbazar area. Rohit, after obtaining all assurances about the secrecy of his identity, informed us about the arrival of a beautiful girl in the said para. She is Joba Rani, a young, vibrant, and gorgeous prostitute but of a class. Not only is Joba Rani beautiful, but she is also equally gifted in singing and dancing. Upon settling in Santirbazar area, she soon set up an establishment like kothas. People with money could go to her kotha to enjoy singing and dancing, and further entry into the interior section of the kotha was dependent on the relative weight of the purse of the person and the yearning of Joba Rani.

'Rohit told us that seeing his two uncles, one from paternal and the other from maternal sides, talking with sense of both caution and amusement, he could not help eavesdropping. The paternal uncle visited Joba Rani's kotha the previous night as a guest of one his friends from Agartala. That was the wonderful experience he was craving to share. He found the apposite person in my visiting maternal uncle. The description covered the entire gamut from vital indicators related to physique, beauty, and talent to setting of the place, motif of dressing, style of talking, and other renderings by Joba Rani.

'We listened intently to what Rohit was detailing. Our resultant exchanges were ephemeral by nature. Conclusion was impetuous. We all agreed to visit soonest the kotha of Joba Rani. The lead was to be taken by Kiran. He, as always, was the most animated one among us but wanted some time to arrange fund. In explaining his predicament, he referred to his experience with respect to getting money from his father. He continued, saying, "Though I never encountered any major problem in getting money, Friday has always been the least irksome to get money from Baba. Being a weekly bazaar day when vendors from different adjoining areas flock around for buying products for subsequent retailing, the business has always been very hectic on Fridays. Baba, unlike other days when he would keep me waiting silently, has always been very prompt on Fridays in giving whatever I asked for. But for our visit to Joba Rani's place, we need a good amount of money. So I need about two Fridays to get needed money from Baba without raising any concern." All of us not only agreed but also voluntarily proposed to put whatever we could to make our planned venture a grand one.

'Days passed by. For all of us, the upcoming event was the first one of the nature and was slated to be most memorable one too. We regularly discussed strategy and progress. Two points were agreed to. First, we decided to visit Joba Rani's kotha on a Saturday, since Friday is a hectic day in Santirbazar with plenty of merchants and other visitors. It was most likely that our visit on a flabby day would ensure relative privacy, more attention, and better interaction. Second, we also decided to send an emissary in advance to advise Joba Rani about our visit. The choice was one named Bhupoti, another young guy of the locality desperate to enter our inner circle. Bhupoti was told to maintain absolute secrecy about our planned visit and to present himself in Joba Rani's kotha as the emblem of an aristocratic young man, son of a local wholesaler who is planning to visit her in the company of four of his friends. Bhupoti was assured that if he could do that job efficiently and would maintain secrecy, then the matter of his entry into our inner circle would be considered favorably by Kiran.

'As planned, Bhupoti went to Joba Rani's place with a beautiful red *benarosi saree* having intricate embroidery work of golden silk thread, some sweets, and flowers. He met the *mashi* (sort of agent cum trusted front person of the establishment), informed her about the proposed visit on Saturday next, and politely handed over the gifts on behalf of Kiran *Babu* (a title conveying both status and respect) and friends as preliminary *nazrana* (offering).

'Sending such nazrana is more of a cultural practice in places like Delhi and Lucknow. That was something unique for a new kotha in Santirbazar area. Kiran and friends had ideas about the setting of kothas and related cultures from Hindi movies of Bombay. We planned everything based on that sort of exposure.

'Those nazrana positively impressed Joba Rani. Mashi returned soon with affirmation and said, "Joba Rani sends her warm greetings to Kiran Babu and friends and will be waiting eagerly to meet them on coming Saturday." Bhupoti merrily reported back the outcome to illimitable happiness of all of us.

Bijoy-da continued his narration, stating, 'Special consideration for and treatment of Kiran were all pervading and noticeable as soon as we stepped into Joba Rani's kotha. That was what it should be, and we all were very happy seeing Kiran, our lead person, enjoying his time in the close company of Joba Rani. For the rest of us, it was a game-changing experience having a deep mark on our future thinking and acts.

'All of us had a wonderful time on that Saturday evening: enjoying songs, dances, light conversations, and casual physical contacts with associated girls of Joba Rani's establishment. Intermittent service of drinks along with snacks under the careful supervision of mashi added patina to the experience. We even did not fail in throwing one *rupee* (Indian Rupiah) note on the body of Joba Rani as a token of appreciation for her rudimentary dance movements depicting popular Hindi songs. Joba Rani was equally happy and flattered by our gestures so uncommon and unexpected in the local setting. We were all astounded when Joba Rani gaily took Kiran inside, signifying an unprecedented act of immense significance on the very first evening. We were left in the outer room to spend time with support actor girls.

Bijoy-da than referred to most agonizing experience of that venture. He said, 'Regrettably, our exhilaration did not last long. To our utter dismay, we saw a beleaguered Kiran literally taking shelter among us, barely holding loose ends of his *dhutti* (unstitched white textile to cover the lower body) with only sleeveless undershirt gracing his upper body. Gone were the trendy hairdo done by the famous local barber, Netai; the graceful crisp crinkle of dhutti attired with the help of Bhupoti; the aroma of aristocracy emanating from the stylish silk *punjabi* (long flowing traditional dress of Indian male gentry) having chained gold buttons that was especially brought from Agartala for the occasion; and the joyful interactions that were the hallmark of jubilation in the entertainment room of that evening. We were stunned. So were the other girls present, while mashi had a relaxed and equally mischievous smile adoring her round plump face. We were at a stage of grappling the preposterous development but did not have to wait long. Soon Joba Rani flung the silk punjabi of Kiran to the entertainment room, loudly saying, *"Morad amar. Shorirey nai takat, a-khane ashechey mastani korte. Ami takar jonno shob kori. Kintu shorirer o cha hida achey. Je purush amar shey cha hida meta te parbe na, tar a kotha te ashar dorkar nai"* (What a man! Has come to my kotha with the air of maleness but do not have physical ability. I do everything for money, but the body has its own demand. There is no need for a person to visit this kotha who can't fulfill that demand and need).

'We left the kotha forlornly having all the opposite facets of our arrival. None of us talked to each other, neither in that evening nor for a few days. Things started settling down with the passage of time. We refrained from inquiring about what exactly happened but individually had clear picture from the loud words of Joba Rani. We made every effort to make Kiran at ease leaving behind for good what happened the other evening.

'But sudden changes in Kiran's behavior were conspicuous. Sometimes he kept bizarrely quiet. Some other times, he would be cranky, screech loud, and get incensed. We all were concerned. Bhupoti, given occasional access to our core group due to previous performance, was still awaiting his full entrance. He seized the opportunity and eventually proved to be much smarter than we thought of.

'We all were sitting in one evening but experiencing, as usual, snag in getting Kiran back to his old self. Bhupoti appeared unexpectedly. Standing at a reasonable distance, he was holding both of his palms together in a gyratory fashion, a local culture indicating the inner intent to say something but has hesitation. Bhupoti's predicament was premised on the fact that he was so near to get cherished entry into the group and thus would not like to commit any gaffe at this stage.

Bijoy-da took a break and resumed his statement after having an intent look at me, saying, 'Observing that, core group member Rajesh asked him, "What is the matter? Do you want to say anything?" Responding to that, Bhupoti, with all hesitation and edginess, softly said that "if Dada Babu (meaning Kiran) permits, I have some information to share." Kiran looked at him with all affection and said, "Go ahead. I won't mind your saying anything."

'Bhupoti, with regained confidence by support words of Kiran, softly stated that "I felt very dismayed by observing you all, especially Dada Babu, since your visit to Joba Rani's place. I think Dada Babu is frustrated by the vibes of that experience. My inkling is strengthened as Joba Rani's market reputation is not that great. She is more known as a hotheaded individual. So I quietly looked at alternatives in the surrounding para of Santirbazar.

"Yesterday, I randomly met an old friend of my elder brother. He was Bhuban-da (brother Bhuban) of Bancharam village, a distance of about twenty miles. He has done well as a *tihkadar* (contractor). Like many of his type, Bhuban-da used to visit para occasionally whenever he was in Santirbazar. It was known to all, and he was not at all embarrassed. He asserted that such visits tote up his physical ability, contributing to more satisfied usual conjugal relations. Bhuban-da's value paradigm would not consider this as infidelity. He considered that as a distraction from daylong hard work away from home and had no hesitation in talking about his visits to para.

"As Bhuban-da was going to have tea with one of his other friends, he also invited me. We sat together. Bhuban-da was in a jovial mood telling his friend about just coming out of the place of the new girl of the para by the name Binati Rani. He continued, oblivious of my presence, saying, 'Young Binati Rani was a prostitute in one of the paras of Agartala and has been in love with her babu (regular customer). Being persuaded, Binati one day eloped with her babu soon to discover that the babu is not as well-off as he used to pretend. In facing the reality of life, both of them moved to Santirbazar para, but her engagement is strictly confined to singing and dancing in both of which she excels. The rules of the agreed arrangements between the two strictly forbid any involvement in prostitution. Physical relationship with any customer is strictly prohibited by her narcissistic *de facto* hubby. He is always there to ensure compliance.' Bhuban-da opined that in spite of all such limitations, she attracts a good number of gregarious people, as her renderings and actions have all the embellishment of performance, elegance, and excellence minus the ultimate physical involvement. He concluded, saying, 'I am very happy and relaxed even without any sex. That is the beauty of her performance.'

"I immediately concluded that our adorable Dada Babu needs something like that. I rushed back today from my family engagements to inform you all about it."

Bijoy-da continued saying, 'Kiran had a puckish smile in his lips. He called Bhupoti near him and softly said that he was very happy with Bhupoti's commitment and sincerity, and informed every one present that "from today Bhupoti is a member of our group." He also decided to visit the place of Binati Rani with his group, and Bhupoti was given the responsibility to finalize all arrangements. Kiran, for the first time in many a days, was evidently very happy, as if he was all set to take revenge on Joba Rani.

'Our maiden visit to Binati Rani's place was instantly pleasing. Presence of her Babu was conspicuous. His presence, though annoying to many visitors, was a comforting one for us, as we did not have any other objective. Our fondest expectation was to spend good time in the company of attractive and equally acquiescent lady with service of drinks and snacks, an arrangement that could make Kiran happy.

'Kiran's cheerfulness was obvious. We started visiting Binati Rani's place intermittently. Soon it became palpable and reached the ears of *Kaka Babu* (Kiran's father). He soon concluded that the only way to get his insipid son on the track was to find a beautiful bride and get him married soonest. That's how you came. When we saw you first, all of us had the same reaction, though we refrained from opening our mouths—what a dreary life this beautiful lady was going to live. You know and understand what we meant. Precisely this is the reason, frankly speaking, that has drawn me close to this house. It is for you that I have developed equally both love and empathy. That is why I am in this house on every pretext.'

"As Bijoy-da started unwrapping facts with swarming emotions focusing on desolation of my private life and his related compassion, I became nervous. To obviate any unforeseen loathsome situation, my inkling propelled me to leave the place. As I stood up and took a step, Bijoy-da grabbed my left hand and bluntly said, '*Bou-di, ar kotto nije ar shatey protarona korbe. Thomar o to jibon achey. Ami shob shomey tomar kachey thaktey and tomar sheba korte prostut achi. Tomake kache pour jonno ami a bari tay ato ashi*' (sister-in-law, how long would you cheat yourself? You have your own life. I will always be with you and ready to serve you. I come to this house so often only to be with you closely).

"Those words said by Bijoy-da with all emotions made me panicky, and I made a deliberate attempt to disengage myself. As I was trying to disentangle me, Bijoy-da suddenly pulled me toward him.Within twinkling, I bumped against Bijoy-da's chest, my head resting in a downward posture. He placed his both hands on my back, moving them up and down. That act was accompanied by heavy breathing. He pressed me hard toward his chest, flattening my breast. I do not know what happened to me. I momentarily forgot my identity: who am I, and where am I? I lost all control on me. I could feel physical responses of my body including the mushy condition of my vital organ. Unknowingly, I also put both my hands at his back and started murmuring, 'Bijoy, Bijoy.' He then pulled me afresh with additional force. That somehow straightened my head with face positioned upward. Without waiting for a moment, Bijoy lowered his face and sucked in both my lips. I was in a bemused situation, but my physiology was enjoying every bit of Bijoy's act. That sensitivity was just unexplainable, as I never ever experienced before such intense embrace from a man.

"At that moment of delight cum guilt, your shadowy self appeared before me, reminding me of your oft-repeated words: 'Indu, to be beautiful is one thing and mostly god gifted but to be able to retain that beauty in its limpidness is the most difficult challenge.' That was a stunning hypothetical encounter with your spectral self at a critical moment of my life. I joggled and forcefully disengaged myself from the embrace of Bijoy and hurriedly stepped out of the house while placing the *anchal* (the rear end of a saree when wrapped around the female body) halfway on my head, as is usually done to demonstrate modesty. Soon thereafter, Bijoy left the house, advising Gokul-da that he had to go immediately, as he forgot an important errand, and there is no time to take leave from me.

"Flustered impulse triggered by the abrupt act of Bijoy continued to have reactions within me. While I felt ashamed for being vulnerable to the ascendancy of Bijoy, my inner self was longing intently for grueling physical interactions. Right at the moment, Kiran unexpectedly returned home and appeared to be in a very affable mood. I was planning to send Gokul-da to a nearby trading place to get a few things. Seeing Kiran returning, I expedited the process. Eventually, we were the only two at our home.

"Unprecedented emotional pressure and physical longing overtook all my thoughts and value judgment with which I grew up. I was not within myself. Taking full advantage of the empty house, I rushed toward Kiran sitting in a chair in the veranda, held his hand hard, and quickly dragged him inside near the bed. I did not waste a single second nor gave time to him to make queries. Positioning him near the bed, I hastily took off his shirt and removed his dhutti, pushed him on the bed, and placed myself on his body. Later on, we reversed our position, and I pressed his head against my breast, ignoring his complaint of breathing discomfort. I enjoyed it so much that I could not control my screaming.

"The tragedy of that short and equally enjoyable episode was that Kiran was never present in my thoughts and follow on actions. It was you who was omnipresent and involved in whatever I did or whatever happened. Since your snapshot appearance in my thoughts during Bijoy's initiation of physical acts, you were all-pervading in my thinking and acts of that evening. The end result was that I conceived that evening, and dear Shetupa was born to the delight of the family.

"The naming of Shetupa was the most delicate task I had to undertake in otherwise a very supportive in-law's family. Except Baba, who always preferred to keep his position unspecified until the moment of final decision, everyone had his preferred name, including even Kiran. But I was adamant to name her Shetupa, closest to Shetu that I could think of. To me, Shetupa is your daughter and hence needed to be named closest to your name. I could achieve that due to Baba's support premised on the logic that 'while everybody's preference is respected, Indrani should have her desire fulfilled being a mother.'

"With Shetupa's arrival, my way of life took a different focus and turn. With about seven-year-old Dhruva (whom I called Dhrub), three-year-old Anjali, and newborn Shetupa, my life centered on their care and well-being. It is 'they' that became important in place of 'me': my right, my expectation, my desire, my fulfillment—all became secondary. Also, what Kiran was doing and where he went did not bother me anymore.

"The challenge of rearing up all the three was significantly alleviated due to very calm, sober, and astute behavior traits of Dhrub even at that tender age. I always remembered that after finishing the special puja that Shashuri-ma organized with the participation of local purohit, friends, and well-wishers to celebrate my pregnancy, I straightway went to Baba, took podo-dhuli, and said, 'Baba, please pray for me and bless me so that I can have a son like you.' Baba happily put his right hand on my head, closed his eyes for some time, and convincingly said, 'Ami ashirbad kori je tomar jeno amar chaite bhalo chelley hoie' (I bless you so that you have a son better than me).

"As the children were growing up, our abode of Shukhipur, otherwise symbolic of containment and happiness, experienced its first major twitch. Shashuri-ma, taken ill due to acute diarrhea (gastrointestinal distress or disorder), succumbed on the fourth day in a most unanticipated turn of events.

"The house and the courtyard were full of people, and that continued for many days. Initially, all present were preoccupied with cremation (burning, vaporization, and oxidation process). Subsequently, focus was on arrangements for *Shraddha* (a much-revered religious and social responsibility) designed to be performed on the eleventh day. The related rites, aimed to nourish, support, and protect the spirit of the deceased, are to be performed by a male descendant and are followed by communal feeding. It is one of the reasons of special desire for a male child in many Hindu families.

"Baba, being wise and methodical all his life, adjusted remarkably well and handled with pragmatism the pain of losing his life partner suddenly. Even during Shashuri-ma's presence, I gradually took over most of the responsibilities pertaining to Baba. I refocused all my attention to Baba so that he had no feeling of lack of attention or care. But obviously, I could not fill the emotional void created by the death of Shashuri-ma.

"Right from day one, Baba treated me as a daughter, sensitive to my hope, desire, and preference. He always was cognizant of the fact that I am someone from the other side of the border having no link with my family. He thus consciously made efforts so that I am at ease in my new setting.

"Initially, I was one of his two daughters. He used to pass on to me his opinion on delicate matters through Aparna before discussing those with me. With Aparna's sudden death, he cited me as the daughter of the house and was forthright in all his interactions. Many of the times, he exhibited his love for me by placing his hand on my head and praying. Those were precious moments of my life and the best reward I could hope for in spite of discontented married life I was having with Kiran.

"Kiran recommenced his evening rendezvous with friends after Dhrub was a few months old. Initially that was irregular and of shorter duration. But after Aparna's departure for her in-law's home, it started taking the pattern of regularity, and the duration increased significantly. Information trickled down occasionally about his spending money and time in the kothas adjacent to the bazaar.

"Another conspicuous change was related to his contact and communication with close friends. The previous close association slid notably after the unpleasant incident of phul shojja night. I was told later by Gokul-da that Baba had focused discussions with guardians of some of Kiran's friends soon after that happening and cautioned against repetition. This had immediate impact. My strategy of making advent of each night a relatively welcoming one without any expressed expectation made Kiran comfortable at home. This, of course, had occasional exceptions but with my consent. I accepted that and tried to adjust my thinking and expectation with that norm of Kiran's lifestyle.

"With the sudden demise of Aparna, the life pattern of Kiran noticeably degenerated. The same exacerbated manifestly after the sad death of Shashuri-ma. My assessment is he took recourse to longer evening outings and periodical visits to kothas as outlets to express his inner frustration with himself for not being able to perform in a way his thinking envisages or others do. Relative notable additions in his rage were losing temper in minor matters and shouting at everyone. He totally forgot to respect elders. Kiran never vacillated in showing disrespect even to Gokul-da and Bishnur-ma, the two individuals who reared him up as son. This pained me, and more Baba, who opted to keep quiet to protect his own honor and dignity. To my utter dismay, it was my considered assessment that Baba's quiet handling of such situations was perhaps premised on poignant realization that it is more important and relevant at the far end of one's life to protect his dignity rather than looking for respect.

"In spite of all negativity Kiran demonstrated in his family relations, I must be candid to admit that he had no duality in his actions and reactions. Kiran walked out of his life closet without leaving a hidden skeleton. He behaved abhorrently with all in the family, and at all times. That was direct, that was equal; and he never suffered any remorse.

"It was probable that Bishnur-ma could not take that anymore. One day she informed me of her choice to leave the job on the plea of both age and health. Bishnur-ma also said that she had already identified a middle-aged reliable and efficient replacement. The replacement was a widow, Dhuni by name, with no one in the family to fall back upon.

"Baba had a very caring discourse with Bishnur-ma in Gokul-da's and my presence. He thanked her profusely for the services she loyally rendered ever since the family settled in Shukhipur and told her that she was not leaving the job. She would continue to be in the job and would come and do whatever she wanted. If she does not come or even not engage in doing anything, that would also be fine. Gokul would visit her at the beginning of each month with honorarium for past services rendered. Baba finally said, 'You can't retire. You are part of the family.' Then he stipulated arrangement for overlapping with the replacement to ensure smooth transition.

"Baba took all of us by surprise when we were about to disperse. He said that 'ever since Ma Indrani told me about Bishnur-ma, I started thinking about Gokul, our first household help and my dear associate for all these years I am in Tripura.' He continued, saying, 'Gokul is neither leaving us nor retiring. He will continue as long as he lives. But time has come to give well-deserved relief to a committed fellow like him. We will soon have his replacements too. Gokul's main job would be to serve me very well-prepared *chillums* (serving of ablaze tobacco cake on the top of a *hookah* [the top holding agent of a hubble-bubble]) at regular intervals while taking care of his smoking urge, which he officially hid from me for so long.' Baba had a nice laugh. We too were very happy. It so appeared that the decision delighted even Gokul-da.

"Dhuni joined the next week to be followed by Chandu, the replacement of Gokul-da. The transition was smooth under the guidance of the dedicated two. To both Dhuni and Chandu, Baba had a position of highest pedestal. They looked at Baba with reverence. Kiran was mostly irrelevant except for his occasional anger and shouting. In the absence of Shashuri-ma, I was the head of the family for both Dhuni and Chandu. For every small thing, they would come to me for opinion or decision. I started enjoying my new status very much.

"A sudden but very pertinent thought engulfed me while observing Dhuni complying with some of my instructions on a particular evening. I wondered about my luck and destiny. With my family setting exacerbated, among others, by poverty, caste, and partition, I could as well be in Dhuni's position. It might be that some of my compatriots were in the position of Dhuni back home. Here,

I am observing someone like Dhuni carrying out my order while seated in a chair meant for the lady of the house.

"It dawned on me out of blue that it is perhaps the inscrutability of nature that an individual is not necessarily blessed with everything in life. Some scantiness between expectation and reality is possibly the norm, and a life is needed to be lived with that. Stressing out oneself with inadequacies beyond one's control not only is self-defeating and amounts to self-torture but also equally deprives life the pleasure of living. The preferred option is to enjoy what one has and not to lament for something that is lacking.

"I was impressed with myself. It made me happy to realize that an uneducated person like me can also think. Perhaps my association with you in the formative stage of life, the companionship that I enjoyed with Aparna, and the love, care, and guidance of Baba had a positive impact on me. I instantly accepted my life with its apparent shortcoming that always disconcerted me. I rededicated myself in rearing up Dhrub, Anjali, and Shetupa as good human beings, having all the attributes of you, Aparna, and Baba—my friends, guides, mentors, and philosophers of life.

"Baba told us earlier that he intends to take Dhrub on some weekends to the business place to promote a sense of familiarity in the latter's mind. We were amazed, and readily agreed with the proposition. It thus gave me immense pleasure when I first saw Baba slowly and steadily stepping out of the home for his business location on one late morning with a walking stick in his right hand, and Dhrub on his left side holding Baba's dangling index finger of his other hand. As the time passed, that became a standard practice for both, giving Baba immense pleasure. Baba often spent a lot of time with Gokul-da sharing the related happiness while enjoying the puff of his hookah.

"In rearing up Anjali and Shetupa, I observed two divergent leanings. Anjali, very responsible but equally garrulous by nature, has proclivity toward household errands and their management. Every detail pertaining to stock position of our daily needs such as rice, lintels, and spices were in her fingertips. She liked to help me and Dhuni in cooking, and in serving food to others. Her open-minded attitude toward diverse visitors and liking for entertaining people were very genuine. Even in that growing-up stage, she was very considerate and responsive to needs and desires of Shetupa. Academic excellence of Shetupa, the resultant good name she earned in the surrounding, and the visible exhibition of love and admiration by Baba never bothered Anjali. She was happy in doing things that were of her interest.

"Shetupa, on the other hand, was totally oblivious of household errands. From the early phase of life, she demonstrated a perceptible penchant for academic pursuit. She was more engrossed with herself, enjoyed interacting with seniors, and was very thoughtful, prudent, and mature in reacting to any situation. Likewise, Shetupa had always been sober and serious besides being equally smart in all her social exchanges and academic pursuits. Neither sweet sayings nor inveigling had any impact on her carapace of thinking, choice of words, and silhouette of actions.

"I observed that particularly in the context of emerging relationship with her father. To my assessment, she avoided Kiran at the early phase of life due to fright syndrome accentuated by his strained relationship with all in and prolonged absence from the abode. Observing that the relationship between the two still being strained even with the passage of time, I designedly took initiative to redress impressions that Shetupa might have in her mind. But that had no impact in terms of objective that I carved out in initiating that sort of effort.

"Dhrub had an attitude of ignoring Kiran on most encounters with no visible other gestures. That was not the case with Shetupa. She, contrary to her persona and as the situation warrants, would react in his presence but always ensured that others notice that too. Not only did I feel uncomfortable but also that made me sad too. I did not have much of father-daughter relationship with my father due to pressures of poverty and other related reasons. It thus pained me observing Shetupa having no father-daughter interactions and feelings with Kiran contrary to what Aparna had with Baba.

"I witnessed for the first time that divinity in relationship between a father and a daughter when I first stepped in Shukhipur. I got my first wink of how supportive, caring, loving, and equally respectful could be such a rapport when I witnessed Aparna interacting with Baba. What a consecration engulfed that bond and relationship? I soon realized how that sort of relationship could contribute to a healthy and enlightened family milieu. Without knowing the challenges that I would have, I promised to myself that if I have a daughter, I will do anything to ensure that both father and daughter are blessed with most heavenly bond.

"That sort of feeling and focus predicated my efforts to have an affable and supportive bond between Kiran and Shetupa. I tried to put up a scenario with imaginary physical and psychological locale to make a dent in her negative frame of thinking pertaining to Kiran. I even did not hesitate to assign blame on me and, to some modest extent, on Baba for Kiran's sort of strange behavior to most of the family members and elders.

"Her reaction to my repeated efforts during the growing-up phase was a very standard one: she would look at me straight with eyes wide-open and then would leave the place without a word. She would come back after some time, but there would be no trace of allusion of what we discussed earlier. I soon concluded that it was not to be in the case of Shetupa and Kiran.

"An event of absolute happiness withered away other family constraints for some time. That was the wedding of Anjali. She did not pursue higher studies after doing her high school certificate examination. She was happily engaged in routine household tasks, which earned a name for her among relations, friends, and the community at large.

"A proposal for her marriage was initiated by one of the community elders who had close relations in an adjoining habitation known as Bhatipara, also in South Tripura. That family is looking for a genial bride from a respectable family for their youngest son who is teaching in a local college. As the process of negotiations was on, Baba was very worried about the outcome, as his own family's overall image had been tarnished due to Kiran's way of life. The strategy was not to keep Kiran discernible during the entire process.

"The paternal family of Anjali had regular interactions with Shukhipur notwithstanding the sad demise of Aparna, and the father used to visit her occasionally. But on top of that, Baba always insisted that Anjali spends some time annually in her paternal place. Thus the relationship between the two families was easy, comfortable, and based on good feeling. That family was kept involved at every stage of negotiation and marriage even though the main identity of Anjali to her in-law's people was that she is the granddaughter of Dhireen Babu of Shukhipur.

"Two other major events coincided with the departure of Anjali for her new home. Dhrub successfully completed his college education in spite of giving full attention to grandfather's business. His devotion and orientation from the growing-up stage were on ensuring that good reputation and name of his grandfather's business traversed through the nook and corner of Tripura state. Observing Dhrub conducting business, Grandfather's satisfaction burgeoned with the assurance that the business he had so arduously established would be continued and would even flourish in the safe hands of Dhrub. That not only made Baba ecstatic but also equally enabled him to overcome the frustration that he had concerning Kiran. I noticed this as he gradually started briefing me about outstanding attainments of Dhrub in expanding the family's business operations. He was, however, always hesitant in opening up in this regard, as he was conscious of the fact that I always wanted both Dhrub and Shetupa to excel in education, which I had no opportunity to pursue. On suitable occasions, I deliberately raised the issue and enjoyed the unwavering happiness that glowed from his face and body language in the course of detailing the accomplishments of Dhrub.

"Dhrub had carved out a way of life for himself. He had been a young man of few words, very articulate in conversation, astutely focused in terms of objectives of his life, respectful to seniors, and conscious of social dicta. There is no doubt that he loves me immensely, but I could never be very close to him. Perhaps our respective orientations of life are so diverse that commonality between us is more exception rather than the rule. He never showed any interest with respect to Kiran except putting up pressure on Baba not to yield easily to Kiran's frequent asking for money. But he had a very amiable open relationship with Baba. I derived happiness from that.

"Shetupa excelled in her high school certificate examination conducted by the state school board. No one from that school performed so well ever. The consensus of the faculty and members of the school governing board was that had she been in a better school, she could have a top-ten position in the examination. Based on such assessment and considering the seriousness of Shetupa, Grandpa decided to send Shetupa to Agartala for higher studies.

"In spite of apparent shortcomings on my part such as lack of education, I consciously focused my attention to develop and nourish a genial bond with Shetupa. In the past, that was partly handicapped, as I was to share same sort of love and care with both Anjali and Shetupa. Some change in our mutual relationship was visible as Shetupa was growing up, and that took further positive turn when Anjali left for her in-law's house. As Shetupa was about to finish her high school, she started showing signs of warmth in our relationship.

"Soon after Anjali's marriage, Shetupa also left for Agartala for post-high school studies. The house suddenly became empty with the burden of loneliness overwhelming my life. The silver lining of that life was my waiting for occasional visits by Shetupa.

"Shetupa's all-embracing but equally explicit change in approach and attitude manifested during the first college holiday visit to home amazed me. She, to my surprise and pleasure, started opening up slickly, became friendly with me, discussed matters of life and living including women talk, viz., health tips, wellness information, conjugal relationship, and so on.

"At this phase, she would no more leave the place in response to my cajoling for a friendly relationship with Kiran. She would straightway ask me questions about my relationship with Kiran: our feelings for each other, our mutual responses to various needs, and our sharing of grief and happiness. I could never be specific in my riposte.

"With the house mostly empty due to marriage of Anjali and Shetupa's departure for college, I had the rare opening for cultivating more caring, understanding, and personal relationship with dear Baba. Because of Dhrub's commitment and interest, Baba gradually assigned more business responsibilities to the former, overseeing from a distance. Thus, he had his time in conjunction with my free time due to Dhuni's taking over full responsibility of kitchen. We started sharing wonderful time, mostly Baba revisiting his ancestral place, growing up, migration, settlement in Shukhipur, and other aspects of his life. In all such discourses, I observed one thing particularly: an intent craving to guide me with equal expectation of passing those to succeeding generation. All that he said or referred to guided me immensely. Things generally were very conducive all around.

But the problem pertaining to Kiran not only persisted but also aggravated. Baba's relatively long presence at home provided Kiran with the excuse to stay out longer. At the same time, Kiran gradually developed a wild attitude and approach in his even routine exchanges to the annoyance of all in the home and absolute dislike of Baba and our children. That hardened the prevailing barrier in having much-desired and valued father-offspring relationship. In spite of efforts on my part, it caused agony in the minds of our children. The more they grew up, the more they distanced themselves from their father because of the latter's reprehensible and simultaneous arrogant personal traits. I continued, perhaps naively, trying to placate them with varied types of reasoning, but they would overtly disagree on all counts.

"Once, Dhrub, who seldom expresses himself on such matters, straightway told me, 'Ma, I understand that no one is perfect. But that can't be a justification for continuing life with disjointed caprices one holds. People do change as they mature, as they have responsibilities, as they are accountable to society. That was not the case with that person. So please do not bother us anymore with hope for us to change our attitude toward him. No cajoling would yield desired outcome. The onus is on him to change. In this context, there is no seniority. One does not acquire respect just because he happened to be our father. He needs to earn it.' I got the message and refrained myself from raising the issue anymore. Dhrub's efforts from a distance to control Kiran's access to unaccounted flow of fund under threat were only partly successful, as Kiran always pressurized Baba for money, and the latter often succumbed to that.

"With somewhat reduced flow of fund, Kiran's evenings were mostly mundane ones, but his close friends, except Bijoy, who left for Agartala on some pretext soon after the incident in our home, were mostly loyal and around him. Even with less money, Kiran was the main financier of all their evening events.

"Kiran's evident preference to stay out and his urge for evening entertainment and fun patently became noticeable with Baba's staying longer at home, demise of Shashuri-ma, the wedding of Anjali, and the departure of Shetupa for higher studies. That continued for quite a while; however, as Dhrub gradually took over the management of business, the flow of fund gradually emaciated. Visits to Binati Rani's place became occasional. Continuous presence of her angel guardian was an excuse too. In a rather limited scope, fun became somewhat secondary. Their main pleasure was from drinking of limited native drink made of rotten rice and reminiscing about some good old days. Friends continued assuring Kiran about the prospect of greater access to fund soon when he inherits the business.

"In such a depressed setting, Bhupoti once again came up with new and equally thrilling information to the delight of Kiran but the reservations of some of the accompanying friends. On being encouraged by Kiran, Bhupoti slowly stated, 'I do not know whether any one of you ever noticed the seasonal visits of *shapures* (snake charmers) in our area. They generally move in a group of three or four boats and stop at various places. The duration of their visits generally depends on the money they earn.'

"As told to me later on, Kiran, to prove to the group that he is generally more knowledgeable about things around, and to minimize Bhupoti's relevance in this case, interrupted and said, 'Many of you are not aware of the fact that Tripura, our third-smallest state of the Union of India, has ten major rivers, besides numerous streams, crisscrossing the state. The more significant among them in terms of basin areas are Gumati, Manu, Khowai, Muhuri, Feni, Dhalai, and Burima. By nature, many of these rivers are ephemeral. The flow in some of these rivers is significantly dependent on rainfall. Because of this characteristic, the surrounding panorama of such basin areas undergoes significant changes during dry and rainy seasons. Several townships of Tripura (like Agartala, Udaipur, Kumarghar, Bishalgarh, Bisramganj, and Jolaibari) are on the brink or in the vicinity of such rivers. Following that pattern, Santirbazar is also located near a riverbank. That is why shapures anchor in Santirbazar, though their captive market is interior village areas.

"Kiran continued his narration saying, 'Snake charming is an inherited profession passed on from generation to generation. Being a nomadic ethnic group known as *Bede*, they prefer to live in settlements and move in small groups during rainy season with their boats to earn livelihood. Besides snake charming, they are also considered as traditional healers and magicians. The people's trust in them varied from area to area, and the interventions sought are diverse in nature: from general healing to treating cold and other ailments, to getting homes rid of snakes, and so on. They sell all sorts of potions and unguents concocted by them. Both children and elderly people enjoy the magic and snake show.

'Mostly the ladies, locally known as *bedinis*, leave their boats in early morning for surrounding villages. Bedinis carry a number of snakes on their head in covered cane containers (baskets) or pots, in addition to other saleable products. They would entertain people with snake dance to the tune of their flutes in exchange of voluntary rewards, mostly in the shape of throwing of coins. Bedinis take advantage of assembly of people for snake dance to sell rudimentary antidotes for snake bite and other illness. They usually return to their boats around late afternoon. That is perhaps one reason why we mostly do not notice their presence. But that is a very normal way of life for them.'

"Kiran then asked Bhupoti to finish what he started. Bhupoti, impressed by Kiran's knowledge about shapures and reassured by his interest, said, 'Such a party has arrived in Santirbazar. The group has four boats. Most of the men stay in the boats taking care of the family. They are very fond of drinks and mostly are tempted by the excitement or escape it offers. Some of them also like other means of addictions.

'The Bedinis, having specific ways to put on their very brightly colored saree with length flowing up to lower end of knee and the tail end draped around chest with *khopa* (updo) generally featuring the hair arrangement, are the ones who toil the whole day to earn livelihood.'

"Bhupoti then paused for a while, assessing the ambiance for the juicy part of what he had to say. He continued, 'This group has a very attractive young girl. She is Dhobila, meaning something akin to fairness, though in reality she is very dark complexioned. But god has blessed her with some beguiling physical features and attributes to outweigh the outward darkness of her skin color. People around her can't help but stop when Dhobila walks past with snake basket on her head. It is very exciting just to see her.

'Considering that Dada Babu is not in his own self in recent times even with occasional visits to Binati Rani's place, I established contacts with the male head member of the group. Offering him *Mrito Shonjibini Shura* (sort of rudimentary local drink marketed as Ayurvedic [alternative medicine] product) in the early evening settings of last two days, I explored the possibility of arranging performance by Dhobila for Dada Babu and his accompanying friends. The proposition of private performance is relatively uncommon and could as well be vetoed by anyone in that group. So I offered a price of ten rupees per performance. I also took additional caution to foreclose possibility of confusion in the future. I made it clear that the performance should strictly be a private one and should initially be arranged at least twice a week and in different adjacent venues unless Dada Babu desires otherwise. Dhobila would be escorted by one of Dada Babu's trusted man, and if so desired, one male member from the boat could accompany her. I also said that I would confirm all these once I have the opportunity to talk to Dada Babu, the only as well as busy son of a big wholesaler of the area. The status of Dada Babu, the price offered, and the drinks enticed the head of the group, and he impulsively agreed with all that I stipulated.'

"Kiran was very impressed by the sincerity, care, and commitment shown by Bhupoti as well as his emblematic initiative to have sensible discussions with the lead person of Bede group but kept it concealed. He looked around his more trusted and regular friends who normally did not spare any opportunity to ridicule Bhupoti as a *chamcha* (sort of obedient dumb follower). His friends were uncertain as to the proper mode of response, as their prime aim was to keep Kiran happy and in good mood.

"Rajesh, one of the relatively better-informed friends, opened up, saying, 'I think that it is totally a loony proposition. Bedes normally are very standoffish and shielding by nature in their interactions. Moreover, as I have seen from a distance, the vibes around the setting of their boat-based nomadic life is usually a very morose one. They do not identify with any place or person. Their principal identity is their snake and boat, and a lifestyle surrounding that.' Rajesh, however, restrained himself from stipulating any conclusive position, as that had always been the prerogative of Kiran.

"A sense of bleakness engulfed the physical reaction of Bhupoti, who always thought that he was doing something extraordinary for his adorable Dada Babu and everyone would be supportive. Rajesh's remarks plausibly saddened Bhupoti, while others present were keeping quiet. Kiran was still maintaining his silence, outwardly giving an impression of casualness, even though the earlier brief narration of the proposition by Bhupoti created an immediate impulse within him. He had a glance at his associates. Except Rajesh, all were reacting like obedient fools, awaiting signal from the leader. Kiran enjoyed loyalty from his group fellows, more so when that is padded with obedience. The silence of this evening did not have any negative impact on his thinking at all. He sensed definite excitement in Bhupoti's proposition.

"Kiran, in an exhibition of elegance and command, repositioned himself and took a big sip from his glass and swirled the liquid inside his mouth for a while before allowing that to pass through. He then looked at Bhupoti with a lot of admiration. Kiran slowly started responding to Bhupoti's proposition. But before doing that, he retracted, noticing a propensity among group members to keep Bhupoti on the fence, and recalled occasional sordid comments about him. It dawned on Kiran, as an acknowledgement of Bhupoti's loyalty and commitment, that time is appropriate to make clear the need for a change in that sort of mind-set. He concluded within himself that there is no need for Bhupoti to hunker down his presence anymore. Kiran decided to make two points very clear to all: first, no one should demonstrate any inclination to disparage Bhupoti on any context and, second, that, from now on, Bhupoti deserves to be treated with decency. He immediately acted to make those loud and clear to all present.

"Kiran noted with happiness the silent approval of what he said, but still thought it relevant to justify his position. So he stated, 'I am impressed by Bhupoti's commitment and sincerity. Not only that. He always was concerned about my discomfort and unhappiness. Bhupoti is the only one to take an initiative, however mundane it might be, to do something to make me happy.' Kiran then continued, saying, 'I have noted what Rajesh has just said. But we are not acting on the proposition to achieve something permanent. Their loyalty may be with their snake and boat. But our objective is confined to merriment in divergent setting. So there is no conflict, and nothing to lose. I have therefore decided to enjoy one or two private presentations of snake dance by Dhobila as outlined by Bhupoti, and would decide the future course of action based on the levels of our enjoyment and happiness.'

"Kiran authorized Bhupoti to make necessary arrangements, saying, 'Life has become a dreary one for me with the slide in cash flow since Dhrub has taken over the management of the business. I feel small to approach Dhrub for money. Baba still passes on some money occasionally but most of the time expresses his inability to give what I want with Dhrub as the excuse.'

"Bhupoti, assured by earlier comments of Kiran and conscious of his elevated position in the group, made his maiden statement on the issue without any charade. He, drawing the attention of Kiran, said, 'Dada Babu, I had occasions to mix with some nomadic people like Bedes. Rajesh-da is correct in putting forward some of the challenges of interacting with such ethnic people. To them, money is the only thing that matters. Everything else is secondary. With money, they are like tamed snakes. Without that, they are both unpredictable and vicious. I kept that in view in initiating the discussion. I also had in my mind about temporary constraints that Dada Babu has. So I started with ten rupees per performance. That may seem to be paltry sum compared to what Dada Babu spends even for a visit to Binati Rani's kotha. But those ten rupees is much more than the group of ladies makes in a day and is therefore quite attractive. If Dada Babu so prefers, he can always give more. But the flow of each additional sum should be gradual and should be seen as the result of graciousness of Dada Babu rather than reward for performance or of physical attraction.'

"Kiran palpably was touched by the depth of Bhupoti's thinking and genuineness of concern about his well-being. He had a very affectionate look at Bhupoti and asked him to be close to him. By putting his right hand on the shoulder of Bhupoti, a symbolic gesture of love and tenderness, Kiran stated without inhibition, 'I have committed a big mistake. So did the group as a whole. We inordinately delayed according due recognition to Bhupoti. He is a real gem. He is our black diamond.' He also said, 'I sense some vibes in the proposition of Bhupoti, and I am feeling sort of a strange zing within me.'

"After such conclusive statement, Kiran authorized Bhupoti to proceed with arrangements for private performance by Dhobila. Kiran, for the first time, also said that Bhupoti would have responsibility to monitor the aptness of his actions while interacting with Dhobila and might privately be forthright in drawing his attention.

"That evening gathering ended relatively early with all-around happiness, and for sure, Bhupoti was the happiest one. He not only was the full and equal member of the group but could as well earn the trust and confidence of Dada Babu, who patted him while departing with short but equally important side comment, 'Well done.'

"Kiran returned home early that evening with glow of vibes, but he was taken aback observing a sense of happy mood all around. In a rare display of family amity, all three male members (grandfather, son, and grandson) were having their dinner together while I was serving them. During the service, and keeping in view my one-on-one discussion with Baba just before dinner, I said, 'Baba, what a good news that is! The recent letter of your friend, Moni Mohan Kaku, proposing matrimonial relationship between our Dhrub and his granddaughter Nandita is a very welcome one.'

Dhrub, to begin with, was not comfortable with the setting of that night's dinner and finished it early. He left the dinner assembly soon. But I decided to pursue the matter positively as, to my quick assessment, the proposition is likely to be good for all in the family. With the objective of drawing Baba's specific attention as well as to keep Kiran informed, I continued saying, 'All my efforts of the recent past to convince Dhrub about getting married was unsuccessful. He always demonstrated reluctance. Dhrub's principal logic is he needs time to pursue the target of expanding business to make you happy.' My poised follow-up was for Baba to try to convince Dhrub. Baba, in his self-assured posture of interacting, had glanced at both Kiran and me and possibly had the feeling that Kiran might think that both Baba and I were getting his son married without keeping him informed.

"To obviate that sort of impression, Baba started to respond to my suggestion, highlighting both preliminary and noncommittal status of the proposition. Baba said, 'This friend of mine is also an emigrant. In the early years, we struggled a lot and had regular exchanges on challenges and options of doing business in a new setting. Moni Mohan soon opted out of our area and relocated his business in Agartala proper where his extended families settled earlier. We did communicate with each other regularly. I visited and stayed with him whenever I was in Agartala. Of late, our communication has become irregular, and frankly rather exception. The other day, Moni Mohan came to my thoughts repeatedly. So I wrote a letter inquiring his well-being and mentioning about Dhruba: how good he is and how proud I am of his achievements so far in fulfilling my dream. He responded quickly and suggested that I should consider a matrimonial relationship with his family as his granddaughter Nandita is equally talented, attractive, well mannered, finishing her intermediate college education. Her aptitude for cooking is noteworthy besides ability to paint. So it is a surprise proposition from the other side, and I need time to talk to Dhruba.'

As I expressed my unspoken astonishment to what he just said compared to what both of us discussed awhile back, Baba wanted to put a coating on his statement, probably for the sake of Kiran. He said, 'Ma Indrani, in life, one should just not take a position on anything solely based on relationship or seniority, or one's judgment. If I or Kiran tell Dhruba about this proposition, he would take it as a command and may agree just to please us keeping in view our relationship. But I would not like to do that. We should also respect his desire. Thus, I will wait for a convenient time and situation, being emotionally susceptible, to place the proposition in a way where he would have the feeling of choice in taking the decision but can't say no. One can say that the approach amounts to blackmailing, but I would not agree. To me, it is a strategy to achieve something in a sustainable way. Moreover, we need to recognize that the time has changed. Present-generation sons and daughters would like to have a say in important events of their lives. Rest assured I would not take unnecessary time either.'

"Everyone in this burgeoning drama was happy, each for a different reason, but refrained from sharing with others. In family contacts, Baba became more correct than cordial with Kiran. I tried to be polite but gradually distanced myself, even to the extent of sleeping on different beds. Neither Kiran needed me nor did I have any attraction left. Dhrub maintained his earlier stance vis-à-vis Kiran while maintaining a fragile frame for need-based rare contacts. Shetupa refrained from discussing with Kiran anything relating to her academic pursuits and future plan. As a poised personality with absolute clarity as to what she wanted to become, Shetupa shared her hopes and aspirations with Baba and Dhrub during her visits from Agartala. She nurtured her very congenial relationship with me, and soon we became good friends. In that unblemished friendship with my dear daughter, my only regret was I could never answer her repeat question of 'Do you have anyone in your life for whom you still live? Your eyes always say something different.' I used to smile, look the other way, and briefly revisited life and events in Anandapur. Progression about Dhrub's marriage proposition made her happy, but her main concentration was on preparing for the All-India-based competitive civil service examination, about which I had no inkling.

"I sensed something positive soon notwithstanding what Baba said in the presence of Kiran. This dawned on me as Dhrub himself initiated discussion for the need to have an additional house to meet future demand. That was contrary to Dhrub's character. He did never initiate any discussion on matters pertaining to material things. I concluded that the need for more living space had its root to Baba's possible dialogue with him concerning marriage. I was very happy and promptly informed Shetupa, emphasizing secrecy.

"The universal truth is that no secret ever remains so. The more it is emphasized, the quicker it travels. That happened in this case too. Notwithstanding quiet diplomacy of Baba and my secretive approach, every one of the household, including Bishnur-ma, Gokul-da, Dhuni, and Chandu, was very happy, but no one would share the reason for happiness. Sort of total happiness was all pervading for the first time in that home since the sudden demise of Aparna and sad death of Shashuri-ma.

"Kiran too was happy but for a different reason. He was happy that he is not being bothered with respect to marriage of his only son in view of the delicate relationship between them. Kiran knew it well that Dhrub's early withdrawal from joint dining a few days back was not that he felt embarrassed about marriage proposal but more for the reason that Dhrub felt uncomfortable in having dinner with his father, an event seldom experienced before.

"The more germane reason for Kiran's happiness was that the marriage proposition of Dhrub provided him with a window of unmitigated opportunity to pursue and enjoy Dhobila's snake dance and company. Bhupoti worked out everything but, as a strategy to win confidence of boat people, proposed to have first two private performances in one of the boats while other members of Bedes would be in other boats. He also arranged sending some advance drinks to the patriarch on the day of the maiden visit.

"As arranged, Kiran, accompanied by his friends and attired dignifiedly with a classy walking stick, more as style and status symbol, in right hand and the tail end of starched dhutti in his left hand, stepped into the boat wearing a mysterious smile to be greeted by the patriarch of the boat people. The patriarch left the boat after greeting and said Dhobila would be in the boat soon.

"That was the twilight hours of the day. The mystic sunset setting against the backdrop of nascent darkness around the rural boat location soon transformed into radiance of color and attraction with the sounds of stepping by Dhobila in a bright saree and khopa decked with flowers. Like all others, Kiran was impetuously husked by Dhobila's amorous youth and attraction. The physical attributes are so beguiling that the dark skin tone was not a matter of attention. Everyone was bemused. Kiran exchanged a supportive look with Bhupoti, conveying his approval of the latter's choice.

"Dhobila sat by the side of Kiran and smiled, transmitting loads of unspoken words. As a bedini, she was very open and at ease in having discussions with and in the company of men. She commented that neither the boat nor the hour is suitable for snake dance. But she could have one, pointing to the cane basket by her side, if they prefer. Kiran said that they would have a snake dance on another occasion but 'let us know each other.' It was difficult to gauge exactly what Dhobila understood, but she moved close to Kiran and served his first drink, while Bhupoti took care of others.

"The presence of Dhobila made Kiran instantly more buoyant, and he started indulging in sultry expressions to the amusement of his friends. Bhupoti, sitting at some distance, could assess the nascent direction of discourse, tried to caution Kiran by sign language, and proposed quietly that the first meeting should not be overstretched. He also clarified his understanding with the patriarch and observed that nothing should be done to derail the agreed understanding of private performance.

"The first meeting on the boat was followed by similar other gatherings in nominated safe places, but the snake dance never took place on one excuse or the other. Presence of Dhobila: her words, her

JAHED RAHMAN

smile, her touch became more treasured, enchanting, and desirable to Kiran. And a happy Kiran was what his loyal friends wanted in the ambiance of free flow of native drinks. Male members of the boat were equally kept happy by astute increase in supply of drinks. Selective grading of gifts kept the ladies of the boat happy too. Bhupoti excelled in doing all these to keep the road clear of bumps. Young Bhupoti was optimistic and unflappable during the course of this journey.

"Bolstered by regular kudos received from the group, intimate access to private emotions of Kiran, and successful discharge of responsibilities more with emphasis on keeping the boat people happy, Bhupoti slowly assumed a mind-set of doing things in proper priority and sequence. In the process, he ignored a young guy of another boat, Ghettu by name, who was always standing with arrogant stature at a safe distance from the boat or other locations of performance with enraged anger and hate oozing out of his face. The totality of expressions was reflective of a mental state prepared to take revenge if anything unwanted happens to the young girl of the boat for whom he had tremendous feelings.

"As rapport warmed up, Kiran worked out an arrangement for his friends to be seated at some reasonable distance while he and Dhobila enjoyed intimate private moments of light talks, physical touch, and sporadic lustful advances, being insensitive to his physical ability. He appeared to be totally oblivious of what happened in Joba Rani's kotha a few years back. Kiran was swamped by panoptic beauty of Dhobila. To him, the dark skin tone of Dhobila was something analogous to emblematic portrayal of enchanting beauty.

"In that sort of exclusiveness, Kiran also started occasionally passing on small amounts of cash. Dhobila was illiterate but knew well how to attract money. Each time Kiran passed on money eluding the vigilant eyes of Bhupoti, Dhobila would put that inside her top, deliberately making posture, which would unveil half of her bulging firm breasts. That amused Kiran very much.

"With the passage of time and intimacy that evolved over time, Kiran's calculative focus was to intensify the emotion and expectation of poor and rural bedini based on panoramic illusion of what the future holds for an attractive girl like her. She started believing every word uttered by Kiran. She developed trusting every proposition

Kiran made. Dhobila was enamored when Kiran confidentially suggested her leaving the group and had a kotha–type setting in the bazaar area where each evening, she could earn by dancing, just with her flute but not the snake, more than what she earned in a month. The life will be easy. Kiran was smart enough to caution that she could reasonably expect initial fury from her family and group. But the inflow of unexpected cash would soon be able to mollify alienated family and other group members.

"Similar discussions were pursued until Kiran was sure of unwavering eagerness of Dhobila and secretly worked a plan for sudden escape. Kiran, acting for the first time in taking the decision alone, hired an accommodation in the para locale adjacent to the bazaar and recruited a help. He regularly updated Dhobila about the progress, more to ensure and strengthen continued trust in him. A place near the wayside public temple contiguous to the huge banyan tree, relatively close to the boat location, was agreed to for the meeting of both. That was to be the staging stone for Dhobila's ramble to the world of affluence, solely trusting Kiran. The agreed time was about an hour after sunset of the appointed date to ensure proper cover. The time was also considered apposite, as by that time, most elders and some young occupants of the boat were normally intoxicated. To obviate possible suspicion and as a strategy, both agreed not to have private performances for a few days. That was specifically agreed to minimize possible apprehension in the minds of some premised on their intimacy.

"Dhobila passed those few days dreaming about independent life as a dancer with inflow of cash and enhancement of prestige in the close company of Kiran. The thought of leaving her family, and inevitable loss of face and resultant embarrassment the family and the patriarch would have to face and endure within the nomadic Bede group, pained her internally. Thus, she was somewhat unmindful periodically. Elder ladies of the group used to enjoy that sort of scenario taunting Dhobila for missing her evening babu (resourceful evening man), as no private performance was taking place. The group as a whole was, however, happy as Bhupoti, under instruction of Kiran, not only maintained the flow of drinks but also increased the quantity.

"That was not the case with Ghettu, the bucolic young boat guy. He always had close watch on Dhobila during private performances and kept her under his silent and systematic surveillance. He monitored her every word, every move, every reaction. All these were reflective of both emotional attachments to Dhobila as well as trepidation about the intent of Kiran. Above every conceivable reason, the pride and prestige innate in ethnic nomadic living as a concerted group and consternation regarding possible dent in that due to Kiran's advances bothered him constantly.

"Friends noticed changes in Kiran's usual social behavior. He was comparatively quiet but, contrary to recent behavioral pattern, relatively friendly. One conspicuous change was his leaving the gathering sooner than usual often. Though a bit of exception, that did not cause any anxiety within the friends' circle. They ignored it as something due to family matters that Kiran would not like to share. He was equally very affable with everyone in his house without tangible response from any immediate family members. Both Dhuni and Chandu, who had little time to know the real Kiran, were obviously responsive to his gestures.

"Friends assembled as usual in the evening for relatively dull natter in the absence of earlier excitements while spending time in Joba Rani's kotha, Binati Rani's place, and snake dance evenings in the company of Dhobila. They were thus happy to see a jovial Kiran joining them after some days of controlled and equally fretful behavior. He appeared to be very happy and similarly munificent in entertaining his close and trusted friends. That was a memorable evening in all respects.

"The group was both surprised and overjoyed with Kiran telling them to wait for him around late hours of the following evening in Binati Rani's place, as he would be late in joining them. He then instructed Bhupoti to make arrangements for the visit and to send some advance nazrana (gifts) to Binati Rani, as the visit was being planned after a gap.

"The following day was a beautiful one with bright sun, clear blue sky, and a gentle south-to-north breeze. Absence of rain during last few days made the setting dry and sultry. That made the gentle breeze so welcome. Taking the pretext of discomfort, Dhobila opted out of daily trip for snake dance and trading. She instead spent all her time to cook a good dinner for her parents while serving her father frequent drinks that were made available by Kiran.

"Both parents were happy observing Dhobila in a pleased mood, but they unwittingly failed to take note of the inner strife causing soreness within her. As Dhobila was passing the earthen plate full of rice, *dal,* and some fried vegetables, the mother noticed the teary eyes of the daughter. On specific query as to the reason for that, Dhobila bypassed the issue, saying she had difficulty in ensuring steady fire in the *chula* (generally a clay cube with a round hole in front to facilitate putting firewood with hole on the top acting as a burner. It can have one or more such burners). Dhobila explained that due to wetness of some firewood, she had to blow the *chunga* (a flute-type bamboo piece to push air below forcefully by mouth) regularly from proximity to ensure fire. Thus, the eyes got irritated. That was a satisfactory response, and no further discussion followed. Prior to that, Dhobila fed her snakes for the last time with all love and care.

"As all daily chores were completed and people settled in their respective boats following standard practices, Dhobila put a small packet, containing one each of her saree, petticoat, and blouse, under her left armpit. She took cautious steps to the rear of their boat in proximity to the landing area. Dhobila was about to take her first step out of the boat but suddenly felt something emotionally distressing. The thought of snakes was the reason for her pensive adagio. Dhobila turned back, opened her basket, patted the snakes, and carefully left the boat after scanning the surrounding areas and the conditions of closely parked Bede boats. All these she managed and did with enormous amount of confidence and gusto.

"Dhobila's immediate feeling on stepping the shore was contrary to the echelon of confidence predicated her leaving the boat: the emergent darkness of the night suddenly became still darker; her firm physique for which she was the envy of many started tattering under coerce sense of haziness of the journey she was undertaking; her determined push for big and rapid steps resulted in smaller and slower ones; the relative little distance of the place for meeting Kiran appeared to be a long one. Dhobila poised for a while, revisited the equations engulfing her thought, and decided to overcome the diffidence. She dragged herself toward the destined point even though overwhelmed by negativities caused by fear, uncertainty, infidelity, and sense of guilt.

"Her physical breakdown was almost complete as she saw Kiran waiting in the shadow of emerging darkness. Nearing him, Dhobila just stooped on the chest of Kiran, oblivious of the fall of the small bundle containing the saree that she held so cautiously in her armpit. Kiran, in spontaneous effort to protect her, extended his arms and held her firmly. He instantaneously experienced the spark of sexual sensation, even at that mature age, as taut and bulging breasts of Dhobila, under her loose top without any support, braced his chest for the first time. He quickly surveyed all that he had chances of contact in the past and was charmed by the ones of Dhobila.

"But that was a fleeting spark for Kiran at that moment. His main objective was taking Dhobila away from the immediate vicinity of Bedes. He never forgot Bhupoti's repeated caution about the ferocity and brutal nature of response by most tribal people, more so Bedes. Kiran soon detached himself from Dhobila, held her left wrist firmly, and resolutely said, 'There is no time to waste. Let us move fast. We will take an exit by the side of nearby primary school, negotiate a few farm blocks, and then reach the main road at the southern end of the bazaar area. A *rickshaw* (man-driven tricycle) has been stationed there. He is my trusted rickshaw puller. He will take us to your new place.'

"Ghettu had been very watchful about responses and movements of Dhobila once Kiran's presence in the life of boat people became conspicuous. He could not openly disagree with the patriarch or relay his reservations. That was against values and cultures of nomadic people like Bedes.

"Ghettu developed the habit of positioning himself continually under the huge mango tree slightly far away from the anchor site of their boats. This he used to do at a time most boat habitants were enjoying postdinner drinks coinciding with the advent of darkness. His arduous isolated sitting was not premised on any particular apprehension. It had no intoxication of expectancy. He just did it for his own sake: enjoyed peace of mind without any specific concern.

"Ghettu used to sit there generally up to early hours of the night and then quietly go to his boat for sleep. The only distraction he had in these hours of quiet stay was to have a few *biddis* (locally made smoke of dry tobacco leaves). For that, and complying with common traditions of the clan, he had to take the cover of the tree to conceal his smoking from others. On that evening and at that hour, Ghettu took cover to smoke. After finishing smoking, he was about to reposition himself in the normal place of sitting.

"Ghettu's vigilant eyes noticed unusual movement at the landing site of the boats. Suspicion brewed in his mind, refocusing unabated attention in monitoring the discernible movement of a shadowy image. He did so from obscured position behind the tree without creating any commotion. As the shadow figure disembarked from one of the boats and stepped on the shore, Ghettu bashfully thought it as the being of Dhobila. As he had some doubt in mind due to descending darkness, Ghettu refrained from making an outcry. He was certain that his earlier premonition about the intent of Babu was not only correct but also reinforced many a times as he saw that shadow taking cautious steps toward the temple side even though it was relatively dark.

"Ghettu decided to follow the shadow but as a precaution wanted to carry something to defend him or the honor of the clan, if and as it would be warranted. His brief search in the neighborhood was unproductive to identify anything of significance. As recourse, Ghettu decided to take one *boitta* (an oar—a long pole made of wood with flat blade at one end) from his boat. By the time Ghettu disengaged the boitta and came to the point he saw the shadow last, there was nobody around. He thought for a while and decided to proceed toward the main road. As Ghettu took steps, his feet came into contact with the packet that fell from the armpit of Dhobila. The contents of the packet were sufficient evidence as to the identity of the shadow and conclusive revelation of the intent of the secret journey. His shock and suspicion soon turned into an outrage, as he had no doubt that Dhobila, being propelled by the evening babu, was on her way out, betraying their nomadic tribe.

"Ghettu intently scanned the close surrounding and setting with focus on structures, shadowy escapes, and approach to the main road. He soon identified two shadows bypassing the primary school periphery on their way to connect with the main road at the southern end of the bazaar through adjacent paddy field. The approach chosen was a shorter route to the bazaar, used by some mostly during dry season. That was obviously a choice of detour to avoid public contact during Kiran and Dhobila's brief travel to the point of the main road.

"Ghettu quickly started running toward the main road and decided to take a shortcut while halfway through to confront the shadows in the remote setting of paddy field, and at the earliest. He left the alleyway at the meeting point of the main road and commenced crisscrossing the paddy field blocks of different sizes and divergent conditions to avoid attention of the suspects. He soon positioned himself ahead of the shadows and opted to deal with them in the paddy field before they could be on their way to ascend the main road. His expression of emotion, his manifestation of anger, and his determination of vengeance were all omnipresent in his body language and the way he held the boitta.

"Kiran, not being aware of the existence of such young man among the group of Bedes, was annoyed seeing Ghettu in front of them obstructing their journey. But the reaction of Dhobila was more of shock and severity, as she had clarity as to the consequences of confrontation emanating from similar situations.

"Kiran, in a pressed but threatening voice, asked Ghettu to step out of the way and said, 'Do you know who I am? My father is a very influential person of this bazaar. We can have even police on our side in case of any charges, fake or genuine. So please step out of our way and leave us alone.' Ghettu surprised Dhobila by responding most sensibly in a calm voice, 'I am not interested to know about you or areas of your influence. Dhobila belongs to our clan. Nobody takes our girls like this. This involves the honor and dignity of our tribe. If necessary, we will do anything to preserve and protect that honor of our tribe.' He paused for a moment and continued, 'I do not wish for any bedlam. Release the hand of Dhobila and allow her to return to the boat. We will not create any problem for you.'

"Kiran was infuriated observing the composed nature of and listening to the words of the illiterate Bede young guy and shouted back, 'Go to hell. I am not taking Dhobila anywhere. She decided to pursue her destined path, and I am only helping her. No one can stop me from doing that.'

"Ghettu once again pleaded, 'Babu, please listen to me. We do respect people like you. Your area helps us in living. I do not like to create a scene to draw public attention that might dishonor you or your family. But in response to your last utterance, also please note that no one can take Dhobila anywhere but the boat as long as I am here.'

"Kiran just could not control himself anymore. He distasted both the words of patronization and those of assertiveness and, as a reactive response, slapped Ghettu firmly as a gesture to teach him for life. In the process, and perhaps unknowingly, he released Dhobila's hand. She instantaneously took a few steps back and stood neutrally at a safe distance. Dhobila's motionless and speechless silent posture was indicative of possible violent consequences, and she froze within herself. None of the other two persons was aware of Dhobila's instant disposition.

"Ghettu once again pleaded and said, 'Babu, no one slaps a shapure's (snake charmer's) son. We are to make a retort, if necessary even by deploying a snake. But I am not inclined to take any such action. You are much older than me. I take your slap as a blessing. But I beg of you. Allow me to return to the boat with Dhobila, and I assure you that no harm will befall on her.'

"Both the tone and texture of Ghettu's message appeared to be sordid to Kiran. It was just impossible for him to remain hunkered down and see Ghettu walk away with his prized possession. His reactive exorbitance was manifested in a sudden kick aimed at the left thigh of Ghettu. That was the ultimate limit for Ghettu to contain his temper. His youth and ego revolted. The robust and rustic left hand of Ghettu held the neckline section of Kiran's silken *punjabi,* and whispered, 'I had no intention to hurt you. You asked for it. I can kill you now or in your bed by deploying a snake. I will not do that, but I would make you pay for what you did.'

"After saying these, Ghettu did neither waste any time or word, nor was he bothered about any reaction of Dhobila. He took a step backward to create enough space, dangled his boitta held firmly by his right hand, and hit Kiran hard repeatedly below both the knees. Kiran, shocked and shattered by the suddenness and severity of response, fell on the ground, groaning with pain and visible bleeding.

"Dhobila continued to stay frozen. She did not move to stop Ghettu by words or deeds, or positioned herself on the top of Kiran's body as a cover. In that situation, she was overtaken by an advice of her father: 'not to take any action to restrain Ghettu once he is angry.

At that moment, he can even kill you, though he loves you most, and even though we helped him to live and grow after the demise of his parents in a boat fire. Being enraged without control is the trait of his character since early childhood, but the best part of that is his mastery in managing that anger.'

"Ghettu took possession of the left wrist of Dhobila, and took definite firm steps toward the boat. He did not utter a single word or accuse Dhobila during the walk. He broke his silence in a very personal conversation with the father of Dhobila and the patriarch of the group detailing what happened.

"On-the-spot consensus was to leave the place soonest, to get out of *khal* (canal) area at the earliest for better maneuverability and defense strategy if the group is attacked: to be in the main river trying to find and line up with other Bede groups, to keep snakes handy in case of any need to use them, and to have the venom in possession in case any sporadic retreat is necessary.

"But not a single negative word or acquisition was hurled at Dhobila. By his body language, the patriarch advised all concerned to be supportive of Dhobila at this time of her mental condition with enough time to talk to her once they were out of the current vulnerable spot. He also raised his clasped both hands up to his forehead and promised to *Ma* (mother) *Manasa Devi*, the snake goddess worshipped by Hindu population of India for the cure of various ailments and prevention of snake bites, to hold a grand *puja* (ritual) in expressing gratitude for saving the group from a calamity.

"Kiran was lying in the paddy field groaning with pain and weakened by continuous bleeding. Normally a few local people only traverse that way after the dark. They generally take that unconventional short route more for convenience and familiarity, if the weather is good and dry. One of them was the Sanskrit teacher of the school. Known popularly as *shonsh krito sir* (Sanskrit teacher) rather by his name of Chiranttan Das, he was in the habit of taking that walkway more regularly, as he was tutoring in the house of a bazaar elite with side benefit of dinner.

"Shonsh-krito sir was returning to his one-room accommodation in the school structure. That accommodation was specially made available for him, as it was difficult to have a local teacher capable of teaching Sanskrit. Seeing an empty rickshaw parked in an isolated place like that, he stopped for a while and asked the rickshaw puller whether he had any problem. The rickshaw puller merrily responded that he had no problem and was waiting for his *babu* (gentleman) who hired him and asked him to stay there.

"A man of few words, Shonsh-krito sir proceeded toward the walkway and descended from the main road without any further comment. Proceeding the way he usually takes, Shonsh-krito sir's attention was drawn to a groaning sound, symbolic of both pain and exhaustion, from a nearby location of the farm field. Even though scared and nervous, he took cautious steps to find a well-dressed gentleman lying there. His careful eyes roughly identified, even in that setting of darkness, significant lower-leg injuries bleeding profusely. Shonsh-krito sir shouted for the rickshaw puller, seeking his immediate presence and help. The rickshaw puller did not waste any time and responded promptly. He came near the injured person and identified him as the babu who hired him and he was waiting for. The rickshaw puller disclosed the identity of the injured person and requested the fellow gentleman (Shonsh-krito sir) to be by the side of his babu while he would paddle quickly to inform the family.

"As the rickshaw puller was taking the northwestern alley of the bazaar area toward Shukhipur, he noticed the friends of his babu who just that time came out of Binati Rani's place. Since it was past usual evening time already and late hours by local standard, the friends assumed that Kiran, constrained by family or other reasons, would not show up. They thus decided to leave. The rickshaw puller suddenly took a U-turn, stopped his rickshaw in front of his friends, and hurriedly narrated the situation. Soon three friends of Kiran managed to be on the rickshaw with one sitting on the puller's seat, while the rickshaw puller was paddling in a standing position. Bhupoti was sent to Kiran's house to inform the family.

"Since Kiran left the house in a good mood, the general feeling around that setting of Shukhipur was one of ease and serenity. I was resting after finishing my usual *shandha annik* (sunset puja consisting of offering of lit lamps, touching of objects and feet of deity, the ringing of bells, uttering of chants, and smelling of incense, followed by tasting of blessed food known as *proshad*). Baba leisurely finished his early evening smoke of *hookah* and waited for Dhrub to join him for dinner, a practice dating back to many years. Gokul was relaxing, keeping his eyes nevertheless fixated on both Dhuni and Chandu, ensuring that all relevant household things were in place and positions preferred by me. Bhupoti reached Kiran's house at that point in time.

"Bhupoti was pensively worried and nervous by the sudden turn of events about which, and its severity, he had no knowledge except what the rickshaw puller described in a jumble clutter manner. He had the feeling of being beleaguered in facing the family. Bhupoti was confused in approaching the open courtyard of the house, which he cheerily negotiated many times in the past on the way to meet his Dada Babu. Within his nervous self, he was exploring options in breaking the news. Bhupoti, disembarking from his hired rickshaw, called Gokul-da in a very compliant voice. Gokul-da listened to what Bhupoti had to say, asked him to wait, and went to the adjacent new home where Dhrub started living for some time. Gokul-da narrated to Dhrub what he was told earlier by Bhupoti. Forgetting all intent feelings of distaste and dislike for his father, Dhrub rushed to meet Bhupoti and inquired about the incident. Bhupoti said, 'We do not know anything. The rickshaw puller reported to us that someone bodily injured Dada Babu below his both knees in a farm field on the southern side of the bazaar. The local schoolteacher (Shonsh-krito sir) noticed him and sought the help of the rickshaw puller, who was waiting slightly far away on the main road per Dada Babu's instruction. On identifying Dada Babu, he rushed to the bazaar area on his way to Shukhipur and met us on the northwest corner. Our other friends boarded that rickshaw to go to the spot, and I was asked to inform you. No other detail is there except that he is bleeding profusely.'

"On being so appraised, Dhrub went straight to his new accommodation, got money from the almirah (wooden cupboard), and met me, briefly saying, 'There is some problem with Baba (father Kiran). I am going there. Please finish your dinner. If I need more time, I will send Bhupoti Kaku (uncle) to keep you posted,' and then went to his dadu (grandpa) to tell that he had to go out on an urgent business and would not be able to have dinner with him that night. Baba remained nonchalant even though he observed all movements of Gokul and Dhrub, had his premonition about things that could happen and be faced, and looked at Dhrub with a blank gaze. Baba's physical movements, to the immense surprise of Gokul-da, were indicative of something ominous even though Gokul-da continuously repeated to himself the same wordings, '*Chinta korban na tahkur. Bhogoban ar kri pae amon kicho hoy nai*' (Do not worry, sir. Nothing major happened by God's grace). He continued to say so, as it is considered impolite under local culture for staff to dispense solace to his employer.

"My abstemious priority has always been to avoid inconclusive discussions on both critical and vicarious matters as often the outcomes may be both confusing and embarrassing. I conditioned myself accordingly and decided to be away from all and sundry. As Dhrub approached me again, apparently to tell the thwarting news about Kiran, I looked at him with wide-open eyes without any wink. There was neither any vocal nor physical burst as was common in the contiguous culture. I drew the anchal of my saree to fully cover my head and started taking unstable steps toward the puja ghar (place/room within the house especially earmarked for placing devi [deity] and performing daily religious ritual). I softly drew the attention of Gokul-da and advised him about serving dinner to Baba properly, observing Dhrub leaving home.

"In the serene setting of puja ghar, I sat on the floor facing the devi, slanting my legs at knee point. I raised my two folded hands up to chest level, closed my eyes, and prayed absorbedly for one who never loved me, cared for me, thought about me, shared any agony or happiness with me, and never even recognized me as someone who gave birth to his two children. I impetuously opted for that as Kiran socially is part of my life, an existence bonded by *saptapodi* (seven circles around fire taking each other as life partner per Hindu wedding ritual). Such Hindu wedding bond is never to be tarnished by neglect, torment, hatred, and so on, and that value element is built in prevailing traditions and practices over thousands of years. The Hindu husbands of ancient India enjoyed, independent of the quality of their conjugal life, so much of esteem and enhanced position that the practice of *sati* (immolation of a Hindu widow on the funeral pyre of deceased husband or burying her alive) had to be banned by the East India Company (British) government by enacting a law as late as 1829.

"I prayed for hours together in the same position notwithstanding malevolent background of my conjugal life. Commonly, this sort of response and behavior were consistent with traditional values and practices. But I had other reasons to do so. I was cognizant of appalling consequences that could be caused by any excruciating happening both on the good name of the family and the social standing of Baba (father-in-law). My worries hinged around Baba's ability to handle and manage such experience if, God forbid, that eventuates. I struggled with myself when such thoughts preponderate my mind despite my eagerness to perform puja. I, in the midst of prayer, started saying to myself, '*Shuv, shuv chinta*' (Happy, happy thoughts). The other pressing trepidation was possible sway on children. Still I continued praying with full devoutness and dilution.

"Gokul-da punctiliously arranged dinner and respectfully requested *Thakur* (as he addresses Baba) to come for dinner: a routine matter of many years that suddenly became so thwarting that it made him edgy at every step. Baba slowly came and sat on his usual seating place of the dining mattress, keeping a space for Dhrub: a standard practice since early childhood of Dhrub.

"Baba fixated his eyes on the cooked rice served in traditional round brass plate with series of small brass bowls all around containing related food items. He raised the brass glass full of water, poured a little on his right palm, and then sprinkled that around the brass plate following Hindu tradition of commencing eating. Gokul-da, who was observing the process, was very happy but soon was taken aback when Baba, after having a long look at the puja ghar, stood up slowly and asked for a fresh service of his favorite hookah. Dumbfounded, Gokul-da had no words and complied with.

"The night sets early in any surrounding like Shukhipur of rural South Tripura. But it was different on that night. With the passage of time, people—family, well-wishers, community elites and elders, and snooping onlookers—slowly started stepping in the open and wide courtyard of Dhireen Babu's homestead. Each had his own version of what had happened without even being near the place of incident. Each one of them excelled in consoling Baba. Most of his responses to those observations were restrained look, nodding head, inhaling hookah, and exhaling limited amount of smoke.

"Bhupoti showed up around midnight and said, '*Nomoshkar*' (Hindu way of greeting) to Baba and requested Gokul-da to inform me (*Bou-di*, as friend's wife is addressed, [sister-in-law]) about his presence. I came out of puja ghar without emotional outburst and stood near the kitchen door. I intentionally did that to create a space so that Bhupoti-*da* (brother, as husband's friends are locally addressed) can say whatever he was supposed to say. Bhupoti-da, carrying in his persona the full burden of associated guilt and resultant embarrassment due to responsibility of detailing what happened, stood in a static position with stooped posture. Both of us were quiet for a few moments. I then inquired, 'What happened?'

"Taking advantage of that opening, Bhupoti-da responded in detail. He said, 'Dada Babu was in a very good mood the last few days. He met us yesterday, desired we assemble in a particular place where he would meet us but a bit late than normal. He also said that he would share good news with us. So we were in that particular location. As it was getting late, we decided to leave, thinking Dada Babu might have an unforeseen problem. It was at that point that the rickshaw puller saw and informed us about the calamitous incident. Our friends rushed toward the spot, and I was sent to home to inform Dhrub.

'As *Dhrub Baba-ji* (local way to address the son of a friend with affection and love) and myself reached the spot, the local teacher, who was still being surrounded by a number of people, told us that the victim had been taken to a dispensary in the bazaar area. Upon arrival at the dispensary, we saw Dada Babu in semiconscious condition with his body experiencing excruciating pain out of merciless bashing of lower parts of his two legs. The attending pseudo physician was of the opinion that continuous bleeding, as was apparent, is the major problem; recommended his immediate transfer to the district general hospital; and was struggling to pinpoint some sort of painkiller to give Dada Babu immediate relief.

'As the spot of the incident was near the place where Bedes (snake charmers) anchored their boats, and as Dada Babu, to my knowledge, was interacting intimately with the Bedes latterly, I rushed to the canal side but did not find any trace of either Bedes or their boats. I had no doubt in my mind about the involvement of Bedes in the incident but opted to keep that to myself.

'By the time I returned, arrangements were finalized to take Dada Babu to the district hospital. Dhrub Baba-ji decided to be by the side of Dada Babu all the way through, and so was the decision of all of us.

'I was, however, told to stay put and inform all the concerned families about the friends' travel to the district headquarters. At that stage, Baba-ji took me to a solitary location and requested me to come to the house to brief you privately about the incident and condition of Dada Babu, and also to tell you that nothing needs to be stopped. Gokul-da was to be sent in the morning with keys to open the business premise and ask Niren (store staff) to come and see you and *Kaka Babu* (father of Kiran) to get necessary advice.'

"Since the briefing was short and lacked clarity, with information good enough to confuse one and create more anxiety, I ditheringly raised my two clasped palms denoting *'nomoshkar,'* also a local way of saying 'thank you' while departing. As I turned toward the inside of the kitchen, a very unusual sound attracted my attention. I turned back to see Bhupoti-da sobbing. Surprised by such outpouring of emotions from a middle-aged man whose basic identity centered on Kiran and his company, I quietly asked Bhupoti-da whether he had anything else to tell. Bhupoti-da waggled his head and pleaded for pardon from me by saying, *'Bou-di, amake khoma kor ben'* (Please pardon me). I was fully aware of Dada Babu's proclivity for the Bede (snake charmer) group, especially the young Dhobila, but never tried to caution or stop him. I am the one who is responsible for what happened to Dada Babu. I can't excuse myself.' He then left the place in a state of total torment. Bhupoti-da even forgot to take leave from his revered Kaka Babu (father of Kiran), a local tradition and requirement.

"The naivety of Bhupoti-da bemused me. Sitting in a corner of the kitchen with only Dhuni tensely staring at me, I, upon reflection, laughed at his comment. Some individuals are born with atypical traits. Kiran is one of them. The family's traumatic migration experience and traditional values repeated by Baba often, Aparna's open-ended love and support, Shetupa's unsolicited guidance and startling reactions, and my initial unreserved submission and total devotion had no impact on his behavior pattern. It had been evident that by staying most of the time with friends outside the homestead, he enjoyed escape from that sort of environment. Nothing else mattered to him. Nothing else registered in his mind. But here was one blaming him for not advising his Dada Babu to refrain from mingling with the Bede group, especially young Dhobila, as if that would have done the trick. Notwithstanding simplicity inherent in his statement, I developed some instant respect for Bhupoti-da as at least being one among friends who genuinely had feelings for Kiran besides drinks and other amusements.

"Exhausted, Dhrub returned the late afternoon of the following day and quietly took his seat by the side of his revered *dadu* (grandpa). He called me to come and take a seat by his side. I took a little time, as I got engaged in preparing *jol khabar* (refreshments) soon after seeing Dhrub had returned. I placed the plate and glass of water in front of Dhrub and kept waiting, fixing my eyes on the ground, both out of shame and embarrassment. I had a premonition about the likely content of what Dhrub was going to say in front of Baba (shoshur moshai).

"Dhrub, quite sensibly and as was expected of him, totally avoided detailing the ugly incident. He straightway narrated the reason for taking Kiran to the district hospital and the prognosis upon arrival. 'As that was past midnight, it took time to get proper professional attention. As Baba's (Kiran's) both legs below the knee level were badly thrashed and nothing could stop resultant bleeding, the initial symptoms of gangrene slowly set in. The attending physician opined that there was no way to repair the battered bones, and the only recourse to avoid any major complication was to cut off the damaged parts of the legs for the healing process to start. In discussions with Baba's (Kiran's) friends, I consented. The operation was done in the early morning. He came to senses around midmorning and recognized all of us. His friends decided to stay with him. I left a good amount of money with them to take care of all eventualities. I told them that I would return tomorrow late afternoon.'

"I slowly raised my eyes and blessed Dhrub copiously but in silence for not detailing references to Bedes (snake charmers), and particularly of Dhobila. I, however, made a specific query about what was meant by gangrene that propelled taking of such a cruel and quick decision. Dhrub explained that according to the attending physician, gangrene happens when a body part loses its blood supply.

That may be due to variable conditions such as injury, an infection, or other causes. If not attended on time, gangrene is a life-threatening condition as a mass of body tissues dies because of it.

"Baba (shoshur moshai) maintained unmitigated silence, puffing his hookah frequently. That was apparent symptom of his internalized anxiety and restlessness as well as a strategy not to get involved in any discourse that could only cause more pain to him.

"The briefing was over sooner than normally expected. That did not reflect any lack of interest and concern on the part of very relevant people in Kiran's life. Each of the persons involved had their respective discomfort in having a detailed discussion on an incident that was full of negative attributes, a premise based on piecemeal and equally variable inflow of information. The need for Dhrub to take a shower, get ready for food, and have good rest provided a convenient window to close further deliberations, and all concerned availed that.

"Like the earlier briefing session, the dinner was short and simple. After the dinner, and following standard ritual, the grandpa and grandson were sitting side by side while Grandpa was busy in puffing his hookah. I slowly moved in and sought Baba's (father-in-law's) permission to travel to the hospital with Dhrub the following afternoon.

"Baba was taciturn for some time and then nodded his head with a casual remark, 'You have my permission if you want to go, but the outcome may not be that pleasant. I know my son. He is one who never thought about and understood the relevance as well as value associated with showing respect to and making other people happy. All his life he just thought that his own happiness is what matters to make life happy and beautiful.'

"Baba (shoshur moshai) then had an intense passionate look at his loving grandson and unleashed, to the surprise of both me and Dhrub, some of his inner thoughts. Those were evidently his frustrations that fraught his mind for a very long time. He bemoaned by saying, 'I am sorry, *Dadu* (a traditional way of addressing a grandson affectionately), that unwittingly I passed on my failing to you in the shape of a bad father. I am beleaguered. I am embarrassed. I seek pardon from all.'

"Dhrub exchanged looks with me and then responded, saying, '*Dadu* (grandpa), I did not discover my father last night. I have observed him from my early childhood, have always been conscious of the agony *Ma* (mother) has been sustaining, and continually cognizant of the inner pressure and frustration you have had. I conditioned myself to carve out a place for me where my father would not have any role or responsibility. Thus, to me, to my comfort, to my contentment, you all, except him, are my identity. I am happy as one being the grandson of Dhireen Babu, son of Indrani-Ma, nephew of Aparna Pishi (paternal aunt), and brother of Shetupa. I do not care about anything else. You can, of course, ask me then why I went out last night and spent most of the day ensuring proper medical care for one who has no relevance in my life. I did not go just because he is my father. I did not go because of social requirements. I primarily went because I was certain that it was my blood-related obligation. Moreover, treating a bad man shoddily during his bad time makes the other person also bad. No mental strain is eased by such action. In any such situation, that only worsens the condition, both in the short and long terms. I am feeling at ease for being positive, and that gives me the strength to talk to you both freely.'

"I went to the hospital the following day in the company of Dhrub and prepared myself to be nice and sympathetic in interacting with Kiran, forgetting the neglect and pain of my entire married life. My mental condition was fortified by the last few words of Dhrub the night before. I argued with myself, 'If my son could respond positively without forgetting anything, then why would I not be able?'

"As I stepped into the general ward (there was no orthopedic ward) of the hospital following Dhrub, I was crestfallen seeing an exhausted man languishing from the sustained pain of the wounds and bearing with postoperation trauma. I was about to express my sincere feelings. But his outbursts took me aback. After impetuously trying to reposition himself on the hospital bed notwithstanding plaster-type bandage below both the knees, Kiran shouted at me, saying, 'Are you not happy to see me in this condition? You did not believe others. So you wanted to see yourself. You must have exalted happiness as Bhogoban has responded to your prayer.'

"I was mortified. I felt all the more miserable seeing Dhrub embarrassed as a few dozen eyes of that ward were all focused on us, forgetting their own pains and tribulations. Dhrub, without uttering any word, put his right hand on my shoulder and conducted me out of the ward. Both of us stood silently in the open veranda looking at the sky. My flustered thought received a sudden joggle when Dhrub very neutrally observed, 'Dadu was so right.' I looked down and wasted an involuntary globule of tears.

"There was apparently no need to tell Baba anything specifically about our visit to the hospital. Observing body language, he poignantly indicated to us to sit by his side, asked Gokul-da for a service of fresh hookah, and plaintively said, 'I knew about the outcome.'

"After taking a few long and quick puffs, Baba complained of some chest pain, and Dhrub and Gokul-da assisted him to his bed. I rushed to the kitchen, poured some mustard oil in a tablespoon, put a threshed garlic in it, and heated the oil until the garlic was brown. Based on my limited knowledge, I took the pain to be a cold-related one. I handed that to Gokul-da for massaging Baba's chest, hands, and feet.

"Dhrub quickly went to the bazaar and brought with him the prominent local physician who knew Baba very well too. The prognosis was something worrisome, as the physician mostly briefed Dhrub outside and generally in a low voice. Both of them left the house together, and Dhrub returned after some time with a number of medicines. As I expressed surprise seeing those and directly inquired as to the finding, Dhrub tried to put up a face of gullibility and hurriedly said, 'No, *Ma* (mother), nothing to worry. Dadu will get well soon.' Jokingly, and while entering Baba's room, he hilariously and loudly added, '*Dadu ke tho tara tari bhalo hotey hobey. Amar biya ache na*' (Grandpa needs to be well soon. My wedding is to take place). Hearing that, Baba meekly smiled and said, '*Bhai, chul gulu amni amni shada hoy nai. Kichu-ta bhuddi amaro ache*' (Brother, I have gray hair for nothing. Also, I have some intelligence). Dhrub did not respond. Treatment continued per advice of physician friend who had brought in other doctors too. Baba's condition did not change in any way in spite of intensive medication and regular follow-up by local physicians.

"Kiran was discharged from the hospital after about three weeks of his admission. All arrangements were meticulously made to ensure due comfort when he returns home. Gokul-da, Dhuni, and

Chandu were eagerly waiting to receive him. Bishnur-ma also came. I remained concerned but was relieved to have him back, as that would minimize problems of Dhrub, and anxiety of all others in our home.

"Things do not normally happen as one expects, or as one likes them to be. That precisely turned out at the time of Kiran's return. As friends of Kiran got him out of wobbly taxi and was carrying him by hand, Kiran started shouting with appalling words to the indignity of Baba, Dhrub, and myself, and embarrassment of others present. All that happened a few weeks back causing the present agony were due to his actions as Bhupoti-da later on admitted to me, but he was totally oblivious of that. Instead, he opted to manifest all his anger as if we present were responsible for that. By all counts, he had an ugly return, a feature of life and living that continued all through.

"Baba's health condition started deteriorating, hastened by continuous gibbering of Kiran. In such a situation, Baba once called me and asked to take a seat near his bed. He slowly said, 'Since we talked last, I exchanged letters with my friend, Moni Mohan. Both of us have an agreement. I also talked to Dhrub. As expected, he too is agreeable. If, by chance, and which is likely, anything happens to me, it would be your responsibility to implement my wish.'

"Baba never had me so close while talking. I was equally frightened by the ominously shaky nature of his tone. Both his gesture and words made me nervy. Baba was having breathing problems in talking to me. So I was extra cautious in responding. I poised myself looking at his trembling feet and politely told him, 'Your desire is a command for me. I will definitely initiate the process soon in consultation with Dhrub and Shetupa, the latter being due home after finishing her examination for a very big job under the government. Rest assured all these will be done, and you would happily participate in the wedding.'

"As I was about to leave, Baba surprised me by affectionately grabbing my left hand and said, 'Ma, I had you uprooted from your surrounding and family and brought you here. You had rare occasions to be with your family. You took all of us as your own. Though you lacked formal education, your sense of understanding, your ability to see things and events from broader perspective, your patience and orientation, your ability to manage pain and frustration all contributed, for me especially, to have a congenial family surrounding. But I am sorry, and would like to apologize, that you did not get what any normal woman would like to have. But look at the brighter side: how many mothers are lucky to have children like Dhrub and Shetupa?'

"I was in a state of emotional distress but reasserted myself and quickly diverted his attention by asking whether he would like to have a fresh service of hookah. For the first time, he answered negatively, looking toward the sky clearly visible through the wide-open window by his bedside. Baba left us for good a few days thereafter.

"After that shattering incident involving Dhobila and the ugly return from the hospital belittling all of us in front of his friends and associates, Kiran remained a pompous blowhard, and his apoplectic behavior pattern worsened to the dismay of all, particularly that of Baba. Being not in good health and unable to resort to his recent pastime of enjoying hookah, he was the one who suffered most by the utterances and behavior of Kiran. Even Baba's subsequent death had no repercussions on his thinking and words. Perhaps his disability-related frustration goaded that as the time passed.

"Moni Mohan *Kaku* (uncle) came from Agartala to attend Baba's *Shraddha*. We had discussions about Dhrub-Nandita's wedding. Most reassuring part of that discourse was Kaku's observation, 'I am not agreeing to this wedding with the identity of Dhrub's father. I am agreeing because Dhrub is the grandson of Dhireen and son of Indrani-Ma. That is enough for me.' That removed one of my major concerns, as Kaku, during the short stay in our place and exchange of pleasantries with local people, definitely formed some idea as to the traits of Kiran's persona.

"Everything was agreed as Baba stipulated except the marriage date was fixed after the end of one year, as local custom do not encourage any festivity in the family in the year of death. It was also agreed to have a small wedding per wish of Dhrub consistent with desolation caused by the death of his dear Dadu. And that happened as planned. Nandita came to our house as our loving daughter-in-law.

"The life after the demise of Baba suddenly became very mundane. A bizarre feeling prevailed all around notwithstanding the frequent pestering of loud outcries of incapacitated Kiran, always uttering foul words. We all carried on nonchalantly. Dhrub's wedding after one year, very successful academic attainments of Shetupa, and her excellence in the competitive examination for service under the government provided intermittent exultant variations, but life was never as before.

"Nandita did not surprise me at all. Her temperament, demeanor, patience, and adaptability are all excellent, and much more ubiquitous than even Baba thought of and we expected. She gracefully adapted herself with the personal traits of Dhrub. That made her perfect match for our relatively introvert son. I advised Nandita not to visit our room at any time, as Kiran was absolutely careless in holding his *dhutti* properly.

"Life moved on, and I started having a strange but gratifying feeling related to my role and responsibility. With the demise of Baba and given the condition of Kiran, I was gradually accorded the status of being the de facto head of the family. Dhrub shared progress and problems of business most of which were beyond my comprehension. I think he too was conscious of that but still then continued the practice, keeping Baba in mind. I would often advise him to share those with Nandita. He frequently did so, as I could gather later on from remarks of Nandita under the impression about my lack of information.

"Baba's death affected all of us in different degrees and forms except, of course, Kiran. But the most affected one was Gokul-da. As there was no need of preparing hookah frequently, he had nothing much to do. He also missed long association with his Thakur (master). In consultation with Dhrub and Nandita, I elevated his position with matters concerning household chores and delegated some supervisory authority on other staffs. Both Dhrub and Nandita's gesture to occasionally share a little information with him pertaining to relationships with other businessmen of the bazaar, intermittent discussions pertaining to socially relevant issues and family estate management matters, made him all the more happy.

"There was, however, a point where Gokul-da had total and pronounced disagreement with all three of us: Dhrub, Nandita, and more specifically myself. He never hesitated to accost me about our total lack of interest, which in his words our absolute indifference, in timely arranging a marriage for Shetupa. He did not hesitate in mincing words in this regard, and that is the only occasion when he would assume the guardianship of the family. At the end of his periodical outbursts, Gokul-da would lament, saying, '*Mae ta ke ki era aiburu ba na be. Boaesh ta ar boshey nai. Kobe kuri par hoyeay che'* (They will like to see this girl as a spinster. Her aging has not stopped. She crossed twenty a long time back).

"I once found him in a very relaxed mood. He was puffing his favorite indigenous hookah (a coconut shell with a standard-sized flute-type adjunct having an earthen container or vessel on the top), holding the same by left hand, and happily fixing and rearranging cookie-type round thin black tobacco cakes occasionally by his right hand. Obviously, this type of tobacco cakes is the one that ordinary people could afford.

"Politely drawing his attention, I asked Gokul-da whether he had a little time to talk to me. I did that deliberately to elevate him emotionally, as I would discuss the wedding issue of Shetupa, an issue very close to his heart and in conversing which he could never control himself. My strategy did work. A very obliged Gokul-da happily responded to my gesture, a unique one contrary to receiving orders all through his life. It also had part recognition of my emerging and sublime new identity as the de facto head of the family.

"Gokul-da gently nodded his head, parked his newly lit hookah in a semiconcealed position, picked up a *mora* (a handmade cane seating item), and sat before me, maintaining a respectable distance. I planned earlier to be direct to him so that his misconception about my lack of interest in getting Shetupa married would just wash away. I did not call him to seek his opinion or understanding. Moreover, my new identity and position were contrary to that sort of approach.

"I told him in a firm but low voice, 'Gokul-da, I am happy for your concern about Shetupa's marriage. But she is my daughter too. I have my worries about her. But please bear in mind that I would not like her to get married just for marriage's sake. You have seen my married life from day one. What did I get in this house from my husband? Had it not been for Baba's illimitable care and affection, Aparna's unreserved love and understanding, and Bishnur-ma's and your support, I possibly would have committed suicide a long time ago. Then Dhrub, Anjali, and Shetupa's existence in my life fortified me with new strength to live. But as a woman, I would not like my daughter to lead such a life. Also, she is a well-educated, intelligent, and considerate young lady. So I told her that she should marry only when she finds one of her liking and the person concerned is respectful to woman. In fact, she unburdened my guilt when she was going to college and said exactly those words herself. I just repeated those.'

"Gokul-da was either convinced or confused by my statement. He looked down and maintained total silence. To give him an opening, I referred to the very early death of his wife without bearing any children, and his subsequent total identification with Baba and family as his existence, as his world. Premised on that, I told him, 'Gokul-da, because of such situation, your thinking mostly is guided by emotion. Innate advantage of your position is not having any bearing with associated responsibility and resultant consequence. Not only do I feel worried when I think of Shetupa but equally I am scared of any probable negative outcome. Shetupa has the same feeling too. We are very frank, and our relationship is based on mutual understanding. She told me that she will marry: marry one who loves her, and would never agree to sacrifice learning just to get married.' I also told him that Shetupa will soon sit in an examination for a very big position in the government. Thus, her present thinking and actions are governed by that. Gokul-da eventually raised his eyes, looked at me, and had a sort of very neutral statement, '*Oh, Ma, tai nake. Atho boro shu khobor*' (Oh, Mom, is that so! That is a good news).

"I had specific objective to raise this issue with Gokul-da. So I told him, 'Thank you very much for understanding. I would not discuss this issue anymore with anyone. But I have a request. Please do not raise this issue in future. You just pray to *Bhogoban* (Lord) so that Shetupa meets one whom she would be able to love.'

"Shetupa finished her job-related examination and came to Shukhipur to spend some time with us. Like all her previous visits since going to college at Agartala, every return of her was a matter of joy and merriment for all of us. This was no exception but a bit more tensed. Shetupa told me that she prepared a lot for All-India-based competitive examination for entry into government service and hopes she gets selected. Thus, she couldn't relax like earlier times.

"Shetupa, on the contrary, appeared to have observed some incongruity in my behavior and inquired from me the reason for that. Since high school days, one of her pet query was 'Ma, I think you have somebody in your early life. A beautiful girl like you must have had suitors in early life. You must constantly be bothered by that feeling. Perhaps your strange marriage accentuated that. Please tell me, who is he and where is he? I want to meet him.' I dodged that query always by an innocent smile or focusing attention to something more relevant.

"She repeated the same query this time too. But this is a different time in my life. It is after unexpected encounter with Joyonto Dada (Brother Joyonto, your friend of Comilla), who came to meet me along with our niece Anjali. That was a visit orchestrated by him pursuing your request of a long time back during his family's emigration to Tripura. I was enthralled when he briefly told me the background and was astounded by his concerted efforts to link information to find me after many, many years. During our brief one-on-one discourse, I could hardly look at him straight, as I always had the feeling that he was trying to scan me through your eyes. His visit refreshed me totally about emotions that permeate my entire life even though occasionally I tried, without success, to surmount that.

"After some thought, I decided to share my inner feelings involving you to my most dependable counselor and reliable well-wisher, my dear daughter: friend, guide, and shield in the thorny process of life. In response to her latest inquisition, I told Shetupa that I had something to share with her, which she would have to document on my behalf in the form of a letter.

"She was taken aback and said, 'So all my past scruple about the presence of someone in your early life was not wrong.' I was hesitant to give her a direct answer but said that 'I will tell you my story. Then you conclude for yourself.'

"We had long discussions between us that night, and intermittently in the days following. At the end, I requested her to put facts of my life, as well as my emotions and feelings, in the form of a letter to be sent through the courtesy of Joyonto Dada. Shetupa readily agreed but wanted a little time to reflect contextually all that I said. She also sought my agreement to arrange things and events from her perspective as a writer and detail certain religious and social practices to make things clearer and relevant to you. I agreed with both.

"Shetupa left for Agartala after a few days. She returned to Shukhipur briefly to personally give the news of her getting into Indian police service, and that she would soon be leaving for training in the Indian National Police Academy located at Hyderabad. Successful candidates inducted in Indian Police Service are trained at this national institute before assigning to respective state cadres.

"Shetupa also told that after the training, she will be a big police officer. I was surprised and told her, 'When village *chowkidar* (guard) used to come to our home, all the ladies would hide behind the door partition and gaze through the opening between the door and the frame. Now you mean me to believe that you are becoming a big police officer.' To convince me, Shetupa said, 'Ma, time has changed. You will see local daroga (officer-in-charge of local police station) coming to your house and salute your Shetupa once I come back from training. You would not have to hide. You would stand in the open door and experience that. I will have many darogas under me.'

After saying that, Shetupa quietly handed over the letter to me with observation that the letter, because of both volume and privacy of content, should not be mailed to Joyonto *Mama* (maternal uncle) but should be sent to him by a trusted person, and must be hand-delivered. I agreed with that.

"Both of us sat side by side for quite a while without exchanging any word. Shetupa then volunteered to read the whole letter, both for information and my endorsement. After finishing the first part of the letter, mostly dealing with life experiences, she paused and made a specific observation: 'Ma, some of the latter paragraphs of this letter capture the events, experiences, and reactions rather explicitly. I have done that after some serious deliberations, as I want them to factually represent your words and reflect the intent of your candid confessions and statements made to me earlier. I considered them necessary to meaningfully conclude the letter. They not only capture your unspoken longing but as well truly reflect and convey your earnest emotion.'

"Shetupa, after finishing her explicatory remark continued reading the latter sections of the letter. Those paragraphs run as under: 'I am uncertain about the receipt of this letter by you at all. I do not have any idea when and how you are expected to receive the same. I am unclear about your probable reactions on going through its contents after so many years. I do not have any idea where you are and how you are. But most of the days of my leaving Anandapur for Shukhipur, I always prayed for your well-being, success, happiness, safety, and good health, notwithstanding my earlier resolve to erase you from my thought. I am certain, wherever you are, Bhogoban will always bestow His eternal bleesings upon you.

'You know, and you understand too, that I had no say in my move from Anandapur to Shukhipur. But I had definitely my baffled but somewhat sublime part in that decision. My singular overarching consolation is that by voluntarily agreeing with that decision, I could make my poor, worried, and helpless parents happy for all time to come. What could a fourteen- or fifteen-year-old half-lettered girl of a low-caste absolutely poor family do otherwise in a position I was growing up?

'During transition to my new identity, I suffered sordid pain every moment thinking about absolute physical separation from you and my surrounding as I was to step into the other side of the border. I fought within myself to stash out such feeling, thinking that as both dalliance and loony. Occasionally I was successful, but most of the time, I had contrary outcome. You were thus omnipresent in most of my subsequent thoughts and actions even though I had no inkling about you, your progression, and your life.

'I left Anandapur's merriment with zealous hope of Shukhipur's happiness in the congeniality of an affluent family and in the warm embrace of a caring husband. While the former was more than fulfilled, the least repeated about the latter is definitely better. I was always conscious of not having a fallback position in life. That perceptibly caused a chill feeling in my reactions characterized by submission rather than assertion. I always controlled my gall about miserable experiences of married life looking at Baba and Aparna, and the growing up of two most loveable children that I have. One can say that in having a family life, I traded happiness with other congealed exhilarations of life. I had not much of options either.

'All my thinking about you was always scraggly and isolated by nature. Mostly, I developed the habit of garnering germane thoughts to get guidance from your earlier utterances. So there was no structure. It was random. It was situation specific. But the vibe has always been there. I must honestly admit that I had an innate desire at the time of leaving Anandapur to surprise you while saying good-bye. I knew, and was very certain, that you would not have any permanent emotional backlash due to my leaving Anandapur. In probability, you would have initial feeling of missing my presence, be sad for a few days, and carry remorse for additional few days. After that, life for you would be normal, and your desired Indu would be out of mind since out of sight, and that too in a foreign country.

'Keeping that innate desire in mind, I prepared myself step by step for a few days, dressed up nicely on that afternoon, ostensibly went to seek Didima's blessings, and spent more time with her than usual, always gazing for opportunity to act in privacy. Sitting with Didima, I emotionally and physically primed myself meticulously, planning various steps in case of unforeseen eventualities. I knew for certain that you would be the silent and shocked partaker in the action I had in mind. I would have to initiate and act on to fulfill my desire.

'After exchanging looks with you and availing a window of space, I rushed to your room armed with supportive willpower and energy. As I was approaching the room, I happily managed to disassociate your siblings. Carefully stepping into your room and without looking for you all around, I quietly closed the door first. It was my plan that as soon as I see you, I would push you near your reading table, embrace you intensely, and would enjoy a physically intimate kiss before leaving. That action will be such an unpredictable one for you, and the shock at your end would be so intense your reactive impulses would be frozen for a little while. By the time you would come to your senses, I would be out of your premise, carrying with me most treasured experience of my life, and burdening you for life with a confused sense of probity.

'But that was not to be. The young poor girl's silent departing desire remained unfulfilled because of your unexpected walking out of the home. It caused simultaneous frustration and anger within me. I tried to put all my frustration and anger in the same envelope to enable me to hate you. But I failed in every respect and on every count. My ultimatum to my parents before crossing Belonia border that 'Indu is dead' was a manifestation of that reaction. But soon after my encounter with Ominesh Mama having toothless front jaw, you reappeared in my thoughts with all your joking observations about my Krishna Kaku (uncle), whom you jokingly addressed as 'Fokla Buro' (toothless old man). Since then, knowingly or unknowingly, intentionally or unintentionally, by choice or by chance, you reappeared in every moment, in every decision, and in every action involving my life.

'I had no idea that my unfulfilled longing for having a physically intimate kiss dating a long time back would still cause thinking and actions in my life. Perhaps it remained suppressed conditioned by a number of factors like matrimonial obligations, social values, and family prestige in addition to persistent emphasis on right or wrong that were taught from early childhood. On a specific day prior to conceiving Shetupa, I had pushy feelings about you. My frozen desire unexpectedly got a zing because of your persistent presence in thoughts heightened by brusque physical advances of Bijoy-da that afternoon. You almost totally took possession of my mind and body for an uninterrupted time of that afternoon. I mostly lost control on my muscles, some of which had involuntary reflexes. The old peeved desire haunted me. That suddenly erupted on the said afternoon when I was unexpectedly alone with Kiran. I dragged Kiran to our bed with panoptic physical posture. When we were in the bed, it was possible that Kiran's perpetual edginess concerning sexual performance was momentarily husked by my amorous youth revealed for the first time in daylight. But I also did not give him any space to think otherwise. To me, Kiran's involvement was only emblematic. I was having intimate physical gush with you. When I scratched his upper backside, it was your body. When I held my breast firmly and put it in his mouth, it was your mouth. When I pressed his face against my vibrating breasts, it was your face. In the process, I kissed you profusely, almost making up arrears. That time and that experience were never ever repeated in my life. I conceived that night.

'When we were blessed with a daughter, everyone, surprisingly including Kiran, proposed various fancy names. But I made it clear that I want to name her Shetupa. I succeeded because of Baba. Nobody knew the inherent inference of that name except me. I just added letters *pa* at the end of your name, as for me she is our daughter. When I confessed to Shetupa about her naming, she did not demonstrate any specific reaction but appeared to be at ease.

Later sometime, she told me that '*Ma*, rest assured that I am, and will always be, happy with whatever makes you happy.'

"Shukhipur (habitation of happiness) did not bless me with what the name stands for, but it definitely consecrated my life with immense satisfaction. Dhrub is a replication of Baba in all his deeds and actions from early childhood. It is what I wanted him to be. That made Baba immensely happy and reassured. Shetupa, in all terms and senses except the gender, is what you are in my eyes, in my thoughts, and in my feelings. She is a dear daughter to me besides being a friend, a guide, a shelter, a companion, and a source of strength. Both of them made me copiously satisfied in terms life's outcome.

"This is where I am. This is what I am. I have no idea about your life and happiness. But I am singularly certain that Allah has abundantly blessed you with both. You were in my thoughts and prayers every moment of life, and that would be continued unabashed as long as I breathe.

"You did not give me a chance to act on my first intimate desire. Though belated, I had emotionally acted on that. So I do not have anger anymore. However, in concluding this letter, I would most sincerely allude to another one. As I do not know your condition and status, I refrain from making a specific request that might saddle you causing needless dismay. But if your condition so permits, if it is feasible and convenient to you, please pay a visit to Shukhipur. Do not think about social propriety. We had adhered to that in the past and will do so in the future too. Joyonto-da could be a convenient cover for your presence in Shukhipur. Except for the three of us, and Shetupa, all others would primarily know you as Joyonto-da's early childhood friend.

"I do not know whether this letter would reach you at all. But I fervently pray to Bhogoban, hoping it reaches you, sooner or later. And I also fervently hope and pray that we have a chance to meet in life, at least once more.

"*Bhalo theko* (Stay well),

"Your Indu."

Shetu slowly and patiently went through the long communication. At the end of most sentences, he used to close his eyes, momentarily feeling Indu in the setting described. Some repetition of events in that letter highlighting emotional paradigm of related feelings were found to be the most pertinent aspect of the communication. By the time he finished reading, Shetu was thoroughly exhausted. Without looking at the watch, he switched off the table lamp and dimmed the *sholtey* (cotton flat stripe) of hurricane lantern. He dozed off, soon to be awakened by the pleasant sound of *Azan* (Muslims' pronounced call for prayer). At the same time, he started hearing the crowing sound of roosters from houses nearby, accompanied by meek sounds in the hotel premise of various types of small early morning birds.

Shetu went out of the room and quietly started approaching the reception desk. The receptionist of that small tavern-type hotel was sleeping in a sitting position with his head gawkily placed on the lower extended section of the desk. Responding to the polite call of Shetu, the receptionist woke up with all surprise on his face and instantaneously stood up, both to make up for unintended sleeping posture and to show respect to the guest. Shetu just said, "It is OK with me. I came to tell you that I am now going to sleep and will wake up at 11:00 a.m. I do not want any disturbance in between." Returning to his room, Shetu attended to nature's call, washed his face and neck a number of times, sipped little water, finished his early morning prayer, and went to sleep.

FINALE

A S EARLIER AGREED, Mikku came to Prestige Hotel in a rickshaw late noontime to meet Shetu Bhai, spent a few minutes mostly talking about old days and events, but astutely avoided any reference to the letters of last night. Both of them then left for Haseeb Bhai's place in a rickshaw. As Shetu was disembarking from the rickshaw, he was pleasantly taken aback seeing Haseeb Bhai standing at the entrance attired in a meticulously ironed crisp white punjabi. That elegant stance was visibly matched by the flowing white beard and white tupi. He literally epitomized what a traditional Muslim gentry of semiurban setting in Bangladesh represents. But what flashed to Shetu's mind was the radical change in his outfit, and possibly in his self, compared to the gregarious Haseeb Bhai he knew earlier: devoting most of his time and energy in stage plays and supportive cultural activities.

Escorted by Haseeb Bhai, Shetu and Mikku went inside and occupied convenient seating places in the improvised living room. Noticeable additional features observed this time were a bed, a reading table, and some handmade toys placed prominently. Looking at those, Haseeb Bhai happily told that the bed was his, the reading table was for occasional use of his grandchildren, and the toys were some snippets of wooden toys that he used to make in youth. Setting was being prepared for a genial discourse but interrupted by the call to go to the dining space for the much-awaited lunch. Bhabi (sister-in-law), as a friend's wife is traditionally addressed in Bangladesh, cooked a number of trendy food items for the lunch. The most likeable one was, of course, the *kochur shag*. The food was delicious, but Shetu's intake was clearly not up to expectation. Both Haseeb Bhai and Mikku observed that as they were frequently exchanging looks but did not press Shetu.

After finishing lunch, all three returned to the makeshift living area. They had service of hot traditional tea, known as *chai* in North America, soon after. That was followed by service of *paan* (betel leaf taken with lime and sliced betel nuts [areca nuts]). Both Haseeb Bhai and Mikku appeared to be ardent paan takers. After putting paan in his mouth with separate application of additional lime mix, Haseeb Bhai inquired about the letters of last night.

Shetu opened up cautiously, and confirmed Haseeb Bhai's indication of last night. He said there were in fact two letters: one from Joyonto and the other one from a lady by the name Indu. Shetu briefly touched base with his request made to Joyonto at the time of migration with respect to Indu. He then summarized the contents but was more willing to share his persistent pressing anxiety.

Shetu continued, saying, "Since going through both the long letters, I started to have an inexorable pressure within me to go to Shukhipur and meet Indu, even though for a while. If I would not do it now, the same might just remain a proposition due to my location in Vancouver and related time constraint. It could as well be an attempt too late." Shetu continued observing, "Due to shortage of time, I really do not know how to act. If I do not do it now, I will always blame myself for not being able to respond to the request of someone who loved me so much throughout her life."

There was total silence momentarily. Neither Haseeb Bhai nor Mikku experienced sudden dearth of oxygen. But each one of them was having his own calculations considering Shetu's inexhaustible emotions and assessing impediments that stand out pertaining to cross border transit. As Haseeb Bhai started murmuring about combination of avowed hindrances and the constraint of time, Mikku had unique pantomime response simultaneously suggesting preference for a desperate try. Shetu's immediate reaction was shifting his eye focus between Haseeb Bhai and Mikku, with eagerness to know what the latter had in his mind.

Mikku spent some more time to recount his stance against the backdrop of implausibility versus a pronounced burden of lack of effort that could possibly remain as a fixture in the rest of Shetu's life. He took another paan, started mincing it, and slowly and carefully laid out his thoughts. He said, "Since Shukhipur is adjacent to Belonia, Shetu Bhai may consider traveling to Belonia tomorrow and negotiate an unofficial entry into Tripura State. I have a very close friend who lives on the other side of the border. I will call him to be present in the immigration outpost of India, trying to assist Shetu Bhai. I am in no position to say that the arrangement would work out, but it definitely is worth a try. You may plead, if so necessary, for permission for a short visit. If you feel like, and if it is convenient, you may plan a longer visit later on."

He then continued, saying, "I thought of sending you to Dhaka tomorrow by my personal vehicle. Keeping that in mind, I sent the vehicle for servicing including long-due oil change. The car is available. My driver had been to Belonia a number of times. He also knows my friend Bhabotosh. So neither logistic nor identification in Belonia would be a problem. It will be wonderful if it works out. If not, we would have the consolation of having an honest try."

Mikku then surprisingly, and contrary to his normal aptitude, took a philosophical view of life, observing, "It may sometimes not be worth to alienate sloppy initiative for veneered wisdom. Unknown outcome is always a good premise for taking conceited risk. The choice is yours."

With Haseeb Bhai's endorsement, the proposition for travel to Belonia was agreed without hesitation. For the first time, Shetu became at ease within himself. The follow-up discourses related to mundane issues over refilled cups of chai. The dinner in Mikku's house the following evening was a delicious one with no effort spared by Roma in preparing typical Bangladeshi dishes including a vegetable item of *Datar Saag* (drumstick leaves).

During the journey to Belonia border, Shetu was engrossed with pervading thoughts of possible snag and implications pertaining to his sudden visit agreed to and planned hurriedly. People are generally not stupid in debating options within self, and that happened in the case of Shetu too. He was happy and at ease with the initial decision. But the multitude nature of variable agony continuously dithered his thoughts and consequently made his mind berserk during the whole journey. To obviate that, Shetu diverted his notions in having a dress rehearsal of different responses in probable varied situations resulting from his presence and in facing Indu.

Shetu came to his senses when the driver announced arrival in Belonia border crossing. After parking at the location used during earlier visits, the driver requested Shetu to stay in the car, as he would be looking for Bhabotosh Babu on the visible other side of the border. This border, demarcated by an artificial line dividing India in 1947, runs through usual habitat, and one can easily either cross to the other side or have a glance of it. Bhabotosh Babu, being a longtime resident of the other side of such tenuous border line and a familiar face known to many on both sides including officials, had the habit of slipping through the border for a while without immigration formalities.

On seeing the driver of Mikku, Bhabotosh Babu passed a signal for the driver to wait. After some time, he showed up, exchanged greetings with Shetu, and advised the latter to have a feline approach during interactions with immigration officials. He, without knowing Shetu's background, unwittingly impressed upon the need to avoid arguments with immigration officials. Bhabotosh Babu emphasized that with our set objective of getting needed dispensation of requirements to enable a short visit in mind, Shetu Shaheeb should remain as calm and as passive as possible. Bhabotosh Babu also told that while he would be on the other side trying to help him, the officer concerned should not have any feeling that they know each other.

Shetu cautiously approached the official of Indian immigration desk and introduced him as a Bangladeshi. To properly articulate his plea, Shetu ventured to state that he was traveling to Dhaka from Chittagong and, on reaching Comilla, received an urgent message from Tripura. In view of emergency nature of that message, he needs to visit a family in Shukhipur. Due to time constraint, it was not possible to obtain a prior visa. So he requested a temporary permit enabling a short visit. He as well expressed willingness to abide by any requirement or guarantee.

With a mischievous facial expression, the officer looked at Shetu with a sense of scanning and coldly inquired about the address he would like to visit. Shetu did not have that and obviously was not prepared either. Maintaining a submissive posture, Shetu gingerly embraced the embarrassment and responded, saying that he did not know the specific address but had the intention to visit the abode of one known as Dhireen Babu.

The officer looked at Shetu once again with hesitant serration and left his chair without any comment. Returning after a while, he said that "I am inclined to help you, but the problem is that some of your people often indulge in deliberately breaking trust, and that creates problem for us." After saying so, he inquired about ready availability of passport. Shetu happily nodded and brought out his Canadian passport with a lot of self-confidence.

Seeing Canadian passport, the officer abruptly reacted with unexplainable gut. He abrasively leveled Shetu as a dubious person. In a very rough voice, he said, "What type of man you are? You pleaded for temporary authorization to visit a family whose address you do not know. You introduced yourself as Bangladeshi. And now you present a Canadian passport. How can I trust you with what you said so far? You know that eastern seven sister states of India are restricted areas, and no foreigner, other than cases from Bangladesh, is given permission to visit them. I went to my boss pleading your case. How can I go to him now with your Canadian travel document?" Short of accusing Shetu directly, the officer observed, "Perhaps you wanted to impress me with your Canadian passport, but that enduringly made your case a convoluted one. The outcome is bound to be negative."

To many, such unpleasant, and equally direct, pronouncements would be akin to exhibition of arrogance and officious attitude combined together. But Shetu had a different reaction. Though frustrated, Shetu, being himself in the recent past a senior functionary dealing with law and security matters, easily aligned his thinking with the rationale of officer's comments. From a distance, Bhabotosh Babu was desperately signaling Shetu to open up with some feelers amounting to suborning, which would likely soften the officer's mind-set. Many border officials often succumb to such inducements, and Bhabotosh Babu alluded to that during the earlier brief encounter.

To Shetu's assessment, fortified by long experience of service background, the officer, though curt in communication, did not look like one who is either a sociopath or a malevolent egomaniac. He thus decided to remain honest and factual in his further submission devoid of argumentation. Shetu, with a polite and equally subservient look, drew the attention of the officer and said, "I am sorry for my mistake. In fact, I put forward the Canadian passport, as I am presently traveling with that. It is in no way meant to impress you. My country allows dual citizenship. So I am legally both a Bangladeshi and a Canadian. I have my Bangladesh passport with me. If you so permit, I can show or give it to you." The officer nodded his head, and Shetu handed over his Bangladeshi passport.

With both the passports in his hand, the officer concentrated examining them. Observing perceptible mellowed physical reaction, Shetu ventured to introduce himself as a retired senior police official of Bangladesh. That setting as the premise, Shetu continued, "I would never expect you to breach any rule or regulation. But in many cases, implementation arrangements sometimes have built-in flexibility, and that depends on your discretion. I would request for that. I am willing to comply with any stipulation that you may have including deputizing one of your staff to accompany me, and I will be comfortable with that. I give my word that I would return by 5:00 p.m. of today."

On completion of his review, the officer looked at Shetu with a semblance of respect and closed his eyes. He suddenly stood up, excused himself, and went out of his office room with both passports in his hand, instructing his staff to get two cups of *garam chai* (hot tea). He returned to his room before the chai was served.

The officer then said, "I have oral permission to allow you to go to Shukhipur, about five miles north. But I am keeping both your passports. When you come back by the time indicated earlier, you are to come to my office, and I would then return your passports. There will be no official entry or any seal in either of the passports." Thereafter, he continued, "No one from my office is going to accompany you. Neither would I suggest that anyone else accompanies you. Sir, I may be a junior officer but have the astuteness not to keep an eyewitness. What I have said is strictly an arrangement between you and me." Shetu was both relieved and happy. He profusely thanked the officer to let him have the visit while enjoying the last sip of garam chai.

Shetu came out, shook hands with Bhabotosh Babu, and hired a decrepit Ambassador taxi (made by Hindustan Motors since 1958 with initial licensing from Morris Motors of England) to take him to Shukhipur. As it crawled out, it became evident to Shetu that the roar of the vehicle was more prominent than its speed. Wrecked-inside condition takes any passenger to the level of chassis once he positions himself inside. Shetu experienced that too but consoled himself for being able to have one.

Most drivers of India-Pakistan-Bangladesh subcontinent have a common characteristic. Often they would engage in friendly discourse with passengers, more to make the latter relatively comfortable. The driver of the Ambassador was no exception. In having such exchanges, the driver inquired the reason for Shetu's going to Dhireen Babu's house. On being told that the visit related to old connections, as Dhireen Babu originally came from the same place in Bangladesh as he was from, the driver was surprised and softly asked whether Shetu was aware of a recent death in that family. Shetu had a blank shocking look. The driver continued, "I am not aware as to who died. But I know and am certain based on what I heard in the tea shop near the border crossing that cremation is slated for any time from now, and the whole family would be in the *shashan* (cremation place) for *Antyesti* or *Antim Sanskar* (Hindu funeral rites). After thinking for a while, Shetu advised the driver to take him to the shashan but did not pursue to know more detail as to who died.

Hindu cremation involves high-temperature burning, vaporization, and oxidation, and normally takes place in a cemetery. Dead body is placed on a pyre before the process of cremation is started.

As the vehicle approached the shashan, Shetu could see scores of people, with many more onlookers nearby. Being so advised, the driver parked the vehicle at a nearby safe distance. Shetu stepped out of the vehicle and was having an intense look to locate Indu in the crowd, mostly dressed in white as a symbol of mourning.

Many among present looked at the parked vehicle but concentrated to the Antim Sanskar rituals. Among them, there was a perceptibly smart, and confident-looking rather tall young lady who had a series of glances to the stationary vehicle with definite focus on Shetu. She carefully disassociated herself from the crowd and took steady steps toward the vehicle. Reaching baffled Shetu, she said, "You are Shetu Mama!" As Shetu nodded, the young lady said, "I am Shetupa. The dead body on the pyre is that of my ma (mother). Mama, you just happened to be too late. Ma had an earnest desire to see you once."

Befuddled, Shetu was speechless with his eyes fixed on Shetupa. With choked emotion, she briefly narrated the incident that caused

Indu's death. Shetupa said, "Our house was full of joy and happiness as Bou-di (sister-in-law) Nandita conceived. She went to her paternal home to share some of the happy moments that engulfed all of us. Then the sad incident happened. It was two days before. The day started as any other day. Around noontime, Ma went to give Baba his lunch served in usual round brass plate. Seeing lunch full of vegetable items, Baba got infuriated. His loud rage immediately created an environment of fear and anxiety in the house. Ma felt humiliated being accused of things not related to lunch, and that too in full knowledge of household helps who treated and respected her as head of the family.

"As always, Ma remained nonresponsive to protect her own dignity. She learned a long time back that arguing with Baba is ignominious in every sense, as with each comment, his voice is raised higher, his accusations become horrendous, and his words turn out to be dirtier. Seeing Gokul *Kaku* (uncle) approaching the house possibly to restrain Baba, she hurriedly opted to vacate the room after having a stern look. As she reached near the door, Baba shouted at her with all enrage and threw the lunch plate aiming at Ma. Noticing that, Ma reacted quickly to dodge the oncoming brass plate, lost balance totally, and hit the door frame with her head. She then fell on the cemented veranda and lost sense. Her hitting of the door frame was fatal, and blood oozed out instantaneously. Her fall on the hard floor in a senseless stance was definitely the final nail in the coffin. Gokul Kaku shouted for help. With housemaid Dhuni's help, Ma was placed on her bed in a senseless condition. Dhuni, following rapid but equally rambling instructions of Gokul Kaku, hastily put torn portion of a clean saree as sort of a bandage to cover the forehead wound. But that could not stop the oozing of the blood.

"Chandu, our male household help, ran to inform Dhrub *Dada* (brother) who, as a routine, was in his business premise. Dhuni's deafening cry soon transcended the premise of the house, and a number of neighborhood ladies showed up. Each one was baffled and had her own analysis of the episode as an expression of sympathy. Other ladies got engrossed in recalling ominous statements of Ma made in the recent past. Kamaikha's ma *mashi* (neighborhood maternal aunt and mother of Kamaikha) was specific. She lamented by saying, 'It was only two days back that I came to see Indrani *Didi* (sister). When I was about to leave, she brought a plate of shandesh (traditional sweet made of milk curd) with a glass of *jol* (water) and said, "Please have this before you go. Who knows whether I could serve you again?" I enjoyed that hospitality very much never knowing that it was going to be the last one by our dear didi.' In a sense, many of them concluded by that time that Ma would not return among us anymore.

"Baba's brazenness continued unabated. With pillows placed one on top of the other against the headboard, he happily pushed himself upward to be in a reclined position. Laughing and shouting rowdily, he said, 'Don't worry. Nothing has happened. She is a clever lady and just pretending to get your sympathy and make me small before you all.' He repeated this statement a number of times. Some of the ladies present started looking at each other with consternation looming large on their faces while some others whispered demeaning comments. Dhuni could not control herself. Defying Ma's standing instruction not to go to Baba's room, Dhuni rushed in a state of tantrum, saying, 'Babu, will you please shut up? Ma is dying there, and you are in your world of ruthlessness. We respected and cared about you so far only because of her. If you utter or shout a single word, I promise in the name of Bhogoban I would do everything to starve you to death so that you could realize what you did to this devout lady.'

"Saying those ungainly words to the master of the house, Dhuni walked out of the room of my parents with anger all pervading in her body language. After glancing at the motionless hemorrhaging body of Ma, Dhuni went to the kitchen to fetch water to wash her wound. While picking up the pail with water, Dhuni felt that she lost control of her body muscle as her body started shaking. Positioning herself temporarily on the lower frame of the kitchen entry door, she was in a state of total tenseness. Dhuni wondered as to how she could utter those words. Dhuni went out of that trance when one of neighborhood mashis (aunts) called her.

"It appeared that my father, for the first time in his life, suddenly experienced a state of shock. He was dumbfounded thinking how his household help, who never raised her eyes even while talking to him, could threaten him like that. Suddenly, he felt nervous. Father perhaps went in a state of total stillness. He felt both feeble

JAHED RAHMAN

and wobbly. Realizing for the first time probably in his life that the unabated abuse he heralded at Indrani so far would not be tolerated by anyone, Father surprisingly went into a state of total silence, placing his head on the side pillow with awkwardly bended position of the body. He did not utter a single word thereafter.

"Dhrub Dada came home soonest accompanied by a local physician. It was immediately decided to take Ma to the district hospital. Gokul Kaku rushed to hire a transport. Ma was placed at the backseat of the transport with her head in the lap of Dhrub Dada. Gokul Kaku held her feet. The accompanying physician was on the front seat. Dhrub Dada's frequent visits earlier during Father's hospitalization made him acquainted and be friendly with some doctors. Because of that and the presence of accompanying physician, medical attention was prompt and intensive, though doctors had reservations about the outcome. Dada informed me, and I rushed from Dharma Nagar of North Tripura, my first posting place. Dada also called Nandita Bou-di and advised her to return to Shukhipur. Gokul Kaku was sent to Bhatipara to inform Anjali and bring her.

"Ma never responded to treatment. Her condition slowly deteriorated. Attending physicians gave up all hope, and Dada was so advised. However, Ma fought with her life. The following late morning and after about an hour of my arrival, she breathed her last. It so appeared that she struggled and waited for my arrival. We brought her dead body in the afternoon."

As Antim Sanskar process was being completed, Shetupa inquired whether Shetu would like to see Indrani for the last time. She said, "Mama, if you decide so, you will see Ma is looking so beautiful even in her death notwithstanding her age and the injury she suffered."

Shetu responded, saying, "Ma (local way of addressing a daughter affectionately), it will not be proper. I will not be able to control my emotions. That will be an embarrassment to you all, and possibly a slur to her noble persona. I would like to cherish her young face as I am familiar with. I would hold her letter as a treasure and would try to recall her, when I want, by reading that time and again."

Seeing Dhrub getting ready to discharge his sacred duty as the chief mourner (being the son), Shetupa slowly raised her hand to say, "*Nomoshkar,*" and took small steps toward the funeral pyre. Shetu looked at her.

Dhrub in the meantime started his religiously mandated three times anticlockwise walk around the pyre, keeping the body to his left and sprinkling water onto the pyre from a vessel. On completion of that, Dhrub lit a small fire inside to comply with ritual of *mukh-aagni*. It symbolizes that the dead is now set as an offering to Agni, the fire. The pyre was then set alight by Dhrub with the help of a flaming torch.

As the process of cremation progresses, Shetu returned to the backseat of his rented vehicle and felt an acute pain for not being able to meet Indu once. He comprehended for the first time in his life that all attributes of personal anguish are essentially internal, and the intensity of pain resulting from that feeling can't be grasped by anyone except the one who is having it. He concluded that pain can never be shared in a consequential way. It is always too personal. Neither the element of time in minimizing pain nor the oft-expressed philosophy of sharing the pain to lessen its impact perhaps is tenable, as both only help in managing the pain but not the intensity of that.

Shetu quickly revisited events of his life, interactions with Indu, and recalled the contents of her letter. He concluded that perhaps the inability to see her once more being so close in terms of time was an ordained one. But Shetu was certain that his decision not to see the dead face of Indu in a totally unknown surrounding and among unfamiliar faces was most appropriate upholding the honor and dignity of the dead.

On getting signal from Shetu, the driver started the engine of his ramshackle vehicle, and the return journey commenced with a fleeting jerk. Shetu looked back but could not see the fire engulfing the pyre, as smoke billows from the exhaust pipe of wobbly Ambassador taxi covered it.

Printed in the United States
By Bookmasters